Seven Summers Ago

GOLDEN GOAST SERIES

STARLA DEKRUYF

SEVEN SUMMERS AGO: A Small Town Romance—Golden Coast Series-Book 1

STARLA DEKRUYF

Editor: Britt Tayler - PaperbackEditor

Cover illustration: Claudia Bonet (@clauins_ on Instagram)

Title page character art: Lero and Vic (@lilytea_art on Instagram)

Digital ISBN: 979-8-9921338-6-8

Paperback ISBN: 979-8-9921338-5-1

Seven Summers Ago

GOLDEN GOAST SERIES
BOOK 1

STARLA DEKRUYF

To all my fellow Endo Warriors and anyone else with an invisible or visible battle:
In the words of Beck - "We all have scars. Some just aren't visible. And scars don't make someone less beautiful. If anything, it does the opposite. Because it means you've lived. You're still living."

AUTHOR'S NOTE &
CONTENT WARNINGS

Hello reader! I'm filled with gratitude that you would pick up and consider my book. Because I'm an advocate for mental health, it's important to me that you have some information I believe is important before you choose to read my book. Without too many spoilers, I want to first touch on the endometriosis representation in this book.

Endometriosis is a condition in which the presence of endometrial-like tissue is found outside of the uterus. Roughly 200 million people have endo. While surgery by a specialist is the best form of treatment—there is no cure. Surgery is also the only way endo can be officially diagnosed.

After receiving the typical gaslighting from healthcare professionals, suggesting everything from yoga, vaccines, therapy, birth control, diets, and more, I finally found a doctor who listened and believed me. She officially diagnosed me during my hysterectomy after 25 years of being undiagnosed and mistreated.

While endo symptoms and level of severity can vary, I wrote the female character—Rosie—based on my lived-experience.

Please keep in mind, if you have endo, your symptoms and experiences can be very different than mine.

Infertility is sometimes a symptom of endo. I used my own personal experiences in this book that could be triggering for you and may not be your experience. (**SPOILERS**) I endured two years of infertility, followed by a positive pregnancy test where I began bleeding and cramping. My husband and I assumed we miscarried until I went for an ultrasound, and it was confirmed they baby was still thriving. Then between my first and second children, I had a miscarriage. The book will touch on these experiences.

Secondly, the anxiety and on-page panic attacks were written with care as they are my lived experience. The portrayal of these conditions doesn't mean they are the only symptoms and levels can be a vast variety. Writing my male main character—Beck—with these conditions was therapeutic.

If you live with endometriosis, anxiety, or panic disorder, I hope this story is healing for you, you feel seen, or you choose to not pick up this book if you feel it will be triggering for your mental health.

Full List of Content Warnings:

- Open door sexual content
- Explicit language/cursing
- Alcohol consumption and smoking
- Death (off page)
- Alcoholic parent and verbally abusive (in past/off page)
- On-page panic attacks
- Endometriosis
- Talk of miscarriage

PROLOGUE

12 YEARS BEFORE

BECK

*A*s Rosie runs into the waves with Stella and Daisy linked to each of her arms, I trudge through the sand barefoot with her high heels slung off my fingers. Her laughter reverberates through the air and rumbles in my chest. It's the sweetest sound. I want to bottle it up so I'm never without it.

The tide is going out, leaving behind seashells and an assortment of sea glass in varying shades. Christian and Jack jog up ahead, tossing a football back and forth. I dig my toe into the sand and from my periphery, a piece of green sea glass nearly in the shape of a heart catches my eye. I pick it up and brush the sand off with my thumb before stuffing it into my tuxedo pants pocket.

I lift my chin just in time to catch Rosie rushing toward me. She's holding the fabric of her long green dress in her fist. Though it's useless. The bottom of it is already soaked. But she doesn't care.

When she reaches me, she launches herself into my arms

and I catch her as she womps against my chest. It knocks the air out of my lungs for a second and I release a chuckle while she laughs and I swing her around.

"You caught me." There's amusement in her expression.

"Of course I did. I'll always catch you."

She grins, and light freckles blend into her cheeks as a blush fills them. "And that's why I did it. Because I know I can count on you."

"Always."

"And forever," she adds.

I lower her back down to her feet and gaze into her green eyes. "Yeah, and forever," I agree, bending press a kiss to her forehead. "I have something for you."

Her eyes glitter. "For me? What is it?"

I stuff my hand into my pocket and close my fist around the piece of sea glass. "You know I love you, right?"

"Beck," she breathes out, and throws her head back. "Of course. It's you and me. Forever."

"That's right." I gift her with a small peck and then open my hand. "I found this for you."

"Oh my gosh, it's so pretty. I hardly ever find sea glass at this beach anymore."

"It looks like a heart, doesn't it?"

"Aw, it does. Thank you."

I shrug. "It felt like a sign or something. Or luck."

"We don't need luck." She wraps her arms around me and pushes up to her tiptoes, leaning her chest against mine. "We've got love, and that's all that matters."

I gaze down at her beaming smile.

"I was hoping you would say that."

"As if you doubted it." She gives me a rueful smile.

A tightness pulls in my chest. The world suddenly slips away, and I don't think, I only act. "Rosie, I love you."

"I love you too." Her brows knit together. "What's wrong?"

My pulse picks up. "Not today...but someday, will you, Rosie Hendrix, marry me?"

Her eyes water as they search mine.

"I'll get you a real ring. I'll do this all the right way. I'll make it special and make it count. But I couldn't wait. I love you, and I want you to spend the rest of your life with me."

She shakes her head. "Yes. Yes, a thousand times, yes. Of course I'll marry you."

Relief fills my entire body. I wrap her up in my arms and lower my lips to hers, kissing her long and hard. When I finally pull away, I close her fist around the sea glass, and say in a whisper, "Promise me you'll keep this forever. That way, when we're old and gray, we'll always remember tonight was the night we decided on forever."

1

ROSIE

*W*hen I went through cosmetology school over a decade ago, I had no idea my breasts would get so much attention. But here they are. On display for my client's viewing pleasure.

As I crank back the stylist chair and my client rests his head over the sink, I spray the water through his salt-and-pepper hair. This is the point when my clients typically close their eyes and relax. But Blake's are zoned in on—you guessed it—my rack. Blake is one of Weston's colleagues, in his late-forties, and apparently "gets laid more than any other guy in the office." West's words, not mine.

When I glance over at Hannah, she has her scissors gripped in her hand and she's giving me the look she always does when a male client checks me out too long. We've been working side by side long enough that her look no longer needs an explanation. She used to mouth the words, gesturing with her dark, expressive eyes and entire body like she was a mime. But now, I know what she's insinuating the second I glance her way. *If he looks at your boobs one more time, I'm gonna cut off his balls.*

My lips curl up to one side at her loyalty, but I give her a stern shake of my head. West won't mind him looking—he'd even get off on it if I told him—but if he so much as lays one finger on me, this guy won't last another day in the office. I clear my throat. His eyes fly up to meet mine. Caught.

"So, Blake?" Hannah calls. "Have you met my client?"

Blake tries tilting his head from where it's perched over the sink. "No, I can't say I have," he mutters, an edge of annoyance in his tone.

Hannah's client is a kind woman in her forties as well. Pretty and recently divorced. But she's not his type. It's all part of Hannah's plan to distract him from ogling me. Which I can appreciate.

Four years ago, I rented this space next to hers in Blush— the most prestigious salon in downtown Seattle—and we bonded almost instantly. She quickly became one of my favorite friends in the city. Okay, she became my only friend. Before her, there hadn't been anyone I trusted. Not with my daughter Charlotte and not with my secrets either.

"Well, my girl here is smart, sassy, and a lot of fun," Hannah yammers on. "You two should go out."

"Oh, yeah?" Blake looks unconvinced. So much, in fact, that he finally closes his eyes. "Sounds great. I'll leave my card. Give me a call."

"Um...yeah, okay," Hannah's client says from behind the shield of foils framing her face.

I smirk, rolling my eyes at Hannah, but she doesn't notice. She's too busy standing straighter with her chest thrust out. Hannah: 1. Rich douchebag: 0.

My workdays usually end earlier than Hannah's because I pick Charlotte up from school. But today I quit even sooner to give myself time to clean up my space in preparation for being gone next week.

"While you're getting a tan, I want you to think of me stuck here getting poured on," Hannah whines, flashing me her sad puppy eyes in the reflection of our shared mirror. Commiserating with her, I pout my lips. "Tell Charlie to pick me out a cute Golden Harbor souvenir."

"I will." After I wipe down the glass shelves to the side of my station, I return the hair products, organizing them by their proper uses. "But you know I'm not gonna have much time to spend at the beach."

Hannah's scissors pause in her manicured hand, and she gives me an irritated look. "Didn't you tell me your grandma's house is literally on the beach?"

"I mean...yeah, I guess." I grab my jacket off the hook on the wall and wrestle it on, and a shock of pain in my shoulder seeps into my arm. "But I'll be pretty busy with my grandma's service and packing up all her stuff."

Hannah sets her scissors down and whispers something to her client. She shuffles over to me and wraps me up in a hug. "Just promise me you'll go out and have some fun with your old friends. As jealous as I am that I can't be there, you need some fun in your life."

I pull back, a little gasp escaping me. "I have fun."

"Sure, you snagged yourself a hot piece of ass. But I can't remember the last time you had fun." She takes me by the shoulders. "Double up on your pain meds and go out to a bar. Drink a beer. Do something wild. Dance. Sing karaoke. Throw an axe." She shakes my shoulders. "Just do something."

"Ugh. Fine, I'll try. But no promises." I groan. "I'll text you."

"You better. Love ya." She hands me my umbrella, and I give her one last glance before I slip out into the Seattle rain.

"*D*on't go," Weston pleads, tugging the suitcase handle from my grip.

"I have to." I wrinkle my nose as I sigh, a wave of emotion rising in me unexpectedly. Shielding my eyes, I turn away from him and snatch my purse from the bed.

With a firm grip to my waist, he spins me to face him. But my mind is elsewhere. It's restless. I've got a mental travel checklist scrolling through my brain. West rests an open palm on the side of my neck, pushing gentle pressure against my skin with his thumb and fingertips. It stills me and my eyes slide up to meet his. Blue and clear. Trustworthy.

"Then I'll come with you."

I give him a lopsided smile. I know he can't. He knows he can't. And yet maybe he wants to. That should be enough. The want. But it's not.

And the intent doesn't matter anyway.

The streetlamp outside flicks on and the light pours through the window where the voice-control blackout roller shades have yet been commanded to cover. It's a reminder of my flight and the time it takes to get through security at SeaTac Airport.

I reach up and squeeze West's smooth hand. "Can you really get the time off work?"

His lips twitch. Like he didn't think I'd call him on his bull-shit. "No. But you know I want to."

"I do." I push up on my toes and kiss him lightly on his perfect cupid's bow lips.

But his greedy hand slides to the back of my neck with increased force and he lengthens our kiss. His mouth moves over mine with determination, his tongue darting out to pry open my lips. He's eager to make me stay.

And it nearly works.

My head goes dizzy, and I hook my fingers into the top of his belt holding up his slacks.

He tugs my bottom lip with his teeth and pulls away to whisper, "Stay. Leave tomorrow." His hot breath combined with the scent of his musky cologne make my head swim. "Alexa, close blinds," he commands, and they slide down. Teasing the hollow of my neck with a trail of kisses, he tells me, "I'll take the rest of the night off."

The reminder of his work turns me off instantly. I love West. I do. But when it comes to work, I will always be second place.

"Mama, I'm ready," Charlotte calls from the hallway as she gallops like a horse into our bedroom, flipping on the bright overhead light as she does.

I step back from West, giving his chest a pat. "Me too, Charlie." I sling my purse over my shoulder and grip the handle of my suitcase again. "We'll be back in a week," I say, gazing at West's creased brow before giving him one last quick kiss.

"I already miss my girls. A week is too long," he whines, and I decide a grown man in a power suit whining is surprisingly sweet. It softens him. *We've* softened him. West's brother told me so. Said if it weren't for Charlie and I coming into his life a year ago, West would've surely been named Seattle's most eligible bachelor. He's probably happy because he's now been given that title in some circles. Including Seattle's *Business Tycoon* magazine.

"It's just a week. That's only seven days," Charlie tells West, pushing her reddish-brown hair out of her face.

My lips quirk into a smile. West crouches and Charlie runs into his awaiting arms. He wraps her up in a big hug and he squeezes her, rocking side to side. "How'd you get to be so smart?"

"I'm smart like you," she says, and her response lights up his expression.

"Nah, you're smart like your mama." He shoots me a wink

then releases her and stands, propping his hands on his hips. "You take care of her, okay?"

"I can't take care of her. I'm only six." She giggles.

"Fine. You two girls take care of each other. Deal?" He holds out his pinky finger and she hooks her little one with his.

"Deal."

"All right, c'mon, Charlie, we gotta go." I nudge her in the back, ushering her toward the hall.

"Wait, Rosie," he calls, and I turn.

"West," I say on a sigh. It really is sweet. Charlie and I haven't been anywhere without him since we started dating a year ago, though he's gone on several business trips without us. We've just never been the ones doing the leaving. I've never had a reason to. Until now. "We can't miss our flight."

"If you need me, just say the word and I'm there."

Part of me believes him. For this relationship to work, I have to.

"Thank you."

"I love you," he says.

"We love you too." I flash him a smile and shuffle out of the bedroom.

Outside, the city lights reflect off wet asphalt, and the scent of rain on a warm summer's day fills my nose. It's something I'm still getting used to after growing up in California.

West's condo is in the ritzy part of downtown Seattle, near Pike Place, meaning it isn't the ideal location to raise Charlie. But the alternative—and where we lived up until moving in with him—causes my heart to race and my breath to go shallow.

Taxis, Ubers, and bikes occupy the street. People flood the sidewalks in packs. At this time of the day, most are heading to dinner or the local bars. I squeeze Charlie's shoulder to keep her close until I finally spot our Uber.

"There's ours." I point and nudge her. "C'mon, get your suitcase."

The driver tosses our luggage into his compact SUV, and Charlie and I climb into the back seat. She looks out the window and is quiet. It's painful how I already notice her struggle with anxiety. She's younger than her father was the first time I comforted him during a panic attack.

My phone buzzes in my hand.

STELLA
Can't wait to see you!

Me too! But we'll be there late

Maybe we should get a hotel tonight?

STELLA
I'll be awake

Come by and you can pick up the keys to Dottie's cottage

I went by there earlier and stocked the fridge with a few things I thought you and Charlotte might need

My shoulders tense. I glance at Charlie and catch her chewing on the string from her hoodie. I tug it out of her mouth, and she scowls at me but doesn't protest.

"Hey, wanna look at pictures of Grandma Dottie's cottage again?"

She nods. "Is it really on the beach?"

"It's just a short walk. You can see the waves from her front deck."

She smiles wide, showing off her newly toothless grin. During the last week, she lost both front teeth. "Is the water cold?"

"It shouldn't be too cold this time of year. Not like when we went to Long Beach."

"Brr." She shivers at the memory.

That was the last full day West spent with us. He let his brother handle the business for their finance company for the day. He arranged everything. Even remembered to bring sand toys for Charlotte. We collected sand dollars and ate fish and chips in town. West let Charlie fill a paper bag with all the salt-water taffy she could fit.

We had needed a day like that. I'd been questioning where our relationship stood and where it was headed. And he rose to the challenge and showed us we were a priority. The next night he took me to a fancy restaurant downtown and proposed. I said yes.

I open my photos app on my phone and find the album I labeled "Grandma Dottie" and hand it to Charlie. After I received word my grandmother had a stroke, I started compiling all my photos of her and her cottage in California. Not just for me, but for Charlie too.

Seeing where we're headed will hopefully calm her nerves. But it's not just where we're going that's got her anxious. She's about to meet a lot of new people for the first time. Including her father.

She just doesn't know it yet.

My chest aches with heaviness from this secret I've been holding in for far too long. I lean closer to Charlie and push her hair out of her face, resting my head against hers. "Let me look with you," I whisper.

I want to soak up these last moments where it's just Charlie and me—before I rock her entire world.

2

BECK

"You know it's perfect," Milo states, stepping back and observing the freshly painted siding as the sun lowers behind Dottie's cottage.

I tug the brim of my hat down to shield my eyes from the sun ricocheting against the powder blue while I study it. This paint color wouldn't be my first choice. But it's what Dottie wanted. And I made her a promise.

The color, along with being back at the cottage, has me daydreaming about past lives. Mine and Dottie's and how they were intertwined. My gut pinches at the memories.

I shouldn't be surprised she chose Rosie's favorite color. It's a popular shade for our small coastal town. It will make resale easier.

"I'm not a house painter." I shrug. "But I guess it will do."

"Well, I'm not one either. But thanks for letting me help out lately. I really need the extra cash." Milo gives me a grim smile and starts loading my tools into the back of my Chevy truck.

I'm not sure "helping out" is the correct term when he's been working full time for me for three years. But I let him live in his dream world. "How's the new album coming along?" I ask my little brother as I fasten the ladder in place.

"It's almost done. Getting some good hype already. Sounds like people are excited for it."

I hand him a corner of the drop cloth and take the other. "That's great. I'm proud of you."

"Yeah," he mutters, blowing the curls out of his face. "Save it till after we release."

I roll my eyes. Milo is worried about nothing. That kid was born with talent others pay big bucks for and spend years trying to replicate. He was made for the spotlight. Definitely not for this small town.

"It's gonna go viral. Pretty soon you're gonna be the one helping me out and loaning me money," I tease, folding the drop cloth and tossing it into the truck.

"Right. Like you'll need money. You're not only the best contractor in town, you're the only one. I'd say you're set." He climbs into the passenger side.

Simple living is the only reason. While some locals clung to their homes and land as big investors from LA started buying everything up, I sold mine and bought a smaller place across town where it's cheaper and less populated.

I glance up at the cottage one more time. The muscles across my shoulders tense as the memories pile on top of each other. Rosie and I spent a lot of our relationship inside those walls. It's where we fell in love.

But that was a lifetime ago.

I duck my head and slide in behind the steering wheel. It takes me a second or two to get my bearings before I start the engine.

"You okay?" Milo asks.

"Fine," I mumble.

"You thinking about Dottie?"

I was. But more, I was thinking about Rosie. I'm a glutton

for punishment. Because going down memory lane is a bad idea. "Yeah," I half lie.

"I know you spent a lot of time over here. With her...and Rosie." He almost whispers her name. Like it's a bad word and he's afraid to piss me off.

"I did. She'll be missed." I say it matter-of-factly and give him a pointed look before backing out of the driveway, so he knows I'm done with this conversation.

"Beck—"

"Hey," I interrupt, "what do you say we call it quits for the day and go to Tacos by the Beach for an early dinner and a beer?"

Milo checks the time on his phone. "Dinner? This is even early for your geriatric ass," he teases.

I'm only three years older than he is. But most days, he doesn't let me forget it. As if I could; I'm the responsible one out of the two of us. The one who had to grow up too fast. Who had to take care of him when our parents were getting smashed or were too hungover to function.

Our childhood turned me into a bitter person for too many years. It consumed me. Until our parents finally cleaned themselves up and got sober a few years ago. Mom moved across the country and started a new family. Dad moved to the island and bought a bar with an apartment above it. Wonder where I get the glutton-for-punishment trait.

"I mean, I was gonna say my treat, but I can drop you off at home instead," I mutter.

Milo lived with me up until I bought my place, then he and his band buddies pooled their money together to rent a small condo only feet from the beach. When they aren't practicing, they're surfing.

"No, no, I'd love dinner and a beer."

I chuckle. Knew that would change his mind. He's a

starving artist. Spends all his money on guitars and recording studio sessions in LA.

I drive down Main Street and pull into the parking lot behind Tacos by the Beach. It's busy already, but not surprising for a Thursday. Ladies' Night. Milo and I sit at the bar. It's easier this way. No fussing with a server and no making eye contact with him if he wants to talk about Dottie again.

Or worse—Rosie.

We order a few tacos and one beer each. I won't be someone who encourages or supports excessive drinking. I won't be an enabler. Not when it's in our blood.

"You think Rosie will show for the memorial?" Milo asks when we're halfway through our dinner.

My stomach corkscrews and it's an instant loss of appetite. It takes extra effort to finish chewing my bite and swallow it down before speaking. "I'd be surprised if she didn't."

"I guess the more important question I should be asking is, do you hope she'll show up?"

Grinding my molars together, I can't look at Milo when I answer. "I hope Rosie does what Rosie thinks is best. She always does."

"You know I've always sided with you. It was selfish of her to leave the way she did. No goodbye even. But...you could've gone with her."

"I couldn't and you know it," I growl back.

The bartender flicks his attention our way before returning to pulling drinks. Milo leans closer to me. "Hey, don't put this on me. I was nineteen. I was old enough to take care of myself."

It's not his fault. And he's right; I can't blame him. It was my choice to stay. But it was her choice to leave. That's my story and I'm sticking to it. Besides, it's been seven years. Why start changing it now.

"I was no good for her. Just a painful reminder. You know she deserved more than I could ever give her."

"But, Beck—"

"That's enough," I bark out, whipping my head to face him. "That's enough," I repeat, but softer now. We've been over this a thousand times. A thousand different conversations about a thousand different scenarios on how our relationship could've gone. But ultimately, we end up right back here. "It's in the past."

"Fine. I'm done." Milo holds up a palm in surrender.

Even if the past has the possibility of rearing its head soon, I'm choosing to live in denial for as long as possible. If Rosie should show up for Dottie's memorial, maybe we won't even see each other. It's a nice thought I have no choice but believe.

Milo's friends pour into the restaurant as we're finishing our dinner. I leave him with them to head home. I'm tired. The job for Dottie's cottage was big. And we were on a time crunch. Originally, she had her upstairs converted from two bedrooms into one big one. But she wanted me to build the walls again and change it back into two bedrooms. It was smart. A three-bedroom would be an easier sell than two.

Besides the work upstairs, all the windows downstairs needed to be replaced. Which meant replacing some of the siding and trim and painting the entire exterior. Dottie wanted me to do all the work, said she didn't trust anyone else. I was flattered, but the deadline was tight.

Dottie hired a real estate agent before she passed, and they wanted the house ready to list at the start of summer. We'd done it. Even if we had to work around Dottie while she was at her weakest following her stroke. She was gracious the whole way through, said she didn't mind at all. If anything, she'd been grateful for the company. The latter made me angrier with Rosie. Where'd she been these past few weeks?

Instead of going home, I pull off Main and turn down Dottie's street. I park my Chevy in the gravel between her driveway and the pathway to the beach. It's idiotic. Like I'm not only forcing myself to feel these bottled-up emotions, but like I want them.

I shut off the engine and hop out of my truck. Peering up at the cottage, it's dark and quiet. Peaceful. That's what Rosie loved about Dottie's. She'd grown up in a busy home where her parents worked a lot and traveled often, and where she and her illness were given no grace. Then she came here. And for the first time in her life, she was free to learn how to live in the body she'd been given.

Sadness washes over me and I shake my head, releasing a rumbled sigh. I yank off my work boots and pants and toss them inside my truck. After rummaging around in the back seat, I find my wetsuit and wiggle it on, glancing over my shoulders as I do. Besides the moon and the row of lamps lighting the pathway to the beach, it's dark. My phone chimes from inside my truck.

JACK

Are you free to meet up at The Sandbar for a beer?

I'm beat

Raincheck?

JACK

Tomorrow?

I have a date

JACK

No shit?

It's shocking to me too. That I got the nerve to ask and that I asked in the first place. I can't remember the last time I went on a real date.

Maybe it was the shitshow with Stella's cousin, Daisy. I

never should've agreed to the date in the first place. We were too good of friends and too much alike. But Stella had been persistent. And after she let it slip that Rosie was dating a rich suit in Seattle, I told her to set up the double date. After a desperate and embarrassing makeout session, Daisy and I decided to just be friends.

Unlatching my surfboard from the roof rack, I haul it under my arm and start down the pathway to the beach. I hadn't planned on surfing tonight, but I have an itch that needs scratching. And it was either this or going home to jerk off in the shower while fantasizing about the same woman for the thousandth time.

The tide is going back out, elongating the beach. The ocean glows from the full moon's reflection. I still can't decide if I prefer seeing it like this or in the daylight when the seagulls are flying overhead and the surf shines golden from sun.

I don't get to the beach at night much these days. Even if it is a matter of feet from most places in town. Golden Harbor is growing. Lucky for me, my construction business is growing too. My specialty is framing new houses and remodeling and preserving what's already here. I don't typically take on work outside of my wheelhouse, but I did it on Dottie's cottage as a favor. She was a longtime friend. Some might even call her family.

My brain switches to Rosie. Much like it does whenever I think about Dottie. If it weren't for her, I would've never met the love of my life. But who meets their soulmate at sixteen and stays together forever?

Jogging into the waves, I set my board in and hop onto it, lying flat on my belly. I scoop my arms through the water and paddle fast and hard. Pushing images of Rosie away with each stroke. Her green eyes glittering when I made her laugh, her beautiful auburn hair splayed across my chest, her hips spread while she straddled and thrust against me.

After I catch a few good ones, the water engulfs me once and that's enough for me—I'm done. I prop my board in the sand and drop down beside it to catch my breath. Surfing settled the heaviness in my chest, but my mind is still too busy, whirling with endless thoughts of what might've been.

"Beck?"

My shoulders tense as I jerk my head to glance over my shoulder. It's been so long since I heard the sound of my name from that mouth you'd think I'd forgotten it. But no, you don't forget the voice of your soulmate.

Or...your wife.

Narrowing my eyes, I clamber to my feet and try not to stare at her when I finally find my voice. "Hey, Rosie."

3

ROSIE

Running into Beck the first night I'm back in Golden Harbor was not part of my plan. I had hoped it wouldn't happen until the memorial. But here he is. Sitting on the beach next to his surfboard near Dottie's cottage, watching the waves crash in the dark with nothing more than the light from the moon and stars to guide him.

When he stands and turns, the sight of him steals my breath. He's not the young man I remember. At thirty years old, his shoulders are broader. He's let his facial hair grow out and his dark brown hair is damp and in waves. And when he says "Hey, Rosie," my knees nearly buckle.

"What are you doing here?" My words come out accusative without intention. It's not like I own the beach.

As he shuffles toward me, closing the distance between us, his bare chest and sculpted abs slice into view. His arms are out of his wetsuit, and it's bunched around his waist, showing off his defined biceps. His eyes are darker than I remember, the light from the moon shining in the brown. "I should ask you the same thing," he growls back.

I don't like the insinuation in his tone. Pinching my brows

tight, I tilt my chin. "Seriously? That's a stupid question. I came for Dottie's memorial," I snap. "Did you really think I wouldn't come?"

"Hell, Rosie. I don't know." He hunches his shoulders. "This is the first I've seen you back in Golden Harbor in seven years."

Almost seven. But who's counting?

"Dottie meant everything to me. You know that." I glare, crossing my arms tight.

"Everything? Ha," he barks, throwing back his head dramatically. "Yeah? Then where've you been all these years?"

I stomp toward him and stop when he's only a few feet from me. His chiseled pecs only distract me from my irritation momentarily. "I called Dottie every week."

"Okay. And what about after her stroke? Where were you then?" He's close enough now I can see his brown eyes widen with challenge.

"I couldn't come. I had responsibilities. She knew that."

"Whatever," he mutters, shrugging his broad shoulders again as he walks back toward his surfboard. "What do I care. But sounds like excuses to me."

"What do you know about responsibilities?" I bite out with his back facing me.

He does a one-eighty, his expression stricken with indignation, but just as quickly as it came on, it fades just as fast. "Welp, I'd like to say this has been fun. Let's do it again in seven years for the next memorial, shall we?" He plucks his surfboard from the sand and stalks past me toward the pathway.

I watch him for a moment, partially paralyzed because of his behavior and partially working up the courage. "Beck?" I call after him.

He stops but doesn't turn around, instead he glances over his shoulder to gaze at me.

"Why haven't you signed the divorce papers yet?" The question comes out past the rising lump in my throat.

But he doesn't speak. Instead, he smirks, and anger builds inside my chest like an expanding bubble ready to pop. "It costs a fortune each time my lawyer sends them to you," I argue.

With an arched brow, he says, "Something tells me you can afford it."

I don't get sucked into playing this game by disagreeing with him. "That's not the point."

He approaches me again with purpose, the sand kicking up behind him, and narrows his eyes. "Fine. Why now?"

Releasing an uneasy sigh, I follow it by muttering, "It's been almost seven years. If not now, then when?"

His chestnut-brown eyes are dark as they skate over my face. "Nah, try again."

I pinch my lips together. "What?"

"Tell me the real reason."

I hesitate at first. I've never wanted to hurt Beck. He was my favorite person once. But the truth is, we hurt each other. Neither of us left the relationship unscathed. But the even bigger truth is that we ended before I ever left Golden Harbor.

"I've met someone," I say softly.

He struggles to look at me and it damn near kills me. His head drops to his chest like a bobber in the water. For a moment, I regret saying the words out loud. But then Beck does what he always does when he's hurt but doesn't want to feel it. He deflects.

"Well, congratulations. All your dreams have come true. You're welcome, by the way." He makes an exaggerated show, like he's bowing. Whipping around, he takes off down the pathway again, his surfboard clutched underneath his arm.

But I don't let him off the hook that easily. I hurry to catch up to him, my heart pounding fast and hard in my chest. Because that's what Beck does to me. He gets my emotions racing at a hundred miles an hour. He makes me angry. He makes me want to fight. There's no one who pushes my buttons more than him.

"Are you kidding? You expect me to *thank* you?"

"I don't expect you to, but if you wanted to, it wouldn't hurt," he mutters.

"Ha!" I blurt out in amusement. "It's *no* thanks to you. You know I worked my ass off in cosmetology school, between the pain and flare days and ER visits. It took me a year longer than everyone else to finish. Then I pinched and saved and started my own business. I moved to an entirely different state and had to start my life over. Alone."

"Hey!" He spins around and points a finger in my face. "That was your choice, honey. Don't you ever forget that."

"How could I? It was the last thing you said to me after I left." Intense emotion rises inside of me and tears burn in the corners of my eyes.

"Good. Just so we're clear." He reaches what I assume is his truck. A shiny, newer Chevrolet. He's upgraded since his old lifted four-door with meaty tires.

"Crystal." I glare at his back. "As long as you remember that you're the one who wouldn't leave this place. You're the one who couldn't sacrifice...I don't even know what...this"—I gesture in the air—"to come with me."

He wrestles his surfboard back on its rack. "Don't talk to me about sacrifices. I had to stay and take care of Milo. You know that."

The reminder of his little brother softens my heart some. Since I've had Charlie, I've changed. Maybe all those years ago I would've been different had I known what it was like to take care of someone, to have someone rely on you.

"Whatever," I mutter.

"But you know what?" he says, like we're still in the middle of having a conversation when I've already checked out. "I think what it comes down to is why wasn't this place enough?" He throws up his arms. "Why wasn't *I* enough?"

We stare at one another, and the affliction shining in his eyes makes my heart feel as if it's about to crack inside my chest. I didn't expect Beck to be holding all of this in so many years later. Honestly, I expected him to have moved on by now. Or maybe I just hoped.

"It wasn't about you," I whisper past the agony swelling in my throat.

He shakes his head and presses his lips together. "No, maybe not. But it should've been about us. We were married. *Are* married," he corrects, swinging open his truck door.

"Just sign the papers. Please," I beg. "I don't have a fight left in me."

"I'll think about it." He slides in behind the steering wheel.

"I'm going to marry him." My voice is quiet, but I know he hears me before he slams the truck door closed. "Ugh," I groan, and spin toward the back door of the cottage, not waiting for him to even drive away before I slip inside.

Locking the door behind me, I hurry down the hallway where the walls are filled with photos of memories and tiptoe up the stairs and into the spare bedroom where Charlie is sleeping. She didn't rest at all on the flight or the Uber ride to Golden Harbor. Now, she's snoring lightly, her small hands rested underneath her cheek on the pillow. I tug the blanket up to her chin and brush her dark, strawberry-blonde locks from her face before pressing a light kiss to her cheek.

Pulling the door behind me, I leave it open a crack so the hallway light can still shine into her room. It took her almost a month to finally sleep in her own room after we moved into Weston's apartment. It wasn't until I bought her a night light. Even though we're only here for a week, I make a mental note to pick one up when I go to town.

Downstairs, I pour myself a glass of wine and sit on the

navy-blue sofa with my phone. My eyes take a trip around the room, absorbing all the things that are new and all the things that are the same.

Grandma Dottie was a good cook. The three years I lived here with her during high school, I never missed a meal. Some nights she let me pick what we would have. And sometimes she'd let me help in the kitchen. It's thanks to her I even know how to cook at all.

My own mother never taught me. Her career had been more important than her family. Same thing with my father. It's the reason I came to live with Dottie. I wasn't a bad kid; the reality was my parents just didn't have the time or patience to parent me. Especially since I was sick a lot.

My parents went to work overseas for the entire summer before I started high school and instead of forcing me to go with them, they let me come to Dottie's. After a week here, I never wanted to go home. And I didn't.

I take a sip of wine and tuck my legs underneath me. A memory of Beck assaults my brain. Him and I making out on this very sofa. It's as if I can still feel his strong arm wrapped around my waist, his soft lips pressed against mine, and his hot breath near my ear as he whispered promises about our future.

Empty promises.

I shake my head and send a reply to West's earlier text.

> Here safe and sound

> All settled for the night at Dottie's

WEST

> Good. I'm glad. It's late. I'll check in with you tomorrow

> Love you. Give Charlotte a kiss for me

> I will. Love you too

I text Stella next.

> Thanks again for everything. Especially the wine!

STELLA
I thought you might need it 😏

> You have no idea

STELLA
You okay?

> Beck was here

STELLA
Wait. What? At Dottie's?

> He was at the beach

STELLA
How'd that go?

> Exactly how you'd imagine
> 0 out of 10
> Do not recommend

STELLA
I'm sorry 😔

> Tonight was nothing compared to how the memorial is gonna go
> Maybe I shouldn't have brought Charlie with me

STELLA

You gotta rip the Band-Aid off at some point, sweetie

Yeah I know 😭

⌘ ⌘ ⌘ ⌘

Stella arranges for Charlie to come to her place and stay with her two-year-old son, Max, and his grandma so I can go out with her and her husband, Jack. In her words: "the quiet before the storm will do you some good."

I don't argue. A night out with two of my oldest friends is exactly what I need. Jack ran around in our same friend group until he and Stella finally admitted their feelings for one another after graduation and got married a few years after.

Stella is fun, optimistic, and soft when it comes to this world. Everyone needs a friend like her. I only wish she and I didn't live so far apart.

Charlie and I have a rideshare driver drop us off at Stella's, who assures me Jack won't be drinking more than a beer or two and will take both Charlie and me back to Dottie's tonight. Their yard is small, but the landscaping is immaculate with topiaries in large gray planters on both sides of the front door.

Charlie lets me hold her hand as we walk up the steps and onto Stella's porch. But after I knock and Jack opens the door, she lets go. She puts on a brave smile even as she twirls the string from her hoodie around her finger.

"Hey, Rosie." Jack joins me on the porch and wraps me up in a hug. "It's been a long time."

"It has. Too long." In Jack's embrace, warmth washes over

me. It's another reminder that Golden Harbor wasn't just Dottie's home. It was mine too.

"Sorry I missed you last night when you came by. I got caught up at the office." He steps aside, waving an arm for me and Charlie to enter their house.

"No apology needed. I'm way too familiar with that."

"I heard your boyfriend is quite the big shot in Seattle, huh?" There's teasing in his tone.

I waggle my fingers in front of his face to show off my engagement ring. "Fiancé."

"Wow." He rubs the back of his neck. "Is this news?"

I breathe out a laugh. "For you, yes. But don't worry. The secret is already out."

"Yeah? For Stella, or Beck too?" He purses his lips and shifts his footing from side to side uncomfortably.

"This is Charlotte." I clutch Charlie's shoulders, using her as a scapegoat to block his question.

Jack smiles and bends. "It's nice to meet you, Charlotte."

She extends her small hand to shake Jack's like she's a grownup and it throws him for a second. West and his manners have been rubbing off on Charlie.

Max zooms down the hallway toward us and runs right into Jack's arms. He's a perfect combination of both parents. Jack's black hair and Stella's big smile. I try not to think about which of Charlie's features resemble Beck. The truth is, there're too many to count.

"Hey, Rosie," Stella calls, rushing down the hall after Max. "Jack's mom is already here, ready to go?"

"More than ready."

4

BECK

The Sandbar has been open for as long as I can remember. Red painted walls, green lighting, and an even darker green carpet gives off a 70's aesthetic. But it's a popular hangout for locals—not quite overtaken by tourists—making it one of my favorite places in town.

Though it probably isn't the ideal location for a first date. But I don't know how interested I am in this date going well. Sasha is smart—she works with Jack at his accounting firm—and she's gorgeous. She's tall with long legs and it's obvious she knows they're her best feature because she's dressed in a short skirt and knee-high boots.

When she bends across the pool table to line up her shot, I get a clearer view of just how short her skirt is. My gaze travels up the length of her legs, zoning in on her backside. My skin heats and I can't resist stepping up behind her.

"Need some help with that?" I growl in her ear, resting my palms on either side of the table.

She glances over her shoulder and her eyes crinkle as a pretty smile stretches on her face. It reveals her age, but I don't mind an older woman. It's sexy. It's different. And different is better than familiar. She just might be the woman to break me from my dry spell.

"I'm confident in my skills with a stick," she replies suggestively, dragging a lazy finger down my chest, stopping at the waistband of my jeans. "I don't think I'm like the young women you're used to dating."

I'm instantly aroused. I wrap my fingers around her hip and grip her firmly. "You're right. You're not. And that's what I like about you."

She rolls her eyes and gives me a playful push in the center of my chest. "You don't know anything about me."

I exhale a breath, smirking, and take a step back. Crossing my arms, I go right back to admiring her round ass while she takes her shot. She's right to be confident. She hits the cue ball at just the right spot. It strikes her striped ball, spinning and gliding across the table before landing in a corner pocket.

Sasha straightens and flicks her wrist. "What can I say? I've been playing pool since you were probably in grade school."

I know what she's doing. She's trying to push me away. But it's having the opposite effect. Age is just a number. And I don't mind her number.

"Then maybe you should be the one teaching me." I lean in close to her, dropping my eyes to hers. "I'll be a good student."

She throws back her head and laughs. "You have a comeback for everything, don't you?"

"I've been known to say the right thing at the right time on occasion, I suppose."

She settles on, "I think you're a flirt," then sashays toward her drink on the table near us.

From the corner of my eye, a blast from my past is suddenly standing in my personal space. Instant dread fills my limbs, weighing me down.

"Tell me, Beck, when have you ever said the right thing at the right time?" Rosie challenges, determination flashing in her eyes.

"Rosie," I groan, glaring at her with intention. "What are you doing here?"

"What? Last I checked, you don't own Golden Harbor. Or the Sandbar. Unless..."

In this moment, dang, I wish I did own The Sandbar. That would've been the ultimate comeback. But sadly, no.

"I didn't mean here, I meant *here*—" I wave my hand between Sasha and me. "Interrupting my date."

She glances at me and then Sasha. "Oh, I'm sorry, I didn't realize this was a date. But why am I not surprised you wouldn't up your game in the last ten years? The Sandbar is after all, your favorite place to take a woman."

"Am I missing something?" Sasha asks, doe-eyed.

"No," I mutter. "She was just leaving, weren't you?" I narrow my eyes at Rosie again, hoping she'll take the hint.

But Rosie glares right back. She never was one for backing down. It's the reason she and I argued so much. The way she used to piss me off...

But the making up? That made it worth it. My skin heats at the memory and my imagination runs wild. I've got her bent over this pool table and I'm tight against her, thrusting deliciously slow, exactly how she likes it. My mouth waters and I allow my eyes to rake over her, pausing at the way her pale yellow top hugs her chest. She always did look amazing in yellow.

Staring directly in my eyes, Rosie says, "Leaving? Of course not, *honey*." She bats her eyelashes at me, her jaw set, and before I know it—we're in a showdown. "Why don't you introduce me to your date?"

"Rosie," I say through gritted teeth, feeling my nostrils flare.

She steps closer. "Last night I was honey."

"Last night?" Sasha's brows lift. "I think I should go."

I take a hold of her arm. "No, no. No. Please, stay." Exhaling a long breath, I mutter, "Sasha, Rosie, Rosie, Sasha."

Sasha puts out her hand reluctantly. Something tells me there won't be a second date. "Nice to meet you."

Rosie shakes it. "It's so nice to meet you, Sasha. I'm Rosie, Beck's wife."

I throw my head back. "Dammit Rosie."

"You're married?" Sasha shrieks, tugging her arm free from my grip. "I knew there had to be something. But married?" She picks up her purse from the chair.

"No. Sasha, wait."

"You're either married or you're not. Which is it?"

"It's...complicated."

"Beck, it's been fun. Really." With a palm to my cheek, she gives it a pat. "But I don't have time for complicated." She storms off.

I watch her go before whipping around to face Rosie, who has too big of a smile on her face. "You happy?"

She narrows her eyes, taking a few small steps closer until the toes of our boots touch and she has to peer up at me. "No. Sign the divorce papers. Then I'll be happy."

"You're unbelievable." I grit my teeth and tear off my hat, running my fidgeting hand through my hair. "What happened, you moved to Seattle and forgot your manners? Forgot how to be a civilized person? Jeez, Rosie."

Stella and Jack approach, and I should've known Stella would bring Rosie to The Sandbar. It's not like there's many options in Golden Harbor.

"Hey, Beck. I thought you were busy tonight. How've you been?" Jack gives me a fist bump.

"Been better," I mutter, shoving my hat back on my head. "Thanks to this one." I hike a thumb in Rosie's direction.

With her hands on her hips, she says, "Nuh-uh, don't blame me for your date going south. You brought it on yourself."

Stella cringes as she mindlessly offers Rosie a beer. "You were on a date?"

"Yeah. I *was*." I glare at Rosie again.

"Tell him to sign the divorce papers and he will be free to go on however many dates he wants." She presses the bottle to her lips and takes a drink.

"Free?" I snap. "Apparently that didn't stop you," I grit out.

"I didn't mean free, of course...Not like that. I just meant, ya know, I won't get in the way and mess up any more of your dates." She stumbles over her words.

For a second I think she might actually feel guilty that she's moved on. That she's shacking up with some rich asshole. But why should she? Just because a piece of paper says we're still married doesn't mean anything. Clearly it doesn't mean anything to her.

"Wait..." Jack speaks slowly, his eyes flicking between me and Rosie, his head tilted slightly. "You two are still married?"

I glance down at my boots.

"It's not like I haven't tried. Beck won't sign the papers." Rosie tosses a hand in my direction.

I can't help but look at her, as though I'm waiting for her to continue spilling our business to everyone at this entire bar.

"You knew?" Jack asks Stella.

"No," she blurts. "Not until today. And don't give me that look. It wasn't my place to say anything. This is their drama."

"We don't have drama. It's just this one thing. And then after the memorial, I'll be gone."

Leaning in closer, I narrow my eyes at her. "Is that a promise?"

"But I thought you were going to stay in Golden Harbor for a while. Dottie had Beck remodel the cottage," Stella interjects.

I swing my gaze to Stella. "Are you kidding me? Is that why

Dottie hired me? To get the cottage ready for Rosie? She told me it was to get it ready to go on the market."

"I'm sure that's why. Dottie never said anything to me about coming to Golden Harbor to stay," Rosie assures us. "I have a life back in Seattle."

I groan. "Yeah, so you keep reminding us. Ya know what, Rosie? Why don't you do everyone a favor and get back to it already. Get back to your perfect life in Seattle. And leave us the hell alone." I take a swig of my beer. "None of us need your pity or reminders that you moved on without us."

"What? No." She bites on her lower lip and her fingers fidget with the label on her beer bottle. When she opens her mouth to speak again, she looks at Stella. "I never said that. I never said my life was perfect, or whatever it is he's insinuating."

"Yeah? And how often did you come back to see Dottie? How often have you come back to see Stella? Your so-called best friend."

Rosie sniffs and her eyes water even while she's trying to glare at me. "That's not fair."

"Hey, okay you two. That's enough. We're done taking this guilt trip down memory lane." Stella gives Rosie a pool stick. "Let's all play some pool and get another beer."

"You expect me to stay and hang out with her?" I stab a finger at Rosie.

"I do. Because we all used to be friends. We should be able to hang out together."

"Just like old times." Jack hooks his arm around my neck.

I can appreciate the sentiment, but it doesn't help. I shrug out of his hold. "Fine," I grunt.

Screwing her lips up to one side, Rosie's glare is hard and purposeful. "Fine," she says, looking right at me.

"Great," Stella says with forced enthusiasm. "Maybe you wanna get us some more drinks?"

I swing a cold gaze to Rosie. "Sure. Why not? Does *my wife* want another beer?"

She rolls her eyes, flipping her dark auburn hair off her shoulder. "Don't call me that."

"Oh, yeah, you're right, Stella. This night is gonna be fun," I mutter, then stalk off to the bar.

5

ROSIE

*W*hen Charlotte was born, I started only drinking socially. And I don't drink more than a glass or two of wine. Especially since West and I began dating. He splurges on the expensive stuff and one glass is all it takes for me to get a little tipsy.

But something about being back in Golden Harbor, at the Sandbar, and surrounded by my old friends has me loving the taste of cheap beer and losing track of how many I've had. Stella reassures me Jack is only having one and will get me and Charlie back to Dottie's safely. It's a good thing because every time I see Beck's stupidly handsome face, I have another drink.

It's more stupid than handsome. But even still. It's his face. Here, right before me and no longer only haunting my dreams.

Since Beck's date ditched him, Stella thought it would be a great idea to invite him to play a game of pool with us. But one game led to two, and now three. The entire time, Beck and I have managed to only exchange a few words. But the tension in the air is as thick as early morning fog blanketing the ocean.

"Your turn," I call to Beck while he's propped on a stool grimacing with his arms crossed.

He stands and shuffles past me. "Yeah, yeah, chill. Don't get your panties in a wad," he grumbles, his gaze moving over my face with distaste.

"Too bad that's not possible. Because I'm not wearing any panties," I taunt, not backing down. The alcohol is doing its purpose and not only taking the edge off the pain radiating in my low back, but also giving me a sense of bravery.

His brown eyes widen and his jaw ticks. I almost let a smile slip, but I won't give him the satisfaction that this banter between us is amusing me. He glances away and I exhale a sigh. If he looked at me any longer, I wouldn't have been able to resist saying something else.

As Beck readies his shot, he spins his hat backward and the action has me spinning with it. My knees weaken and I'm caught off guard. This simple act has me suddenly feral for a man I'm not supposed to have feelings for anymore.

My gaze moves over his body slowly. The way his back arches, it's not hard to notice the muscles that take shape as his shirt stretches. His bicep swells as he grips the stick and leans across the pool table. I don't know what he's been up to all these years while I've been away, but he's definitely doing something to keep himself fit.

I bite my lip as I continue studying his features, tilting my head to admire the way his backside still fills out a pair of jeans nicely. His brow lifts while he concentrates. It's the same, but somehow different. Because Beck isn't the boy I fell in love with and left. He's older. He's a man now.

He straightens and turns to face me, and I feel exposed. I draw in a breath and the corner of his lip curls up.

But he doesn't call me on it. "Your turn," he quips.

Squinting my eyes, I scrutinize him. But I don't overthink it. The alcohol is numbing my senses, and I won't allow myself to.

I grab my stick and shuffle closer to the pool table. I'm

about to attempt a strategic shot when Milo Stone enters the bar.

He gives me a wide smile from across the room as he makes his way over.

"Rosie Stone," he greets before wrapping me up in a hug I don't feel like I deserve.

"Milo. Hey...it's good to see you." My words come out muffled in the crook of his neck. I don't bother correcting him that I've been going by my maiden name since I left.

"I was hoping you'd come." He releases me but still holds his smile. "Guess I shouldn't be surprised the first place I'd run into is The Sandbar with Beck."

"Whoa," I say, quick to correct him. "I'm not with Beck. I came with Jack and Stella. Beck just happened to be here."

Milo chuckles. "Sure. Whatever you say. And that's why you're playing pool...together." He raises his brows, unconvinced.

"It's true. In fact, Beck was here on a date."

Milo's smile fades. "For real? You didn't mention anything about a date."

"I don't tell you everything," Beck mutters. "You're my little brother, not my therapist."

"Bet you don't tell Dr. Sam everything either," Milo shoots back.

I swing my attention to Beck, my chest tightening. "You have a therapist?"

Beck rolls his eyes. "Don't start feeling some kind of existential guilt or something, he's just busting my balls. Of course I don't see a therapist."

"Oh." I bite the side of my lower lip, unable to stop my brain from feeling remorseful. Like I have somehow contributed to Beck seeing a therapist when he never would have before.

Milo fist-bumps his shoulder. "So a date, huh? Who with?"

"Doesn't matter," Beck grumbles.

"You're not still seeing that cougar from LA, are you?"

I can't help myself; I snort out a laugh.

"The woman with the legs…who Jack set you up with?"

"Like I said," Beck growls, giving his brother a death look, "doesn't matter. It's over with."

"Well, what do you say, Rosie. We should get a beer and catch up," Milo suggests.

Getting a beer with Milo Stone feels all kinds of wrong. Milo was just a boy when I left. He can't possibly be old enough to drink, let alone with me.

"I think Rosie has had enough to drink," Beck states, his tone grating against my skin.

I shoot him a glare. "You're not the boss of me," I bite out.

"No. Maybe not. But you are *my wife*."

He holds my eyes captive. I want to be angry with him. But the way he said "my wife" has my emotions and my body reacting in a traitorous way. My skin buzzes and sends a signal between my thighs in an electrifying wakeup call.

"Okay…" Stella interrupts by stepping in between us and I find myself gasping for a full breath. "I think it's time we got going."

"Already? But Milo just got here," Jack argues.

"I can take Rosie back to Dottie's," Beck suggests. My mouth pops open, ready to argue, but then he continues. "There's some things we need to talk about."

Stella looks at me, her dark brows raised in question. Confusion mixes with the alcohol and causes my brain to overload. Part of me wants to go with Beck. He's connected to every memory I have in Golden Harbor.

But in my current state, I fear I will say something I'll regret. Or hell, *do* something I'll regret. I don't trust my consciousness to make choices for me in this state.

When I glance down to compose myself and shake away this strange desire for Beck, the weight of the sparkling diamond on my finger is the reminder I need. "It's fine, Beck can drop me off on his way. I need to get some sleep. Big day tomorrow."

Stella gives me a hug, but before she lets me go, she whispers into my hair so only I can hear. "We'll bring Charlie home soon."

My mind snags on Charlie's name. Is tonight the night I tell Beck about his daughter? Or will it be better when I can form coherent thoughts and sentences? Do I wait until Dottie's memorial, or tell him afterward so we don't cause a scene?

"Thank you."

Beck says goodbye to Milo, and I follow reluctantly. At the door, he opens it and ushers me out first. I roll my eyes as I pass. Whatever that feeling was for Beck, it's fleeting. Chalk it up to alcohol and muscle memory.

The night is clear, the sky dark and spanning with bright stars. Despite the blanket of warmth in the air, I cross my arms. "I may have agreed to you driving me home, but I never agreed to talking."

"Fine." He bends, sticking his head in my personal space and forcing me to make eye contact with him. "Then I'll do the talking and you can just sit there and listen. How about that?"

"Ugh." I drag out the word on an exaggerated groan.

He opens the passenger door for me. My gaze scans the bold black letters on the side of his truck before I climb inside: *Stone Construction.*

My stomach drops. I want to be hurt at the realization that when Beck finally accomplished his dream job, I wasn't around to witness it. "You actually did it. You started a construction company?" Grabbing on to the handle, I grip it, and when I pull myself up, pain shoots through my entire core, landing in my butt. I audibly hiss and he props a sturdy hand underneath my elbow, helping me inside with the kind of care and gentleness I remember well.

"How?" I exhale a low breath. "With what money?" I narrow my eyes, my legs still hanging out the door. "Are you selling drugs or something?"

Beck barks out a laugh and it rumbles in my chest. I purse my lips. "You're not the only one who made something of themselves, ya know?" He shoves my legs inside the truck. "Some of us didn't have to leave Golden Harbor to do it." He shuts the door and stomps around the front to the driver's side.

"I didn't go to Seattle just to start a career," I argue after he slides in behind the wheel. "I needed a change of scenery. I needed to start over."

"Yeah, I don't need the reminder," he bites out.

"I thought you wanted to talk?"

"I did."

"Then, about what?" When he doesn't speak right away, my brain goes to Charlie. My stomach flip-flops and a wave of nausea washes over me. Does he know?

"Tell me the truth."

"What?" The word struggles out.

"Why did you really come back to Golden Harbor? Why come back now? When things are finally going good for me? Are you trying to screw with me?"

When my stomach settles and realization sets in that he doesn't want to talk about Charlie, my eyes go hard. "Despite what you think, Beck, not everything is about you."

"Pfft. I'd never think that. Nothing is ever about me when it comes to you."

This hurts. And it's not true. When I told him it was too hard for me to heal in Golden Harbor, I begged him to come with me. "You know why. I came for Dottie's memorial."

"And that's it?"

"That's it." The lie slips out easily.

"I don't believe you."

"Fine. Don't believe me." I turn my head and focus my

attention out the passenger window at The Sandbar's neon sign flickering.

"If I find out I remodeled Dottie's cottage for you to live in…"

"Ha!" I scoff, whipping my head back in his direction. "Don't you worry. I have no plans of staying in Golden Harbor."

"Good."

As he finally shifts into drive, I hesitate at first, but finally manage, "But, Beck…"

"That's all I needed to know," he interrupts.

It's less than a five-minute drive to Dottie's cottage but we spend it in uncomfortable silence. Beck doesn't even have the truck in park when he says, "I'll see you tomorrow. At the memorial. Good night."

I push open the door, climbing out slowly, my body already grumbling. It's going to retaliate for drinking. I fear it will not be a good night, but rather a night hugging the porcelain goddess. Just one of my many endometriosis symptoms. Sometimes all it takes is one beer and I'm sick. Or I can be sick with no alcohol at all.

"See you tomorrow." I shut the door and shuffle toward Dottie's cottage. The headlights from Beck's Chevrolet shine on the back door. I don't turn back around to glance at him. Not even when I get inside and the lights fade as he drives away.

6

ROSIE

Grandma Dottie always believed a cup of coffee could make or break your day. If it tasted off, your day would be off. If it was perfect, your day would be perfect. It's the reason why Dottie's espresso machine is the most expensive appliance in her entire house.

This morning, I say a quiet prayer over the brim of my mug before I take a sip. I need this Americano to taste better than it ever has before. I close my eyes and take a drink. The robust flavor of the beans mixes smoothly with the creamy oat milk. The combination of honey and cinnamon dances on my tongue.

It's good. It's darn near perfect. And I'll take it.

I gaze out the window at the waves curling and crashing onto the beach. It's high tide. My stomach swims with anticipation, almost like the ocean is calling me like it used to. A day spent surfing and lying out on the warm sand feels like yesterday and somehow, like a million years ago.

"Mama, I need help with my dress." Charlie shuffles into the kitchen, holding both ends of a ribbon at her waistband.

"You look so pretty, baby girl." I set my coffee down on the kitchen island and crouch down behind her.

"I'm not a baby," she groans, throwing her head back dramatically.

This is her new thing. Her new era. She thinks she's grown up since she turned six a few months ago. She hates when I call her by the nickname. But I've always called her baby. At least she doesn't seem to mind Charlie.

"I know you're not." I wrinkle my nose and smile, tying the ribbon at her back while forcing away the emotions of the day that stretches before us. And it's not just the memorial.

Her dress is a soft, light pink. Dottie hated black. Having Charlie wear it to her memorial service wasn't even an option. Dottie loved blues, pastels, and coastal colors. Just like me. Or at least, what I used to love.

Now I usually dress in black. It's easiest and the most professional-looking to wear to the salon. The rest of the stylists all wear black and I want to fit in. Plus, West prefers me in black. He says it's flattering and makes me look sophisticated.

While Charlie had plenty of dresses to choose from, I had to buy a new one. I found a flowy periwinkle dress with skinny straps and a V-neck at a boutique in Bellevue. I packed it without showing West. My nerves are already high; I didn't want to stress more if he hated it. Besides that, it isn't my normal style or color. But I like it. It feels like something the old Rosie would wear. And it makes my chest look spectacular.

"C'mon, Charlie, we gotta go."

I usher her out the back door, locking it behind us and carrying her booster seat under my arm. We go around to the detached garage, and I push the button for the garage door opener. A smile spreads on my lips as soon as I see Dottie's Mini Cooper convertible. It's red, it's shiny, and it's so Dottie.

"Oooo it's so pretty," Charlie coos.

Unbridled emotion hits me like a shovel to the face. My

eyes water, and it takes a few swallows before I get out words. "It really is."

I put Charlie's booster seat in the back and she climbs inside, buckling herself in.

"Does the top come off like Weston's car?"

West has a BMW convertible. He almost never puts the top down. For one, it's Seattle. It rains one hundred sixty days a year. For two, he's too afraid the wind will tousle his hair. But if Charlie begs enough, he gives in.

"It does. But don't even think about asking. It's still cold and we don't want to mess up our pretty hair before the memorial, right?" I slide behind the steering wheel and catch her frowning in the rearview. "After the memorial, I promise we'll put the top down."

Her face brightens. "Pinky swear?"

"Pinky swear."

Grandma Dottie didn't want a traditional funeral or a gravesite service, but she did agree to a memorial at the park in the center of town. I squeeze Charlie's hand as she walks next to me. It's more for me than for her. My heart beats too hard, too fast. But she has nothing to be nervous about. Only I know that she's meeting her father today.

As soon as Charlie sees Jack and Stella's son, Max, she releases my hand and ditches me, running toward them. Stella embraces me after I reach her. She may be petite, but her hugs are tight and comforting. She assures me it's fine for Charlie to sit with them. It's probably best this way, then I can prepare for my reading that the minister told me would come toward the end of the service.

There's a song followed by a few words spoken by the minister at the local Lutheran church. Only by the grace of God do I make it through without crying. But now it's my turn. When Dottie and I last spoke, I promised her I would read her favorite poem by Sylvia Plath.

The walk to the podium feels impossibly long, but my brain can't seem to wrap around the fact that's only a few feet. After I reach the microphone, I don't glance at the crowd of people. I can't risk making eye contact with anyone if I want to make it through. Especially not Beck. If we lock eyes, I will combust into a bucket of uncontrollable tears.

But suddenly it's dawning on me that I don't even know if he's here. Maybe I pissed him off last night when I interrupted his date. Or the night before, when I told him I was getting married.

But I can't risk it. Searching for him will only force me to see the solemn faces of those here. Lifetime friends of Dottie's. No other family though. My parents couldn't be bothered with cutting their Italy trip short. I try to put Beck and everyone else out of my mind and focus on my reading.

At first, my words come out shaky, vibrating between the quiet sobs I try but fail at holding back. I swallow and push through it. No one is coming to save me from this or the reality that Grandma Dottie is truly gone.

The rest of the service is a blur after I return to my seat. I don't know if anyone else spoke or sang. Or cried aloud. The only thing I'm very certain of is how alone I feel at this moment.

The park empties slowly, some people filter toward the buffet set up with drinks and snacks, but I amble toward the tribute table. There's a framed photo of Dottie in her happy place. She's on the beach wearing a wide-brimmed straw hat and a blue pantsuit. There are a few candles, a small garden shovel, and even a pound of espresso beans from her favorite roasting company in Ojai, California. My lips pull into a smile at this little detail.

The poem I just read out loud has been typed up and printed and framed. In a smaller frame there's a photo of Dottie and me. My chest expands and my heart threatens to push through my ribs. Tears pool in my eyes again.

I pick up the frame so I can get a closer look. It doesn't take me long to recognize when the photo was taken. I'm wearing a nice but simple white dress, and my hair is pulled up with a few wispy auburn curls framing my face.

My wedding day.

"You looked beautiful that day." Beck's voice sounds from over my shoulder.

I jerk and spin to find him hovering behind me. He takes the frame from me and studies it. A fresh tear slips from my eye, and I quickly swipe it off my cheek.

"I mean, you looked beautiful every day," he continues, but I can't speak, so I just watch him and listen. "But on that day, you were stunning. I'd never seen you smile so much. I thought your face might freeze that way." He chuckles, but his eyes are watering. "And I was perfectly fine with that. Because your smile...was my favorite thing to look at."

"Beck," I whisper on an exhale, except I don't know what else to say. The memories from that day hit me like a punch to the gut. So real and raw, forever carved into my brain. Like a tattoo in my mind.

"I was happy," I finally admit. It's seven years too late. But it's true. I *was* happy then. Though happiness wasn't enough to hold us together.

His Adam's Apple bobs as he swallows. "We were, weren't we?"

I stay quiet at first. His question feels rhetorical. Like he just needs the confirmation. And if I can't give him anything else, I can at least give him that.

"Yeah," I whisper, and another tear slips out.

"Mama?" Charlie calls.

And what has been the sweetest sound since Charlie

learned how to say the word suddenly shatters the fleeting sincere moment we just shared.

I whirl around as Charlie skips toward me. Swiveling my head at Beck, I find him looking at her in a daze. Slightly confused, maybe slightly curious. I sidestep away from the table and into the grass to give us some space I have a feeling we'll need.

Charlie reaches me and hugs my leg. "Can I have a cupcake? Pleeeeease?" The word drags out and hisses because of her missing front teeth. "Miss Stella said I had to ask you."

I sniff and wipe the traces of tears off my face before she can see them. Crouching, I take her by the hand. My heart beats wild and desperate in my chest. This moment has played in my mind countless times over the last six years.

And now, it's finally happening.

I suck in a deep breath as my eyes dance over her angelic face. "Charlotte, there's someone I'd like you to meet."

At first, she looks annoyed. But she's inquisitive, much like her father. She glances up at Beck, who has joined me in the grass, her big brown eyes squinting as she scrutinizes him. I can't help but wonder if he's looking into her eyes too. If he's seeing the familiarity in them. If he's putting the pieces together.

A boulder sized lump sits in my stomach. "This is my... friend, Beck. Beck, this is Charlotte, my daughter."

In true Charlotte fashion, she sticks her little hand out. "Charlie," she corrects me.

I almost breathe out a laugh. She always makes me laugh. But I'm too anxious about this particular introduction.

Beck shakes her hand and gives her a tight smile. "Hi, Charlie. It's nice to meet you."

She purses her lips and tilts her head, and I hold my breath. Does she see it? The similarities between them? Does she feel it? The connection I'm sure they hold even though they've never met?

But she turns and faces me. "Now can I have a cupcake, please?"

My eyes flutter closed while I exhale, relief filling me. "Yes. But only one. And stay with Stella while I finish talking with Beck.

"Okay, Mama." She skips away happily.

It's not the moment I had pictured in my head. But at the very least, it goes smoothly. And I really can't ask for more.

"You're a mom," Beck finally says as Charlie is reaching for a chocolate cupcake off the buffet table.

It's not really a question, more of a statement. But I answer him anyway. "Yep."

"She looks like you."

"Yep," I say, wobbly. Because she does. She has my red hair, but hers is a darker strawberry blonde rather than my dark auburn. And she has my upturned nose. But her eyes are his. And so is her dimpled chin.

"Charlotte huh? As in Dorthea Charlotte?" he asks, still looking at Charlie.

He's putting it all together, I know he is. I fear I don't have much time before he figures it out. Stella advised me to just get it out, rip off the Band-Aid. She said it would be better for him —for everyone—to get it over with. But after holding this secret in for so long, releasing it isn't easy.

I nod, the tears building again and threatening to spill. "I didn't think there would be anyone better to name her after."

"Huh." He scratches at the back of his head before resting his fidgeting hands on his waist where his black belt is clasped, causing his suit jacket to flare backward. "I didn't even know you had a kid. I'm surprised Dottie, or Jack or Stella, never said anything." He's studying Charlie, possibly taking notice of her features. The ones that don't match mine. Maybe he's even doing the math. Counting the years I've been gone.

I don't speak. I can't. My voice, my words, have vanished.

Finally, he rips his focus away from Charlie and gazes at me. "How old is she?"

The tears escape from my eyes, racing down my cheeks, and I break. My body trembles and I cross my arms to try to stop it, attempting to hold myself together.

"Rosie." He mutters my name quietly but sternly, and it rattles me. "How old is she?"

I shake my head and quietly sob, hugging myself. This is it. The moment of truth.

7

———

BECK

$\mathcal{M}$y skin heats. It starts at the back of my neck and seeps into my face. The tips of my ears burn.

It takes what feels like an eternity for Rosie to answer. Meanwhile, my body is on overdrive. My legs and arms fill with lead. A whirling sensation crams my thoughts, causing my head to pound.

She swipes a knuckle under her nose and sniffs. "Six. She's six," she whispers.

"Rosie—" Her name comes out broken. I throw my hands up and run them across the top of my head and down the nape of my neck. *She can't be. It's not possible. Can she?* "Charlie...is she...?"

But somehow, I already know before Rosie speaks and confirms it. The undeniable truth is visible on her face. In her body language. Because I know her.

And maybe because I could spot the Stone family resemblance on the little girl. Spot *my* likeness.

Rosie meets my eye, and her gaze sends an ache deep in my gut. With a small, pitiful smile, she wipes her cheeks and finally whispers, "She is."

And now I'm crying.

"Charlotte is your daughter."

"Shit. Rosie. Are you kidding me?" I blurt.

She dips her chin and tucks her hair behind her ear. "I know, I know."

"No," I mutter, "you don't know." I bend to meet her eyes with mine and draw her face upward. "What the hell?"

"I'm sorry," she says on a sob.

"You're sorry? You're *sorry*? Rosie." I clench my hands into fists and whip around, stalking away several feet before spinning back and pacing toward her again. "We had a baby, and you didn't tell me? I thought...I thought we lost her."

"I know. But—"

My vision blurs and I scratch at my stubbled chin. "This doesn't make sense. You...the bleeding...and cramping...you miscarried?"

She shakes her head. "That's what we thought. What we assumed. But about a month after I left, I missed my period, so I made an appointment. And they did an ultrasound and... there she was."

"How could you do this? How could you not tell me?"

She reaches for my arm, but I wrench it out of her grasp. "I meant to. I planned to. I was going to call. Then I thought it would be better if I came to tell you in person. But then one month turned into two, and two into three, and so on. And you knew I was in Seattle. Dottie told me she told you. And you never came after me. You never even called."

I stab a finger at her. "No. Don't blame me for this."

"I know, I'm sorry, but please calm down," she hisses like a warning.

I pinch the bridge of my nose as I pace back and forth again. "And now, you show up here, six years later. What am I supposed to do with this?"

"Please," she pleads.

I stop in front of her, my eyes hardening as a sharp pain shoots through my chest. "No. You don't get to tell me to calm down."

"Please don't cause a scene like you always do."

"Excuse me? *Me*? I think you've got that backward, honey." I glare. "But at least I've got a good excuse. I just found out I have a kid. That I'm a father."

"I know. And I know you probably have a lot of questions, but this isn't the place or the time for this conversation."

I exhale a long, low breath. I gaze into Rosie's eyes. The pain and regret I see in them doesn't compare to what I'm feeling.

"Did Dottie know?"

She nods and I shut my eyes tight, pushing out a traitorous tear.

"It wasn't her place to tell you. And I asked her not to."

"Yeah," I mutter, "and I guess she was quick to bend to your demands." Charlotte and Max run past us with Stella following behind them, trying and failing at being nonchalant.

"Did Jack and Stella know?"

She purses her lips. "Yes. But then that's it. Other than my parents."

I run a palm down my face and groan. "I'm such an idiot. This whole time...I thought you miscarried. And everyone knew you didn't but me. And I bet they all think I'm some kind of deadbeat dad, huh?"

"No, of course not. They know you had no idea you're a father."

"Ha!" I scoff. "That's the thing, Rosie. I'm *not* a father. You can't be a father when you never knew a kid existed. You took that away from me. Don't you get that?" I turn and stalk away.

"Wait," she calls. "I can reintroduce you. So she'll know too."

"Don't bother," I grit out over my shoulder as I stalk off.

If I was like my father after receiving bad news, I'd be taking a twelve-pack of beer and my shotgun up to Golden Pointe. There were a few times I had to drive up there and rescue him. I'd find him near passed out, empty cans shot up and scattered. He'd curse at me while I forced him into my truck and buckled him into the passenger seat. Like somehow, his screwups and bad life choices were my fault.

But I took it. Him shoving me around and the verbal abuse. I couldn't risk Milo being taken away. I had to protect him, protect his childhood by keeping our family together.

And now I have this other family I couldn't protect because I didn't even know she existed.

I drive to the beach and park on the street against the curb. Before I hop out of my Chevy, I strip off my suit jacket, and wish I had my surfboard with me. I slip off the black dress shoes and socks and amble onto the sand barefoot. The beach is about the only place that works to clear my head and give me clarity.

My feet reach the cool sand and a shiver races up my legs. I keep walking until my toes dip in the ocean. The rush of frigid waves focuses my thoughts and feelings. And they're ones I don't want to face.

Rosie had so many health issues we didn't think it was possible for her to have children. The painful cramps came on days outside of the typical week-long periods I'd learned about in school. Rosie was facing something entirely different than the average girl.

Some days her body was too exhausted to even get out of bed for her cosmetology school in LA. I tried to help when I could. Be there to drive her or cook for her. There had been a handful of late-night ER trips filled with tears, ultrasounds, and unanswered questions.

A few years into our marriage, I'd accepted that I wouldn't ever be a father. And if I'm being honest with myself, I was okay with that. I have too many painful emotions tied to the concept of fathers. When I thought Rosie miscarried and our relationship ended, my dreams of ever being a father ended as well.

But like it or not, I *am* a father.

In my periphery I see Milo heading down the beach. He's changed out of his suit and is back in his typical gym clothes. When he reaches me it's hard to hold back from expelling everything I just learned.

"How'd you know I was here?"

"Because you always come here when you're pissed off at the world." He picks up a seashell and chucks it into the waves.

"And how'd you know I was pissed?"

"I saw you talking to Rosie. More like I *heard* you talking to Rosie."

"Yeah? And what did you hear?" I grunt.

Milo shrugs. "Not much. But it sounded like a heated discussion."

"Did you hear that I'm a father?" I rush out.

He jerks his head to look at me, his eyes huge. "What?"

"Yep. Apparently the little girl with Rosie...is my...daughter."

"What the hell?"

"I know. I had the same reaction." My skin tingles as the earlier conversation replays through my mind.

"How is that possible? She's been gone for, what? Six or seven years? How old is the girl?"

I look at him—deadpan. "Almost seven."

He props his hands on his hips. "You're sure she's yours?"

"Milo," I mutter on a released breath. "Have you seen her?

She looks like me. Hell, she looks like you. That girl is definitely a Stone."

Milo lets out a low whistle. "I can't believe she had a baby and never told you. What are you gonna do?"

I shake my head. "I don't know." I dig my toes into the wet sand. "What can I do?"

"I hate to say it, but now that you know, bro, you can't just be an absent father."

Of course I can't. I won't. But I don't know how this is going to work. "Her life is in Seattle, mine is here. What am I supposed to do? Just move over there and start over? I don't even know the girl. What if she wants nothing to do with me? What if she hates me for not being around these last six years?"

Milo glances out toward the ocean and shakes his head slowly. "I don't know. But what I do know is you're not gonna let this go. You're too good of a person. Even if she ends up pushing you away."

"What if I don't have a choice?"

"Don't give her the choice."

"What if I suck at being a dad?" I finally ask the question that's been haunting me since I heard the news. "We didn't have the best example."

He turns to face me. "You're gonna be an awesome dad. You know how I know?" But he doesn't wait for me to answer. "Because you were an awesome dad to me," he admits, the honesty of his words hanging in the air between us. "You stepped up to be a father figure for me. And now, you get to do it for this little girl. *Your* little girl."

"That was different. I had to."

"That's bullshit. You didn't have to. And you need to stop saying that. What you did was selfless. Not just anyone would do that, but you did."

My eyes burn.

"But now, I'm good. Thanks to you. And Dad is coming

around. Now that he's sober, he's trying to make up for lost time. We'll get there."

"What are you suggesting? That I move to Seattle? Because that's crazy." I shove my hands through my hair and slide them to the back of my neck, interlocking my fingers.

"I'm not saying that. All I'm saying is maybe keep an open mind. But you need to start with getting to know this little girl. Because you're probably right, she's going to have a lot of questions."

Turning to face the waves, I stuff my hands in my pockets. A few seagulls swoop down to the sand to peck at a crab that's belly-up. "Yeah, and how am I supposed to answer them?"

"With honesty. That's what I would want of our dad."

Sounds so simple. But it's anything but. "How'd your ass get so wise?"

"I had a great role model."

I glance at him and he's looking at me, grinning. I hook my arm around his neck and haul him into my side. He allows a second of brotherly love before he retreats, breaking free from my hold and then tackling me from behind.

He may be grown up, but he's still my kid brother and I know him. He'd rather roughhouse than get emotional or affectionate. So I let him lighten the mood.

He nearly takes me down, but I've got a least an inch on him and use it to my benefit. I escape and he chases me before hopping onto my back to try to take me out that way and we both end up in the water.

8

BECK

"Thanks for squeezing me in this morning." I jiggle my knee while my fingers fidget in my lap. The scent of cucumber melon filling the small office triggers unwelcome memories of my mom to flicker into my mind.

My gaze takes a trip around the room, trying to look at anything but Dr. Sam Bailey. The office is void of color. The couch is beige, her desk and chair are both white, the boho artwork on the walls vary in shades of ivory, white, and light beige. My brain fixates on the wonder of why this is. Maybe to avoid distracting her patients. But it's having the opposite effect on me.

"You're welcome," she replies. She crosses her legs in the white pants. *Enough with the white already*, I want to shout. But instead, I suck in a deep breath and release it. "You said it was urgent. Why don't you tell me what's going on?"

"So...yeah," I begin, though not really sure where to start, so I go back. "Remember when I told you about my wife and I... miscarrying?"

She nods, and her brunette hair pulled back in a smooth, tight ponytail moves with the gesture. "I do."

I prop my ankle on top of my other thigh and rest my elbows across my legs so my fingers stop fidgeting. "It turns out...she didn't."

Dr. Sam tilts her head, her brows pinching together.

"Right?" I toss one of my hands up. "My reaction exactly."

"So, you're telling me she didn't lose the baby?"

"Nope. And now, that baby is six. I have a daughter who is six. And my wife just showed up here with her. In Golden Harbor. And I don't know what I'm supposed to do with this. With her." I shoot up to my feet and swipe a palm across my forehead. I begin pacing the room, my brain scrambling when I know I should find something to focus on. But maybe everything in this damn office shouldn't be white.

"What you're feeling right now is valid, Beck. These thoughts of confusion are expected when you receive news of this capacity."

No shit, is what I want to say.

"Why don't you sit back down and let's explore these feelings you're experiencing."

I stop pacing and prop my clenched hands on my hips, looking at her. She's here to help, to listen, I remind myself. "I don't need you to placate me, Sam," I grumble out.

I've been coming to see Dr. Sam Bailey for about four years. It took some badgering from Stella and my dad, which is ironic on its own. But if a guy like him, an abuser, an alcoholic, can come out on the other side, I figured there was hope for me.

"Fine." She sits back in her chair. "Let's get down to the nitty-gritty. For starters, that little phrase you mentioned that I couldn't help but snag on."

"Yeah? What's that?"

"The *wife* phrase." Her brows shoot up when my expression hardens and I don't give her an explanation right away. "Beck, you've been coming to see me for years and not once during our sessions have you mentioned that you and Rosie are still married."

I grunt.

"I want to help you, but if you keep things from me, you're making it difficult for me to do so."

"Guess I just forgot to mention it." I finally drop back onto the couch and it's so stiff it doesn't even give out a little from my weight. "When did you get this couch?"

"I don't know," Dr. Sam answers, flustered. "A few weeks ago."

I run my palm over the cushion. The material is soft, almost like velvet but faux velvet. "I liked the old one. It was more comfortable. And it was blue. It suited you better."

"Beck." She says my name on an exhaled sigh. "Let's get back on topic. You and Rosie got married when you were twenty years old, and she left three years later. She's been gone for seven years—why haven't you two got divorced?"

It's the same question Rosie asked. It's the same question I ask myself.

"I don't know, okay?" My voice rumbles in my chest and I shake my head as the regret slides through me. "Sorry. But...I don't know. Maybe part of me held on to hope she'd come back and...we'd get back together."

There's a hum in the room. Maybe it's the diffuser she's got on a side table that's emitting cucumber melon–scented vapor into the air. Maybe it's the sound in my damn head.

"I think, deep down, you knew that wasn't a possibility. You can't expect to live happily ever after without putting in the work. You've got to communicate and go through the hard stuff if you want the reward of the good stuff. Of the good life."

This is why I came to see Dr. Sam today. Because since Rosie left, she's the only person to help me sift through my thoughts and make sense of them.

"So now she's back, with my daughter...and she's engaged." I grind my molars.

Dr. Sam's mouth pops open and a frown line appears between her brows. "That's big news too. So not only did you learn you have a daughter, but that Rosie has moved on."

I hunch my shoulders.

"Let me ask you a question." She looks pointedly at me. "Do you want Rosie to be happy? To be satisfied in her life? Even if it means a life without you?"

That's a loaded question, though she asks it like it's anything but. There are many facets to an answer to a question like that. Of course I want Rosie to be happy. I guess I always thought—

"Say it out loud," she instructs. "What you're thinking, say it out loud."

"Fine," I growl. "Yes. Of course I want her to be happy. I just wanted to be the one she'd be happy with."

"But if you two don't end up together, will you be able to let her go?"

My skin itches below the surface and my knee starts jiggling again. My gaze swings toward the door and as my breathing quickens, I gulp down some air. But all I want is to run out that door.

"Beck?" she calls, her voice sounding distant.

I bring my attention back to her. "Fine. Yeah, I guess I have no choice but to let her go. If she thinks this rich douchebag can make her happy, who am I to stand in her way."

"Good." A small smile appears on her lips, and I can't help but feel like she's won, and I've somehow lost.

"But I didn't ask to see you today because of Rosie. I mean... not really. I needed to see you because I have a daughter. And I don't know what the hell I'm supposed to do with her."

Dr. Sam blinks at me.

"I didn't mean it like that." I push my finger and thumb into my eye sockets with too much force. "I just mean...I don't know how I'm supposed to react. I don't know what to do or say. And what if—?" I stop talking while a thousand scenarios spin through my brain and my heart rate picks up. "What if she doesn't like me. Or worse—what if I don't like her?" I feel like an ass the second the words escape me. Dropping my head, I scoot to the edge of the couch and contemplate my abrupt exit strategy again.

"Those concerns are justifiable. Having a child, being a parent, is a tremendous responsibility. And with your background, it's rational to be apprehensive."

Clasping my hands together, I rest my elbows on my knees and glance up at her. "I never wanted to have kids." Guilt rips through me. "I mean, with my dad, my childhood...And Rosie didn't think she could even have kids what with her medical condition. But then she told me she was late, and the test was positive. She had it confirmed by a doctor. And I was...excited. We swore we were gonna be different than our parents. We would be better." My eyes burn as they gloss over. "I mourned that baby."

There's silence in the room, only that damn diffuser humming again.

"Now that you know, that she survived, what do you want to do with this information, Beck?"

I scratch at the scruff on my chin and sniff. "I think...I think I want to meet her. And maybe get to know her." I shrug. "She looks like me. Maybe she has some of my other traits too."

"I think that's a good idea."

I nod.

"I'm glad you asked to come see me today. And I think we should follow up next week."

"Sounds good. Thanks." I stand and make my way to the door, but then take a detour and yank the diffuser cord from the wall. "This isn't a fucking Bath & Body Works," I grit out.

Dr. Sam's laugh trickles out the door after me.

***

*M*y knees lock and I wipe my sweaty palm down the front of my pantleg while I stand on Dottie's back porch, stalling. I loosen and tighten the grip on the stuffed mermaid doll in my hand. I purchased it from the Seashell Bookshop before I headed over here.

Glancing down at it, suddenly it doesn't feel right. It doesn't feel like enough. How do you show up to meet your daughter for the first time with only a doll?

The door creaks open, the result of saltwater air and time. I startle, jerking my attention up, not knowing if it will be Rosie or the little girl. *My* little girl. It's Rosie who is standing in the open doorway. She smiles and my racing heart stalls in my chest. And dammit, just her smile can help calm my rattled nerves.

But it doesn't take away the years of anger and deep hurt I feel.

She tucks a strand of dark auburn hair behind her ear as she pushes the door open fully. "Come in." It's the same hair I'd once pushed my own fingers through, except it's a bit darker, the red tone muted, and I'm not sure I like that.

She steps aside, allowing me to enter. Dottie's home is filled to the brim with not only memories of her, but of my youth. Of Rosie and me. I glance around but don't see any sign of Charlotte.

"I know I should've called first, but ya know, you should've told me I had a kid," I say harshly, flicking her a stony look over my shoulder.

"Okay, guess we're even then." Even though I know it's sarcastic, it still scrapes my skin.

"Not even close, honey," I grit out, narrowing my eyes.

She folds her lips in, and sadness passes across her expression.

I nearly flinch at my cruelty. But I don't. Any chance Rosie and I had at reconciling ended when she revealed the truth to me about this secret she's been keeping.

"Where is she?" I glance around inside the cottage. Even though I've been here recently, having Rosie here too forces the memories to bleed into the present.

"She's out on the front porch."

I spin and head in the direction, not bothering to take off my boots. I can almost hear Dottie's voice saying *when you're in my house, it's a home. And shoes don't belong in a home.* My chest rumbles with each step I take, and my heart threatens to break free.

"Wait," Rosie calls out, scampering behind me.

Heat fills my cheeks. "What?" I bark, whipping around. "What could you possibly have to tell me now?"

Her brows slant over glassy eyes. "Don't you want to know what I've told her about you?"

Exhaling a long sigh, I run a palm over my stubbled face. The ocean peeks through the slice of the open front door. It's like a calming reminder in this chaotic moment. I do have questions. A lot of questions. But my guess is, that little girl out there has more. And my feelings don't matter as much as hers.

"No," I finally reply. "Because it doesn't matter. I just want to meet my daughter."

"Yeah, okay," she agrees, shaking her head and fidgeting with the cuffs of the sleeves of the yellow sweater she's wearing. "Did you want me to leave you two alone?"

"Something tells me she'd be more comfortable with you

there, and so what I want doesn't matter." Gesturing my chin for her to follow me, I turn and step through the open door.

Charlotte is lying on the porch swing, coloring. The sight of the swing hits me like a blow to the chest. There were many makeout sessions with Rosie on that spot. Many late-night conversations, sunset gazing, tears shed. It's the place I proposed—the first time. And it's the place Rosie told me she was bleeding and cramping, and we assumed we lost the baby.

Now I'm standing here, nearly seven years later, and staring at the very baby I thought I'd lost. The one I mourned. Alone. Because my wife left me.

The irony is not lost on me. That I'd meet Charlotte here. That she'd learn I'm her father in this place. It's a full-circle moment for my and Rosie's relationship.

I push away the nerves threatening to unravel me. "Hey, there, Charlotte," I mumble.

The little girl glances up at me, her crayon stilling in her hand. She gives me a curious look. A slight frown appears on her face.

"Charlie," I quickly correct myself, remembering she prefers the nickname over her given name. That grants me a smile which eases my anxiety somewhat. "Um, hey, do you remember me? From yesterday?"

She bobs her head and sits up, crossing her legs. "From the park."

"Yeah, that's right. I'm Beck."

Her gaze drops to the stuffed mermaid in my sweaty hand. "Is that for me?"

"Charlotte," Rosie hisses from behind me.

"No, no, it's all right." I wave off Rosie. "Yeah. I got it at the bookshop. Do you like mermaids?" I offer it to her.

She pats it, probably wondering why it's damp, but hugs it to her chest anyway. "I love them. Thank you!"

"You're welcome." I exhale a shaky breath, the tension

rolling off my shoulders a little. The sound of seagulls squawk, reminding me why I'm here. "Mind if I sit?"

Charlie shakes her head and scoots over to give me more space.

Rosie leans against the porch railing across from us. "Charlie, Beck has something really important he wants to talk to you about."

I smile at Charlie, taking an extra moment to admire this little girl who has my shade of brown eyes and my dimpled chin.

Here goes nothing.

9

ROSIE

The sound of the waves crashing onto the beach in the distance is muted by the terror battling inside of me. The secret I kept buried and clung so tightly to is about to be revealed to the very person I worked tirelessly to keep it from. Part of me is desperate to put a stop to this before my whole world explodes. But another part is craving the freedom of having it out.

The truth is, Charlie has been asking about her father for years. When she'd see other men with their children at the park, or see her friends being picked up from school by their fathers. The day she asked if West was her dad, I figured she was old enough to learn the truth about hers.

Though I still didn't tell her everything. And not because I didn't think she could handle it. It was because I couldn't.

At such a young age, children's minds are precious. I wanted to protect her from having to grow up too quickly. But I suppose, with my chronic illness, she's had to learn more than most her age.

"So, you know yesterday...when we met at the park? Well, that was the first time I'd ever met you," he begins, his knee shaking so violently the entire swing is responding as if it's in an earthquake simulation. I want so badly to still it, but I keep my distance, the wood railing digging against my back.

She frowns at Beck but she's curious, and by the way her brows pinch, it's obvious she's trying to listen intently.

My heart hammers in my chest while I watch and pray this doesn't turn into a complete trainwreck.

"And that was the first time you'd ever met me," he continues, running his palms across the top of his thigh, and it finally settles to rest. "You knew that I existed before today, but I didn't know about you. I want you to know, that if I had, I would've loved to have met you sooner."

Charlie glances at me and I force a smile to ease any of her apprehensions. Seeing the two of them, side by side, and knowing their anxiety conditions, has my own nerves spiking. I'm not sure how I will be able to calm them if this explodes.

"Your mom just told me...that I'm your...dad," he finally gets out, and the relief on his face is evident. I feel it in my own chest, the tension dissolving. I exhale a long, low breath. "I didn't know about you. I didn't know I had a kid. I didn't know I was a dad." He's sputtering, and by the sounds of it, about to spiral.

I lean in and say, "Remember when you asked about your daddy, Charlie?"

She looks at me and nods her head.

"And I told you that you'd never met him but that you would when the time was right."

"And now the timing is right?" Beck interrupts with a scoff, flashing me a loathing glare.

"You're my daddy?" Charlie ignores us both and stares at Beck, a skeptical look on her face.

There's a delay in Beck's response and for a moment, I worry he's going to deny it. I worry I might have to punch him in the gut and comfort my dejected daughter. But he quickly reminds me of one of the reasons I loved him.

He smiles and nods while propping an elbow onto the back of the wing, then leans closer to Charlie. "Do you see this dimple on my chin? Or is it too hard to see with my beard?"

She gives a slow shake of her head.

"Sorry, I guess I should've shaved. But in my defense, I didn't know I'd be meeting you."

She gives him a little smile.

"Do you know something your mom used to do?" He glances at me and for the first time since being back in Golden Harbor and seeing him, there's a tenderness reflected in his chestnut eyes. Warmth spreads down my limbs. "She used to put her finger on my chin and push it into my dimple."

Charlie giggles and pumps her legs while they dangle off the edge of the swing. "Mama does that to my chin too."

"Really? Well, then see, we've got the same chin."

"What else?" Charlie asks, biting her lower lip.

"Our eyes. You've definitely got my eyes."

My throat constricts as I resist the tears that want to break free. I blink hard to hold back tears. No matter how many times I imagined how this conversation would go, they both surprise me by changing the scenarios I rehearsed.

"Mama says my eyes are beautiful. Did she ever tell you that?" Charlie asks.

When Beck turns his head to look at me, his gaze is soft as he takes me in. I can't resist any longer. The tears well and roll down my cheeks. His eyes lock with mine and my stomach flip-flops when he smiles genuinely at me. It's a smile that used to make my knees wobble, and now, after all these years, I hate to admit it still has the same effect.

"Yeah, Charlie, she did." He finally returns his focus back on her.

"What else?" she asks again, eagerness in her voice.

"I don't know. But I'll bet if we spend some time together, we'll find all kinds of stuff we have in common. Would you like that?"

She smiles and bobs her head excitedly. "Yes! I've been waiting to meet you for my whole life!" She launches herself into his arms, shocking both me and Beck.

And if Charlie's actions weren't enough to completely wreck me, it's his response that does me in. He puts his strong hands on her little back and brings her in close to his chest. It's gentle and reserved. Like he's taking into consideration her boundaries. Afraid to fully wrap her up without her permission.

"Me too," he whispers.

It's faint, but I hear it. And my chest caves inward. Because after learning he didn't lose her when he thought he had, I suppose he has been waiting for her too. I've held on to the guilt of keeping her from Beck all these years. I'm not proud of what I did. I had myself convinced that it was best for not only Charlie and me, but for Beck too. I had no idea what it would do to his life if he learned about her existence. When he never came after me, never attempted to work things out between us, I assumed he'd moved on.

But witnessing this interaction now...The guilt is blaring, front and center. There's nowhere to run or hide, and it threatens to break me. I swipe my finger underneath my running nose, wishing I were anywhere but here.

Charlie pulls away and gazes at Beck with sparkling brown eyes. I watch with intent what she'll do next. She brings up her little pointer finger and puts it up to Beck's chin. Her eyes go big and round and she exclaims, "Ahh, I feel it. I feel your dimple." Beck chuckles and it rumbles in my chest. Now, she takes his long pointer finger and brings the pad of it to her chin so he can feel her dimple too, and my exhale is remorseful. "It's the same."

"Yep, told ya," he agrees, and smiles. But his eyes are watering, and it guts me. He swivels it in a circular motion before bringing his hand down and returning it to his thigh.

Charlie's smile is so big. "Can you sleepover?"

"What?" I shriek, catapulting off the railing like I'm trying to stop a collision. "No, no, Charlie...he can't."

Beck runs a trembling hand over the back of his neck and his eyes dance around. "Uhh, yeah...probably not."

"Probably not?" I whisper-shout, turtling my neck in his direction. What was that response? Not the kind you give a little girl. She's smart. You have to be direct with her.

Pouting, Charlie whines, "Why not?"

"Yeah, why not?" he challenges, crossing his arms.

I glare right back at him. "Because, Beck has his own house to sleep at. But"—I try to come up with a solution fast before she points out that I used to sleep at West's when we had our own place—"he's going to stay for dinner."

He glances up at me and gives me a lopsided grin. "Sure. I'll stay for dinner."

"Fine," Charlie relents, dragging out the word.

"But hey? Maybe tomorrow I can show you one of my favorite places in Golden Harbor. Would you like that?"

Charlie hops up and down on her knees, making the swing shake again. "Yes! Mama, can I go? Please?"

Nerves twist in my stomach. I glance down at my bare feet on the stained wood deck. There's only a handful of people I trust to leave Charlie with. Letting her go with Beck, her father, should be easy. But she doesn't know him. And the truth is, I don't know him anymore either.

"Your mama is welcome to come too, of course."

I lift my chin and mouth, *Thank you*, once his eyes meet mine. "Sounds fun. I'd love to come." It's a pity invite. But he knows me well enough to see my reservations.

"Yay!" She hops off the swing and reaches for Beck's hand. "C'mon, wanna see my room?"

"Um...yeah." He lets her take his hand but is repressed as he follows along behind her. "I'd love that."

"Mama, I'm gonna show my daddy all my stuffed animals, okay?" Her big eyes blink up at me as they pass.

But her use of *my daddy* has a boulder-sized lump lodged in my throat and I can't answer, so I simply dip my chin.

"Mama let me bring six from home. I have an orca and a sea lion." She continues chatting fast while dragging him into the house. "Have you ever seen an orca? Like, in person?"

Beck glances at me over his shoulder and we lock eyes. I dreamed but never truly believed I would hear Charlie refer to Beck as her *daddy*.

I swipe at the fresh tears that race down my cheeks and turn to face the ocean, my hands gripping the railing.

***

It takes an extra book and an unusually long prayer at bedtime before Charlie settles down. And I had to do it all with an audience. This isn't typically something West sticks around for, so it feels new and awkward.

But Charlie insisted Beck stay after dinner and all the way up until she went to bed. Lucky me. Though while I might be overly sensitive and irritated by his sudden presence in Charlie's orbit, it dawns on me that maybe she's worried he won't be here tomorrow.

Beck follows me down the stairs toward the front door. We pass photos on the walls hanging haphazardly. Photos I'm going to be responsible for removing and dispersing somewhere. But my mind can't handle the never-ending list of things I need to take care of during our week here. Not tonight.

The weight from the emotions of the last few days sits heavy on my shoulders and coils around my gut. We reach the landing, and I can feel Beck's eyes on me, steady, resentful. I can almost hear his questions piling on top of one another.

We turn and finally get to the door, and I stand here, crossing my arms while he reaches for the knob.

But he pauses, and I hold my breath. "Thanks for letting me hang out tonight."

My words come out scratchy, when I reply, "Of course. I'm glad you wanted to come. I was worried. Ya know...yesterday, when you said you didn't want to meet her?"

Spinning around, he throws up his hand. "I was upset. Rosie, c'mon, what did you expect? You dropped this bomb on me. Out of nowhere. I go from not having a kid one day to having a six-year-old."

"No, I get it." Mindlessly, I rub my arm while they brace tight against my chest. "I can't imagine what you might be feeling. But I'm glad you changed your mind."

"I don't know what I'm doing." He scrubs a palm down his forehead and the front of his face before wiping it in the air with a swat, making me flinch. "I don't know where we go from here. Or what happens when you leave." He takes to pacing back and forth in the entryway. He's spiraling. "I don't want her getting attached. Hell, I don't want to either. But I do want to get to know her. And she deserves to get to know me."

The pull of the string attached to my heart is persuasive. It always has been where Beck is involved. "She does. And you deserve to get to know your daughter too." My throat throbs as the remorse threatens to unravel me. "I'm so sorry. I should've never taken these years from you."

At my words, his eyes harden, growing sharper with each second that passes. "But the fact is, you did. And an apology doesn't take that away. It doesn't erase what you've done." He swings open the door with so much force it slams against the wall. I don't even have time to worry about the possible damage to the sheetrock of a house I'm going to have to sell soon.

He stomps outside and I hurry after him onto the porch and stay in the open doorway, my heart racing in my chest, and the tears I've been trying to restrain break free once again. "I know."

Spinning around, he clenches his hands into fists. "Do you? Because I don't think you understand the kind of whiplash I'm experiencing right now. After I thought we lost the baby, and then after you left, I made the decision I didn't want kids. I didn't want to risk being a bad father. And then you show up here...with *my* kid."

"What are you saying?" I sniff, wiping a knuckle under my nose.

"I'm saying, you set me up for failure. I'm already a bad father because I've been absent for the first six years of her life."

"You're not," I cry out in protest.

"Don't," he snaps, holding up a trembling palm. "Nothing you say right now is going to help." He gazes at me with indignation for a moment, and maybe a little regret too. "I need time. But I don't have it. Because again, you took that from me. And you're leaving. I only have a few days to get to know this person. This child. My daughter. This fucking sucks."

"You're right," I mutter softly.

"And you agreeing with me isn't helping either."

"What do you want me to say?" I step out onto the porch fully, peeking over my shoulder as I close the door behind me. "That I messed up? That I'm sorry? That I didn't mean to hurt you?" My words rumble from my chest through the heartache, through the tears that are violently streaming down my face.

It's not only me who is hurting, I know. Beck's pain is far worse than mine and I caused it. He shakes his head solemnly. "You don't get it. You didn't just hurt me. You hurt Charlie. You took something from both of us that we can't ever get back. You don't get time back. You of all people should know how important time is."

"You're right." I swipe at my wet cheeks.

"Rosie," he growls.

Wrapping my arms around myself again, I cry out, "What? I mean it, you are. You're right. What I did, keeping her from you, keeping the truth from you, it's unforgivable. You have no idea how sorry I am."

He stabs a finger at me, the glaze in his eyes obvious. "There it is. You're right. It is unforgivable." With that, he whips around and hurries down the porch steps.

I watch him go, sobbing silently, my heart shattering once again.

10

ROSIE

He hates me 😩

STELLA

He doesn't hate you. He loves you!

You didn't see him

You didn't hear what he said to me

STELLA

He just needs to remember that he loves you

You don't just forget you love someone

STELLA

I promise after you spend some time together
he's gonna remember

But what if he can't forgive me?

STELLA

He will 😊

When Beck shows up at Dottie's to pick Charlie and me up, he doesn't speak to me, but he's talkative to Charlie. That's all that matters. But I won't lie, my heart is bruised over the fact that he's giving me the silent treatment. There was a time when we could talk for hours.

You'd hardly notice the unspoken silent treatment because Charlie is speaking a mile a minute from her booster in the back seat of Beck's Chevrolet. She's flying through questions for him. He entertains some and dodges the ones he doesn't know how to answer. I suppose he could've looked to me for assistance while I sat staring out the windshield, but he didn't bother. It should surprise me how easily they're getting along, but it doesn't. Because I knew they would hit it off.

Beck's dressed in jeans today and a plain black fitted T-shirt. From the passenger seat, I only allow my eyes a few seconds to travel over his stature. The same defined biceps I couldn't help but notice the night at the beach when he had his wetsuit bunched around his waist. The corded forearms that flex each time he grips the steering wheel tighter. It's this simple detail that reminds me of his anxiety. This time caused by me and the impossibly difficult decisions I made years ago that have now brought us to this point.

Beck parks against the curb in front of a row of pastel painted buildings. I hop out and open the back door for Charlie while I peer up at the sign on the closest building, shielding my eyes from the morning sun. *Seashell Bookshop*. It's new since I lived in Golden Harbor.

We enter the shop, me following on their heels because Beck is trying his damn hardest to make it clear I'm the third wheel today. His point is made clear when I nearly do a face-plant into the glass door because he doesn't hold it for me. Guess I deserve that. And far worse.

Inside, there's a coffee bar and a glass display case with baked goods on one side of the shop. It smells like freshly ground coffee beans mixed with cinnamon and a hint of maple. There are books on tables, on display in the windows, and on shelves throughout the entire space. I haven't made much time for reading lately. The only books I've read are ones for children or non-fictions about endometriosis.

But I find myself drawn to the colorful spines and organized stacks of illustrated romance covers. Though me and romance? Pfft. I shake my head. "Not in this lifetime," I mutter under my breath, and drag my palm across a cover regretfully.

"Charlie, want a treat?" Beck pipes up.

"Yes!" She jumps up and down.

"They've got the best sugar cookies." He waves us toward the coffee bar and I follow behind. "Any food allergies I should know about?" he asks over his shoulder.

It's the first words he's spoken to me today, so I almost don't realize he's directing the question at me. "No...no food allergies."

Charlie skips to the display case and peers at all the delicious baked goods. My mouth practically waters at the sight of the cinnamon roll. But at the same time, my brain recoils. As much as my taste buds would love it, my stomach would make me pay for it later if I indulged.

Beck crouches next to her and points out all his favorite treats. My heart can't hardly take the image of the two of them interacting. It's small and simple. But to them, and me, this is new. This is a first.

I try not to hover over Charlie and give them a little space. Even if it is hard. I know it's important for them. I peruse the books stacked by the windows. I recognized several covers.

Romance and thrillers that have been circulating on social media. I pick one up and skim the back cover.

"Did you want anything?" Beck calls from the register.

"Um, no, I'm good. Thanks," I reply, taken aback. But as I observe how chummy he is with the woman behind the counter, I have to assume he's putting on an act for her.

"Their cinnamon rolls are gluten free," he finally adds.

"Really? Then yeah, I'd love one." I shuffle over to join him at the register, unzipping my purse to retrieve my wallet.

He shoves me away, his elbow brushing against my bicep. "I got it." He taps his card on the reader.

"I'll pay you back," I mutter, blinking back my disbelief over his unexpected generosity.

"Don't worry about it." He gives Charlie her big pink seashell-shaped cookie.

Her eyes go big, and her smile matches it. "Ooooo thank you," she squeals.

Beck chuckles and my stomach swoops at the sound. A flicker of memories follow it. I haven't heard that genuine laugh in so long. And I'm not sure how it's possible, going so long without hearing a sound that used to be one of your favorites.

"You're welcome," he says to her. To me, he gestures toward the counter. "There's yours."

"Thanks," I mumble.

By the time I snatch my cinnamon roll and spin around, the bell above the door chimes as Beck and Charlie go outside. I twist my lips to the side and sigh, grabbing a couple of napkins before following behind them once again. Guess I deserve this. I'm only here because he knows I wouldn't allow Charlie to go without me.

The two of them sit at a colorful square table with two bench seats that rest partially on the cinder pavers in front of the shop and partially on the sidewalk. There's a seagull circling overhead waiting for some crumbs.

Charlie hasn't taken a bite of her cookie yet. She's still admiring it. "Mama? Take a picture of me with my cookie." Her smile is so big it's like she's swallowed a hanger.

I can't help it, but I smile too seeing that wide, toothless grin. "Oh, right, almost forgot." This is something Charlie and I love to do. When we eat something new, we always take a picture first. My phone is full of food photos.

Sliding my phone free from the back pocket of my denim shorts, I position it while the seagull squawks above my head and distracts me. I hope he knows getting pooped on is not on my bingo card today. I hurry and snap a few pictures of Charlie smiling and holding up her big cookie.

"Send it to West," she says sweetly, and my gaze darts at Beck, but he drops his head before we can lock eyes. "Now you need to get one of my daddy's cookie too."

"Oh. Um...I mean, maybe he doesn't want a picture." I bite on my lower lip; the easy way Charlie refers to Beck as her daddy is still new and a bit unsettling.

"Please, it's fun," she coaxes, pulling up her legs and tucking them underneath her on the small wood bench. I scooch in next to her and sit down on the edge of it so only one of my ass cheeks is hanging off.

"Sure, I'd love a picture," he agrees.

"Me and Mommy do it all the time."

Beck gives me a crooked smile, and my core tightens without warning. He holds his cookie up close to his face. His is a blue seashell. I take the picture and when I bring my phone down, his smile has already vanished.

I eat my cinnamon roll and try to refrain from moaning at how decadent it is. Finding a gluten free cinnamon roll that actually tastes good is a challenge. So far, I've only found one café in Seattle. Most of the time, I skip sweets. They're too hard to trust and there's no telling how my body will react.

While Beck and Charlie chat, I scroll on my phone mindlessly, not paying attention to anything that comes across my screen. Even if one post is a baby announcement from my cousin and another is a sale post by the brand I buy my black tees from for work. It's too hard to give my focus to my screen when my baby girl is chatting with her father. The man who once held my entire life while giving me the space to grow.

A text comes through from West. My initial reaction is to swipe it away. Which—what is that about?

WEST
Morning beautiful! How are my girls?

Morning! Charlie found herself a cookie that's almost as big as her face!

I send him the picture of her.

WEST
Bet she's enjoying it!

She is. I'm sure she'll be talking about this cookie for weeks

WEST
Think you'll be able to come home sooner?

I need to meet with Dottie's lawyer. Could be here a little longer than I originally thought

WEST
Try your hardest to wrap things up. I miss my girls

We miss you too

Maybe we could talk later?

WEST

Sure. I should be free after Charlie goes to bed

Perfect.

West doesn't know who Charlie's father is. He never even asked if he lived in Golden Harbor. My guess is, he doesn't want to know. But if I'm going to marry him, I owe him the truth. Especially now that Beck knows.

It will be a tough conversation that I would've preferred to have face-to-face. But time didn't permit. There were so many decisions to make right after Dottie passed. Not only for the memorial, but she had specific afterlife plans. Some I haven't even heard. I imagine that is the conversation I'll be having with her lawyer.

"Mama?"

I flip my phone over on the table and glance up at Charlie just as the annoying seagull comes in for a landing a few feet from us on the sidewalk. "Hmm?"

"My daddy wants to take me to the beach. Can I go?"

Turning toward Beck, my lips slip into a frown as my stomach coils. How did I miss this part of their conversation? Is he wanting to take Charlie without me?

"Daddy says it's a special beach. Please, Mama," she begs.

I trace my fingers down the front of my throat. "I don't know. I'm not sure we have time to go to the beach."

"It's close," Beck assures me with grit in his tone, his expression stony.

Charlie's got her little hands clasped while she straightens on her knees. "Pleeeease."

Beck holds eye contact with me. In his I see the pain and anger that I caused. The very things he could hold over my head to get me to agree to anything he suggests or asks for.

"Sure," I give in, faking a strong smile for Charlie. Just like

I've been doing for the last six years, even when my heart is about to shatter and my chest threatens to collapse.

11

BECK

osie is Charlie's mom, so I'm not an idiot; I know she calls the shots. Legally, I've got no rights here. Not yet anyway. But shouldn't Rosie be bending over backward to make up for keeping her from me all these years? Instead, she's choosing to be difficult. She's treating me like I'm a criminal with supervised visitations with my own daughter.

Daughter.

The word, the idea—all of it—is still strange. But as far as six-year-olds go, Charlie seems like one of the good ones. She's polite, happy, smart. Hell, maybe she's the smartest Stone yet.

After I park my rig, Rosie releases a strangled sigh from the passenger seat. I roll my eyes. She can complain all she wants, but out of all the beaches along the coast, this one is still my favorite.

"This is the special beach?" she questions in an accusatory tone, the corners of her lips downturned.

"I thought Charlie would want to see it." I give her a tight smile.

She leans across the console just far enough that I get an eyeful of her cleavage. A rush of hot air pushes between us as this moment holds by a thread. "I don't know what your angle is," she whispers, "but upsetting Charlie is not an option."

Clamping my jaw tight, I lean too and lower my voice, narrowing my eyes at her. "Too late for that. You already deprived her of six years of knowing her father."

She tilts her head, maybe out of shock. A sour taste forms in my mouth. It's not like me to be purposely cruel. Especially not to her. If you'd ask me seven years ago, I would've never dreamed I'd talk to Rosie like this.

"Fine. I deserve that. But for this to work, you're going to have to forgive me eventually."

Instead of her words softening my heart, they only harden it further. "Yeah, eventually," I growl. "It's been less than forty-eight hours. Sorry, honey, I don't downshift that fast."

Her mouth pops open to speak and I find myself eager, awaiting what could possibly come out after that. But Charlie has already unbuckled from her booster and is poking her head between our seats. "C'mon, let's go," she whines.

As the three of us start walking, Charlie hurries to catch up to me. Even though Rosie shuffles behind us and she's quiet, her presence is blaring. Part of me wishes she would've just stayed in my rig.

But then again, I don't know Charlie all that well. Besides learning she doesn't have any food allergies, I have no idea if she has any medical conditions. I don't know her favorite things. Her pet peeves. Spending time with her is like being with a stranger who oddly resembles me. Just thinking about that last fact causes my skin to heat and reminds me, once again, why my daughter is like a stranger.

"What's so special about this beach?" Charlie asks, interrupting my thoughts. Her little raspy voice calms me.

"You'll see." I grin at her.

We take our shoes off and walk in the sand. Charlie heads straight for the waves and a smile pulls on my lips. She slows and is cautious when she dips her toes in the water. When a wave rolls onto the shore, reaching further than anticipated, she squeals and spins around, running away while it chases her.

Charlie returns to us and gives Rosie her sandals to carry but I reach for them. "I got them."

Rosie gives me a half smile.

Charlie skips up ahead, stopping to bend and pick up a seashell. I don't initiate conversation with Rosie and thankfully, she doesn't either. A memory comes to my mind of a time she and I were here together.

It was after senior prom. When the dance ended, a bunch of us came here. That was back when they used to allow bonfires on the beach. I carried Rosie's high heels while she, Stella, and Daisy went wave jumping. Rosie looked beautiful that night. Her hair was shorter then. She had it half pulled up and in curls. The shiny dress she wore was strapless and made her tits look amazing.

But that's not the memory that sticks out in my mind. It was the color of her dress. It was green and brought out the green in her eyes. Especially when the light from the fire reflected in them. She was stunning. Even as an eighteen-year-old boy, I knew I was a lucky bastard and didn't deserve her.

"Look!" Charlie runs to us and holds up a large white spiraled shell with knobbed ridges.

"That's so pretty," Rosie says.

I bend and admire it. "You know what? It's rare to find snail shells on this beach these days."

"Can you keep it safe for me?" Charlie's brows lift in question.

"Sure. I'll put it in my pocket."

She smiles big.

"Charlie, see that wood boardwalk?" I point up toward the grassy hill and she looks. "That's where we're heading."

Without hesitation, she runs in that direction.

"Beck," Rosie whispers. "I haven't told her that we were married."

Her use of past tense grates on me even though it shouldn't. Because why do I care? "Are," I correct her. "*Are* married." I shoot her a hard glare before taking off in a jog after Charlie. If Rosie and I stay here any longer having this conversation, I'm positive it won't go over well.

Charlie reaches the boardwalk before I do, her long braids whipping behind her. But when I take the steps, the memories of the night I proposed to Rosie rush at me unexpectedly. My heart races. I reach out and grip the weathered railing while it feels as if the ground quakes beneath my feet.

Charlie climbs onto the wood platform and peers over at the ocean. "You can see the whole beach from here," she calls, her small voice echoing into the wind.

My breathing is ragged while I try to concentrate on each inhale and exhale of my lungs. "Yeah...be careful." My words come out strangled. *Did they even come out at all?*

Rosie whooshes past me, and I take a second to let my heart slow once she reaches the top with Charlie and I know she's safe. I take the steps slow, feeling winded despite being in shape. I lift weights three days a week at the small gym in town. I run five miles on my off days and go surfing at least once a week.

When my feet finally hit the platform, I slump against the railing in relief and pinch my eyes shut for a second.

"Hey, are you all right?" Rosie's voice is soft, distant.

The pressure from her hand is suddenly on my back. It sinks against my skin and I force myself to suck in a breath.

"You're burning up." Her eyes widen while they skim over me.

From my periphery, Charlie's lips pout and she fidgets with the hem of her shirt.

"I'm fine," I rush out. "Don't worry." I say this as I look at Charlie. "Just gotta catch my breath is all."

Rosie purses her lips, still gazing at me with concern. I give her a threatening shake of my head. I don't want Charlie to worry about me.

"He's okay." Rosie shields her eyes from the sun as she peers at Charlie. "Probably just needs to exercise more to get that heart rate going, right?"

"Yeah," I breathe out, nodding, and mouth, *Thank you.*

Rosie gives me a half smile and rubs my back, her touch soothing and gentle, and it awakens something inside of me that's been dormant for so long. Shock jolts through me and I stiffen, causing her to flinch and shuffle away, leaving me alone. I'm not used to having an audience while I'm spiraling, and a panic attack is coming, so I'm grateful for the distance—a few seconds to catch my breath and compose myself.

Rosie stands next to Charlie and leans into the railing while she faces the ocean. My heart strains in my chest at the sight of them. "Do you know why this beach is so special?" Rosie's voice carries over the sound of the wind.

Charlie shakes her head. I straighten and exhale a long breath as I shuffle to join them. Gazing at Rosie, I'm slightly dazed from the near panic attack I just had as well as from the anticipation of what she's going to say. Is she actually about to tell Charlie about me proposing? About the shells I collected for weeks so I could spell out: MARRY ME, ROSIE? Or that we're married?

"This is the exact spot I was standing in when I told your daddy that I was pregnant with you," she confesses, turning her head to look at me.

As her lips pull into a smile, for a second, I'm transported to a time when Rosie and I were literally floating on top of the world. A time we were so fucking happy. Her smile is beautiful, but it shatters my heart all at once. Because the memory of that level of happiness only reminds me of the despair that followed.

Even though Charlie is here now, it's still somehow the same. Because it still feels like I lost her. But I didn't just lose her that day. I lost both of them.

"Yep, that's right." My words claw out of my throat, past the anguish. "This is where I learned I was going to be a dad. It was the best day of my life." The confession is true, even if I've tried denying it for years.

I never wanted to be a dad. Not unless I was planning on having kids with Rosie. She made me want to be a dad. She made me believe I could break the cycle and be a good one.

"But I thought you didn't know about me?" Charlie asks, and I whip my head in her direction to find a little pout on her face.

Shit.

"I didn't. Well, I did. But then…" Okay, as much as I don't want to admit it, Rosie was right—bringing Charlie here was a bad idea.

Rosie crouches in front of her, brushing her braid back and curling her fingers around her shoulder. "Charlie, you know how there are some days when Mommy is in a lot of pain? And sometimes, I'm in so much pain, I need to go to the hospital?"

"Yeah, and I get to go to your friend Hannah's?"

"Yep. But sometimes, you stay and you bring me my medicine and my heating pad and we have our girls' nights?"

Rolling her eyes dramatically, Charlie says, "Yeah, I know, Mommy because you're an endo warrior."

A smile brightens Rosie's face, but my gut twists. The instant reminder of her illness has me feeling guilty because I haven't been here for her. I didn't even know she'd received a real diagnosis for her symptoms until a few years ago. But I have no reason to feel guilty. It's her fault.

"That's right. Well, a few weeks after I found out I was pregnant with you, I was in a lot of pain. So much so, I thought we lost you." When Rosie glances over her shoulder, her green eyes are glossy. My heart throbs. "It wasn't until a few weeks after that when I learned you were just fine and growing in my belly perfectly."

"But I thought I was born in Seattle?"

"You were," Rosie agrees.

Charlie frowns. She's processing. And honestly, same, kid.

My head is still trying to figure out how we got here. How seven summers ago I stood in this same exact place and knew my life would never be the same.

"And now I'm not in your belly anymore. I'm here. With my mama and my daddy." She smiles so big, so genuinely, that it nearly splits my heart.

"That's right, baby girl," Rosie says, her voice cracking and her eyes watering.

I should enjoy the purity of this moment, of coming full circle, being with Rosie and Charlie. But it's tainted by my thoughts of all the things that have been taken away from me.

I swallow. "We should get going."

Rosie nods and luckily Charlie doesn't resist. She squeezes between Rosie and me and takes each of our hands in hers. A tingle shoots up my arm at her touch. Rosie flashes me a look of —surprise, I think?

My chest throbs. I don't speak.

Maybe bringing Charlie here was a mistake. Bringing Rosie here was definitely a mistake.

12

ROSIE

*D*ottie's cottage never felt quite this big when I lived in it as it does now. With seventy years of accumulated knick-knacks, furniture, photos, and memories, it all compresses onto my shoulders like a heavy weight. I glance around the open concept kitchen and dining room and scratch my fingertips against my scalp. A few empty boxes surround me, and I don't know where to start.

My phone vibrates from where it rests on the dining table. I glance away from the empty boxes, honestly a little relieved. It's Stella again.

She's been harassing me all day to come out for a girls' night with her and her cousin, Daisy. A night out with the two friends who helped make sure I graduated high school sounds amazing. But that would mean leaving Charlie with a sitter or Jack's mom again. The single-mom guilt that is all too familiar rears its ugly head and presses into my chest.

STELLA

You know how much Charlie already loves Max. Where's the harm in letting them play together for a few hours?

How about you bring Max here and you and Daisy go out?

STELLA

I can go out with Daisy any time. But when was the last time the three of us got to hang out?

Besides a brief exchange at Dottie's memorial, I haven't seen Daisy in seven years. When we were teenagers, the three of us used to hang out every chance we got. It would be good to see her.

I glance up at Charlie who's sitting at the dining table coloring in a book from Dottie's collection. She's got the stuffed mermaid Beck gave her sitting next to her on the bench. She's carried it around since he gave it to her the other night. I had to practically wrestle it out of her grip so she wouldn't take it into the bath with her.

Charlie lifts her chin, and her curious eyes meet mine. I smile, but she squishes her lips. "What's wrong, Mama?"

This girl is too perceptive for her age. Or maybe this is what happens when you've been a single mom and the two of you have spent so much time together. I exhale a sigh. "Nothing, baby."

But her brow scrunches. She's not buying it. Or maybe it's because I called her baby again. I can't help it.

I purse my lips while she continues to study me like she already knows I'm about to spill what's swirling around in my head. A few more years alone together and ours might be right up there next to Lorelei and Rory's relationship. Minus the takeout. My body could never.

"How would you like to play with Max tonight?"

Her brown eyes brighten and the crayon in her hand goes slack. "Really? Can I?"

The excitement is a little surprising. Charlie doesn't warm

up to strangers too easily. "Do you want to go to his house and hang out with him and his daddy, Jack?"

"Yes!" She rises on her knees and her crayon is abandoned in a heartbeat. She clutches her stuffed mermaid to her chest. "I'll bring my new mermaid to show him."

My lips tip into a bigger smile. "I think he'll like that."

I text Stella.

> I'll bring Charlie by around 6. Does that work?

STELLA

> Yessss!! You won't regret it, promise!

Yeah, we'll see about that. The ache that began in my lower back this morning has decided to wrap around to the lower part of my stomach to radiate pain down my thighs. The wave of energy yesterday gave me false hope today would be the same. But I'm never that lucky.

My phone vibrates again but this time it's West. I roll my eyes to myself. We were supposed to talk on the phone last night, but he never called. I waited for longer than I'm inclined to admit before finally taking a bath and going to bed.

WEST

> Hey sweetie! Sorry I missed you last night. Let me make it up to you tonight. FaceTime?

I don't reply.

These empty boxes aren't going to fill themselves. It's the downside, once again, of being the only child and only grandchild when your grandma passes away. And the damn reality hits me even harder in the chest—I'll be doing this again when my parents pass. For the hundredth time since receiving the news that I lost Dottie, I think of how selfish my parents are.

Anger coils around my stomach, meeting my pain and giving me the nudge I need to start packing and sorting through Dottie's things. My gaze zones in on the wall that has an assorted mix of coastal artwork in canvases and frames, and I begin yanking them down. I stack them one on top of the other, ignoring the roll of bubble wrap and paper, and they scrape against each other. I don't care about the scratches or the dents to the canvas. What does it matter? These were treasures to Dottie but what do they mean to my parents? Nothing.

I go to the next wall and do the same. And the next. Tears build in the corners of my eyes. My breathing accelerates and it must be audible because when I glance over at Charlie, she's watching me, lower lip stuck between her teeth. I exhale a breath even though my pulse is anything but calm.

"Do you wanna take your coloring outside to the front porch?"

She bobs her head and even though she smiles, I know she's worried about me. Wordlessly, she gathers her crayons and coloring book and hops off the bench. Her little hand reaches for the stuffed mermaid and my heart heaves in my chest. I force a pained smile as she slips out the front door.

I blink back the tears. There's no time for crying. But as I stand there, in the dining room, staring at the bare walls, I can't fight them any longer.

Sniffing, I wipe my fingers across my cheeks and open the china cabinet that's overfilling with silver platters, a pristine sixteen-place setting in a pastel floral pattern, and several mismatched teacups and saucers. Memories assault my mind as I empty the cabinet, the stacks of plates clattering against one another.

Dottie loved hosting afternoon tea with the other ladies in town. Sometimes Daisy's mom, Hazel, and Willow, the owner of Peace of Cake, would come. There was a time or two I came home to find the old biddies high as a kite and scarfing down the cake Willow always brought with her. A bubble of laughter breaks free from me. It's the exact memory I need to shake me from the anger plaguing me. The next stack I retrieve from the cabinet, I take into my arms with gentleness and care. I owe Dottie that much.

❧❧❧❧

It's nearly six when I pull into the driveway of Stella's gray-and-white modern two-story beach house. The construction is new. There used to be a set of old fourplexes here. But my guess is some rich developer from LA snatched them up only to tear them down and build these. Dottie had warned me this was happening often.

Charlie has already unbuckled herself by the time I round the Mini Cooper to open her door. She hops out clutching the mermaid in one hand and the loop of her backpack in the other.

She's racing ahead of me and up the steps toward the front door. Guess worrying whether she'd be okay if I left her tonight was silly. The girl acts as if she can't wait to get a break from me. So much for our Gilmore Girls bond.

Stella opens the door as I reach the porch. She smiles wide at both Charlie and me and welcomes us inside. Her long, dark brown hair has a fresh cut, showing off tapered bangs. Glossy pink paints her lips, and strappy high heels show off the red nail polish on her toes. Two clear signs that she's ready for a night out of fun. A black tank top and a red leather mini skirt showing off her muscular thighs finish off the ensemble.

And now I'm feeling both modest and underdressed as I glance down at my flat sandals, jeans, and green sleeveless top. But this shirt is flowy and hides my bloated stomach. The notorious endo-belly has struck at the worst time. Not that there's ever a right time.

"Hot damn, girl. Where've you been hiding that cute figure?" Stella blurts.

I wave off her compliment, knowing full well it's bullshit, but sweet, and step inside the house. "And look at you? That top and skirt are hugging your curves perfectly."

She gives me a little spin, her face lighting up like a glow-stick, and I snort a laugh. "The perks of breastfeeding."

"Well, it's working wonders for you. I don't think it had the same effect on me." I glance down at myself and purse my lips. The girls still look good, despite pregnancy and a year of breastfeeding Charlie. But they're definitely not what they used to be.

"Are you kidding? That color with the low neckline and your gorgeous auburn hair? You've got it going on, believe me. Hey, Jack," Stella hollers over her shoulder to somewhere in the house. "Look at this smokeshow!"

"Okay, that's not necessary," I sputter, fire pooling in my cheeks. "I don't need confirmation from my friend's husband."

"You stop that talk right now, Jack is not just your friend's husband. He's your friend too." A glimmer of pain flickers in her eyes.

"Right, I know," I mumble, tucking my hair behind my ear, which isn't easy with how big it is. I never noticed the humidity in Golden Harbor while I was living here. But now that I'm back, my hair looks like it's the before picture in an advertisement for an anti-fizz hair product.

Jack shuffles into the entryway, black hair perfectly styled, and I find myself envious of him. Little Max is latched to his leg and Charlie is already on his back. He lets out a low, loud whistle. "Looking good, both of you. Now, go, have a good time. I got these two rascals."

Rascals? Who is this guy? Once he was the resident weed

dealer in Golden Harbor—probably even supplied it to Willow's hippy gang—and now he gives piggy-back rides and lives in a two-million-dollar beach house and says things like *rascals.*

If I wasn't feeling guilty over leaving Charlie with him, I'd tease him. "You sure?"

"Go, Mama. Love you." Charlie giggles when Jack starts galloping in a circle and she womps up and down on his back.

"Okay." I laugh too, my anxieties lifting. If I can't trust one of my oldest friends, then who else is there? "Have fun. I'll see you in a few hours."

Jack gives Stella a little peck on the cheek before spinning around and galloping back down the hall. Stella watches them, but I observe her. There's something going on there. Maybe it's nothing. Maybe they had an argument before I got here. West and I have had our fair share before brushing them off and stepping into a business-hosted cocktail party.

Shuffling my feet, I interrupt her gazing. "Everything okay?"

She turns and snatches her purse from where it's sitting the entryway table. "C'mon." She grabs my arm. "Daisy is out front waiting for us."

I allow her to lead me out the door and back down her front steps until we've crossed the yard. We stand in front of a 1977 blue Volkswagen Slug Bug with a recent paint job and a surfboard rack on top. My eyes widen. "Wait. Daisy still has her Slug Bug?"

"Yep," Stella says. "Crazy right?"

Daisy hops out and lunges for me, wrapping me up in a tight hug as soon as she reaches me. "Oh my gosh, I can't believe you're actually coming out with us," she says, following it up with a little squeal.

"And I can't believe you still have your old car." I breathe out a little laugh, gazing at its near perfect condition.

Daisy runs a palm over the shiny paint on the hood. "This

girl hasn't let me down yet. At this point she's more reliable than the men in my life. And now she's a classic."

"Save the male drama for the taco bar." Stella shoves the passenger seat forward and climbs into the back of the tiny car.

I glance over my shoulder at Dottie's Mini Cooper. Daisy's Slug Bug isn't much bigger, but it's got to have more leg room. "You sure you don't want me to drive?"

"I drew the short straw, meaning I only get one margarita tonight because I'm driving." Daisy slides behind the wheel. "Get in," she calls to me.

I chew on my lip. Cruising around Golden Harbor in Daisy's little death-trap in high school was one thing, but I've got Charlie to think about now.

"Hey?" Stella hollers. "The margaritas aren't going to drink themselves."

Exhaling a sigh, I give one last reluctant glance at the red Mini Cooper and get into the passenger seat. After I click the seat belt in place, I glance in the rearview mirror and Stella is smiling back in it, her hazel eyes sparkling. She's right. Tonight will be good for me. Good for us.

"So margaritas, huh?" I ask.

"There's this really cute margarita and taco bar right on the beach. It's literally called Tacos by the Beach. You're gonna love it." Stella coats her full lips with another layer of pink gloss.

"Clever," I mutter. Except I don't drink margaritas. At least, not normally. But I don't say this out loud. Because tonight, I will. The last thing I want is to be accused of being the designated Debbie Downer.

A few minutes later, Daisy pulls into an angled parking spot, turning some heads from the sidewalk at the rumble. At this point, her car is considered a classic. But the stares don't affect her one way or another. She slides her sunglasses up to the top of her head, pushing back her long, blonde hair.

After Stella unfolds herself from the cramped back seat and

adjusts her short leather skirt and top, being sure the girls are tucked in, the three of us strut down the sidewalk. A shiny black Jeep with the top off takes its time driving past us, and a few shirtless men send out catcalls and raucous whistles. I retract my assumption upon closer look—these are boys not men. The three of us let out a bark of laughter in unison.

"Damn, we must look good," Stella says as she opens the door to the restaurant. "Those guys were at least ten years younger than us."

We usher inside and it's bright and colorful. Decorated in shades of oranges, teals, and pinks. Banners and canvases cover the walls, blown glass dishes adorn tables, and paper lanterns hang from the ceiling. There's '90s music streaming from the speakers overhead and the servers are young and vibrant.

Stella was right—I love it.

"Let's check for a table on the deck." Stella brings up the rear as we weave through the bar.

"Already on it," Daisy says in singsong.

She finds us a table in the corner of the patio with exactly three stools. Perfect. No uninvited guests can join us. No shirtless twenty-year-olds.

I drop onto a teal metal stool and glance to the side of me. The ocean stretches farther than I can see. The sun sits low in the golden sky just above the waves. The sunsets in Golden Harbor are known across California for how gorgeous they are. A warm tingle shoots across my bare arms and I shiver. I guess I hadn't realized how much I've missed them until now.

"What can I get ya ladies?" a woman's voice chimes, pulling me from my thoughts.

"We will take a pitcher of your finest mango margaritas. By finest, I of course mean your cheapest," Stella says under her breath with a smirk. "And frozen most definitely. And we'd like three of your taco flights, each one a different taco, please."

Stella hands back the menus before I've even had a chance to look at it.

"Oh, um...I don't think..." I attempt to clutch at a menu before the server can whisk away with them but Stella shoos her away.

"That's right, don't think. I got you." She winks.

Has she always been this assertive?

"Just trust her." Daisy lifts her phone out of her purse. "Every taco here is delicious. And if one of them has something on it you can't eat, we'll trade."

"Okay." I give a slight nod, still off-kilter. But it's comforting that Daisy remembers this detail about me.

"Picture time, ladies," Stella announces as she hops off her stool. She taps the guy's shoulder next to us and after a few words are exchanged, she gives him her phone. "What do we think? Taco bar in the background or the beach?"

"Beach," Daisy and I say at the same time.

We crowd together, me squished in the middle, and my heart gives a sigh in my chest. I still fit between them, like I used to. For this brief moment it's as if no time has passed. We smile and luckily the guy takes several pictures so we can sort through them in hopes of finding at least one we can all agree will be Instagram-worthy.

The pitcher of margaritas arrives with three blue, blown glasses. My first sip is heavenly. It's tart and sweet, the citrus hitting my tastebuds just right. Maybe I'll be forgoing the wine and ordering these next time West takes me out.

Shit. West.

I pick up my phone from where it's been lying face-down on the table. The unanswered text from him doesn't sit there lonely. It's now been joined by two more. I purse my lips as I open them.

WEST

Please don't give me the silent treatment.
FaceTime will be better anyway. We haven't
got to have phone sex yet. Thought that might
be kind of fun. What do you think? Nine?
Charlie should be in bed by then.

If I FaceTime you at nine and I'm naked and
you're not, that will be awfully embarrassing.

That would be embarrassing. But I suppose
your apology is good enough and I won't put
you through the humiliation

I'm out with my friends. I'll call you when I'm
back at Dottie's

WEST

Friends?

I tilt my head and my brows pinch together. Is he...jealous?

Yeah you've heard me mention Stella? And her
cousin Daisy

WEST

So no guys then?

He *is* jealous. I'm not sure if I find it adorable or unbecoming.

WEST

Because that would be pretty fucked up

My eyes bulge and a streak of shock ripples through me.

No men. Never any man but you 😊

WEST

Good. That's my girl.

"Earth to Rosie," Daisy is saying, shaking my shoulder.

I lift my gaze from my phone to find her crouching to meet my eye. "Hmm...mm?"

"I was saying, tell us about this Richard Gere guy you've snatched up and are engaged to."

I shake my head, still attempting to clear it from the whiplash of West's words. "Did I...did I tell you I was engaged?"

Daisy's gaze drops to her margarita, and she pinches the straw and fidgets with it. "No, Stella told me." She looks up again, hurt shining in her blue eyes. "But you should have. How could you not tell me you're engaged?"

I hurry to tap out a quick *I love you* text before flipping my phone over again. "I know, I'm sorry. I was going to. I meant to. Everything just happened so fast. And then...Dottie."

Daisy's expression crumples, but now it's for a different reason—Dottie. She might have been my grandma by blood, but she was like a grandma to all my friends as well. We're all grieving her. "It's fine. You're here now. And this is even better, because now you can tell us all the details in person."

"And show us." Stella waggles her brows while she's got the straw in between her teeth shoved in her margarita, like she's some kind of handless creature slurping up her drink.

"Yes, c'mon, mama, show us a picture of this silver fox," Daisy says.

I snort a laugh, the alcohol warming my nerves and easing the tension out of my limbs. "Whoever said he's a silver fox?"

"You didn't have to. You said he was a little older, rich, and owned his own finance business. I'm sorry, but you put all that together and my mind goes straight to Richard Gere in *Pretty Woman*."

"Well, he is a silver fox," I pause for Stella to release a squeal, swirling my straw around my frozen drink. "He's got a nice condo in Seattle that has the best school for Charlie close by. And he's responsible and so good with her."

Daisy and Stella pick up their margarita glasses and give each other a look as they both take a drink. I glance back and forth at them, my gut pinching. "What? C'mon, what is it?"

Stella lowers her glass and licks her lips. "He sounds amazing, Rosie. Really."

"But?" I wait for it, lifting my brows and studying my best friend as she gives me a little forced smile. She's clearly holding something back.

"But..." Daisy begins, and I swivel my attention at her. "Everything you're saying sounds like this relationship is just... for Charlie."

I can't help it; I flinch. "It is for Charlie. And for me. I'm a single mom. I'm never not thinking about Charlie." I don't even bother trying to hide the defensiveness in my tone. What does Daisy know? Last I heard, she doesn't have any kids of her own. How could she possibly understand?

"No one's saying that. Of course what Charlie needs is important too," Stella clarifies.

"Hey, girl. I'm not trying to pick apart your relationship—" And then she just stops talking. Maybe because she sees the annoyance taking up residence on my face.

Shoving my glass away, I whip my head over my shoulder to peer at the ocean. The angry waves thundering against the beach battles with the irritation pounding in my chest and out of nowhere, tears build in the corners of my eyes. "Are you sure? Because that's how it feels."

Two servers breeze up to our table, interrupting the thick tension in the air. They're holding out wood boards displaying the best-looking flight of tacos I've ever seen. My mouth waters as I get a big whiff of spices and my eyes devour the sizzling meat and tortillas.

After they leave, Stella squeezes my arm. "Hey, if you love him and you want to spend the rest of your life with him, you know we'll support you."

If?

Deep down, I do know. But I also know there will always be loyalty to Beck first. He's the one who stuck around after all.

"It's true." Daisy nods and my reservations slowly dissipate.

Maybe mostly because my stomach is already growling and my hunger is growing by the second with the spread sitting before us.

"If you're happy, we're happy. And it's a bonus Charlie likes him." Stella gives me her best genuine smile, her layers of pink lip gloss disappearing and staining her straw.

I give her a lopsided smile back. It should've been expected to have a few awkward moments, and hell, I guess a few disagreements too with how long it's been since the three of us were together.

She picks up a taco from one of the wood boards, sprinkles a spoonful of pico de gallo across it, and gestures with her chin for me to grab one too.

When I do, she lifts hers and taps it to mine in a *cheers*. Daisy joins in too. It's unclear what kind of taco I've chosen, but when I take a bite and my eyes drift closed, it doesn't matter because it's delicious. That will be a later problem. A million different spices call for my attention and my entire body sighs into the stool when I finally open my eyes and chew.

They both watch me before joining in a combined moan. We must be distracting the middle-aged men at the table next to us because they can't take their eyes off us. One stares mid-sip with his glass bottle pressed to his lips as if he's frozen in place. I giggle behind my taco, but we ignore them.

"They're the best, right?" Stella asks.

"Oh my gahh…" I say around my bite. "I feel as if I've died and my soul is leaving my body."

Stella laughs and nods in agreement. "Right."

Daisy holds up her margarita like she's about to give a big important speech. And she may be petite, but she knows how to command a room. Glossy blue eyes like ice and an affective presence. She's got my attention. "Okay, now fess up, girl. Show us a pic of that Silver Fox of yours."

A wave of humility washes over me, and I feel this strange protectiveness over West and our relationship. He's a good-looking man, there's no denying it. But that's the problem. The last thing I want is them thinking I'm with him because he's gorgeous. "Oh, c'mon, you've seen him on Instagram, haven't you?"

"You've hardly posted anything except for Charlie in the last seven years. Now don't get me wrong, Charlie is adorable. But I need to see this man because he must be doing something right to keep you in Seattle."

"What's wrong with Seattle?"

"Nothing. If you don't mind rain and dark skies every day."

"It's not that bad. And despite what the rumors say, it doesn't rain that much." I shake my head and glance over my shoulder at the beach. A few kids play in the sand with colorful buckets and pails. There a handful of surfers straddling boards waiting for the perfect wave. It's probably the same guys from the Jeep.

"Enough stalling," Daisy presses. "Don't make me beg."

I whip my head in her direction and scan her expression. She's not joking. She will beg. And one hundred percent cause a scene. "Fine," I groan, picking up my phone and finding a good picture of West before reluctantly handing it over.

In this particular photo of him, he was sitting across from me while we were out to dinner at his preferred steakhouse restaurant to celebrate our engagement. If I'd been given the option to choose the restaurant, it would've been this cute little Mediterranean place called Seatown Bowls. So good. If I weren't already devouring these delicious tacos, I would most definitely be craving Fattoush from there. I love it for two reasons: one, it's not overrun by tourists. And two, they serve food that fits in with my anti-inflammatory diet, so my body isn't freaking out more than usual.

West did look extra handsome that night though, dressed in my favorite blue suit and shiny blue tie. They both bring out the blue in his eyes. And while facial hair on men used to be my type, West prefers to be smoothly shaven. He says it makes him appear more professional. I'm not sure about that, but it does highlight his sharp jawline.

"Gahhhh," Daisy moans and melts into her stool, facing the phone at Stella. Her eyes bug out and now she's swooning. They look like two cartoon characters with gigantic hearts for eyes. "Now *I* feel as if I've died and gone to heaven. Forget Silver Fox, this man is a god. It's like he's been chiseled from stone. I'm going to call him Apollo."

I give Daisy a shove and swipe my phone out of her grip before we all burst into laughter.

13

BECK

The sound of my phone chiming and vibrating in unison wakes me from a dead sleep. Panic tightens across my shoulders, and an instant dread fills me all the way to my feet.

Milo.

Before my eyes have a chance to register and fly open, I fumble around on the nightstand for my phone. My hand bumps into my water bottle and then the lamp and it topples over. Shit.

I catapult in bed, blinking my eyes open, but it does little for clarity. Besides the faint light slicing through my blinds from the moon, it's dark in my bedroom. Swinging my legs off the side of the bed I quickly retrieve the fallen lamp before I finally clutch my phone in my hand and squint at the screen. But it's not a text from Milo.

My shoulders drop as a small sigh escapes my parted lips. Yet the name reflected on my screen has a similar reaction and my shoulders are right back up again.

Rosie.

Until three days ago, Milo had been my only concern. My

only responsibility. But now there's Charlie. I swipe to open her text.

> ROSIE
>
> Please don't hate me forever

It's now that the time on the screen finally resonates. Two o'clock in the morning. What the hell? I scrub a palm over my face and release a muffled groan.

> We can talk in the morning

I toss my phone back onto the nightstand, but it chimes almost instantly.

"Dammit, Rosie," I growl aloud, my throat dry and scratchy. Running a hand through my hair, I clench my teeth while I reach for my phone again.

> ROSIE
>
> I hate myself enough for the both of us. But if you hated me too, I'm not sure I could live with that 😞

> Are you okay?

> ROSIE
>
> No. I'm so sorry! For everything. If I could take it back I would!

I rise to my feet and pace in my darkened room, the old wood floor groaning under my bare feet. Where is this coming from? Middle of the night texting?

> Are you drunk?

> ROSIE
>
> Maybe a little 🙈

Great. So she's drunk texting me.

> Go to sleep. We'll talk tomorrow.

ROSIE

> I can't. Not until I know you don't hate me

I toss my head back and groan. How am I supposed to reply? I don't hate her. I could never hate her. But am I still pissed as hell at her? Yeah. And I probably will be for a while.

She likely won't remember talking to me. But it's a text conversation—it will be there for her to see tomorrow.

> I don't hate you

> But if you keep me up any longer I might

> I have to be up in a few hours for work

ROSIE

> I'm sorry

I drop back onto my bed, exhaling a gravelly sigh and closing my eyes. My phone chimes again, still in my grasp.

ROSIE

> Tell me something Beck?

> What?

ROSIE

> Tell me how I'm supposed to un-love you?

My eyes widen and I sit up slowly, my mind and dick suddenly wide awake. I reread the text. *She still loves me?* I rub a hand over my head a few times while my mind spirals. I will regret the words I'm about to type. But if she can be vulnerable, then so can I.

When you figure it out, let me know. I've been trying to un-love you for seven years

ROSIE

Does that make us sad and damaged?

Probably

ROSIE

Tell me something else?

Will we ever be able to move on with anyone else?

I don't know

ROSIE

Goodnight Beck

Goodnight Rosie

But it's not going to be a good night. Because after a text exchange like that, there's no way sleep is happening tonight.

༄༄༄

Milo beats me to the job site, which is unusual. I bring him a coffee from Seashell Bookshop as a peace offering. Not that I need it. Milo is habitually late. Or cuts out early. Must be nice to have your big brother as your boss. If he were any other employee, his ass would've been fired long ago.

I park my truck in front of the peach-colored cottage off Oceanview Blvd. A painting crew is already here doing finishing touches on the exterior trim around the windows. I hop out and retrieve the to-go cups, bumping the door closed with my hip.

Typically, working on a jobsite with another crew irritates the hell out of me, but Jessie and his guys work hard and stay out of my way, so I don't mind. Jessie pokes his head out of the back of his van and flashes me a peace sign as I pass. I lift my chin in greeting as I make my way around the front of the cottage. The power saw screams, but it's music to my ears. It means Milo is actually working instead of on his phone networking with music professionals.

Don't get me wrong, I'm his biggest fan. But for now, this is the job that pays his bills. His time is coming though, talent like his shouldn't be wasted on construction. Lucky for me, wood working and building houses are both my passion and my talent. I've been doing it since I was sixteen and started my own business sometime after Rosie left. My life was spinning out of control, but Jack came along with his nest egg from trading stocks and loaned me the money to get started. If it weren't for him, I probably never would've done it.

Milo is on the porch, cutting pieces for the island we're building and adding to the existing kitchen. The cottage is small but with the L-shaped kitchen that opens to a dining room, it has adequate room for an island.

He finishes the cut and glances up at me. "Look who decided to show up for work. Please tell me you finally got laid." He glances at me with a smirk, brows raised.

I shove the coffee at his chest. "Haha," I say sarcastically. "I brought coffee."

Clutching it in his hand, his eyes meet mine, but I tear mine away and face the ocean. "What happened to you? You look like shit."

"Thanks, Captain Obvious." I groan and chug my coffee

while attempting to focus on the distant waves despite the thick morning fog. "Didn't sleep much."

"Want to talk about it?"

"Nope," I grunt, turning back around. "I want to work."

Milo shrugs and takes a sip of his coffee before setting it on the porch rail. "I just cut the last piece for the build-out." He picks up the wood. "The quartz countertop slab got delivered a few minutes ago. I had them put it in the garage."

I'm only half processing what Milo is saying. Rosie's words are still swishing around in my brain, along with what I'm going to do about them. If anything.

"So last night Rosie told me she still loves me," I blurt over the rim of my paper cup.

Milo freezes before he reaches the back door with the cut piece of wood in his grip. "So you do want to talk about it," he snarks over his shoulder, a smirk on his lips.

"She was drunk texting me," I continue, still not fazed by his words. Typically I'd call him out on his smart-assery.

But he groans and that rattles me.

"Let me get this straight. She told you she still loves you, over text, and while she was drunk?"

I tilt my head, giving a limp shrug. "Yeah."

"How is it that you're the married one but I'm the brother who has more experience with women?"

"Pfft." I narrow my eyes at him.

"Right." He drags out the word. "Don't answer that. I get it, you're married. But I mean, I hate to say it…"

"Then don't," I mutter.

"But it's not like you two are actually married. It's just a piece of paper."

"A legal piece of paper," I correct with a cold glare.

He leans the piece of wood against the siding of the house, running his palm down his thigh. "Whatever. You know what I mean. You haven't even spoken for seven years. Hell, she had a kid and didn't tell you."

In my head, all that he's saying makes sense. But in my heart—well, that's a different story. "Do you have a point?" I grit my teeth.

"Yeah, man, I do. Women text all kinds of stupid shit when they're drunk."

I shake my head. "Not Rosie."

"I love Rosie, but yeah, even your precious Rosie. Her man isn't here. She was drunk and probably just wanted to get laid."

My skin prickles as my body heats. "It wasn't like that."

"Fine. Maybe not." Milo swipes his coffee off the railing and puts up his free hand in surrender. "So...what did you say back?"

I adjust the ballcap on my head and tug it lower, feeling some residual regret. "Uh...I may have told her I still love her too."

Milo's eyes widen.

"Yeah," I mutter, then give my head a subtle shake. "Not in those exact words. But something like...I'm trying not to love her."

"Bro," he breathes out. "Do you? Still love her?"

I raise my brows at my brother. Now who is the dense one? I never moved on after Rosie left. I haven't even seriously dated anyone.

"Right," he replies, tilting his head and putting his cup to his lips. "Okay, well that's that, I guess. Now what's your plan?"

"I don't have one. Not one that includes Rosie. That ship sailed." I turn and face the beach. The fog is beginning to thin and there're people running and a kid with a woman building a sandcastle. "The only plan I need to make is with Charlie. Nothing else matters."

"It's a solid thought. But I know you, and the love you have for Rosie isn't going to just go away. Especially since you're going to have to see her more often, ya know, because of the kid."

I spin back around to face him. "I don't have a choice," I say, anguish crawling up my throat. "She's marrying someone else."

We make eye contact and Milo's gaze hardens. I instantly feel like a dick. But Milo and I aren't just brothers. We're best friends. And if you can't snap at your best friend without it rolling off their back, then you weren't really friends to begin with.

He clamps his mouth shut, knowing when to stop pushing me. He picks up the wood again and opens the back door, pausing before going inside the cottage. "I hate to point out the obvious yet again, but she can't marry someone else if she's still married to you."

I watch him go before I move to the railing. Setting my coffee down, I grip the edge and inhale a deep breath, holding it for a few seconds before releasing it. I do it again. In and out. The wood beneath my hands bites at my palms.

The ocean mist touches my face, and I open my eyes and inhale and exhale one more time. My gaze drifts to the water and I study the waves as they crash onto the shore, my spiked nerves diminishing. My brain is telling me that I need to sign the divorce papers that have been sent to me countless times over the past year. But my heart is telling me to hold on.

Hold on for what though, I don't know.

***

We finish the build-out on the kitchen island and get the countertop mounted and I call it a day. The painters couldn't get to it until tomorrow and we can't wait.

Besides having a calendar packed full of jobs, I only have a few days to spend with Charlie before she returns to Seattle.

Milo's got back-to-back voice lessons tonight, so I send him home while I clean up and put away our tools. He'll be distracted the rest of the week. He's booked a recording studio in LA at the end of the week for a single he hopes to release on Spotify. The following day he's got tryouts for some new reality TV show for musicians.

After I slide in behind the wheel of my Chevy, I pull up Rosie's contact info on my phone and blow out a breath before I hit the call button.

She picks up after only the first ring. "Hey? Everything all right?"

"Are you free tonight?" I ask into the phone, then quickly correct myself. "I'd like to see Charlie. If that's okay?"

"Yeah, sure. She'd love that. What did you have in mind?"

I back out of the driveway. "I gotta head home and shower first. But how about dinner?"

"Dinner?" There's concern in her voice.

"Yeah, like 'kid dinner,'" I clarify. "Pizza, chicken nuggets, tacos?"

"No," she blurts. "No tacos, please."

"Okay, Charlie doesn't like tacos—noted."

"No, no, she does. But Stella and Daisy took me to the margarita and taco bar last night, and let's just say as good as the tacos were going down, they weren't so good coming back up."

I chuckle. "Got it. Makes sense. Okay, no tacos." Also makes sense why she drunk texted me too. "There's the pizza place downtown, Golden Pie's. Remember it?"

"Of course, yes."

"I'll pick you both up in about an hour." I drive to the end of the street and wait to pull out into traffic until we end our conversation.

"Hey, um...Beck? Did we talk last night?"

"Talk?" I tug the brim of my hat down, watching the few cars zoom by too fast for our small town. "No."

"Huh..." Her voice trails on the other end of the phone.

Part of me wants to tease her over this, but it's not really all that funny. "But you did text me last night."

"I did? Ack. Sh...crap." She corrects herself and the sound muffles on her end of the phone. "Oh...oh...no. Gahh, Beck, I'm so sorry."

"Guessing you're reading the texts?" I press my head back against the headrest and squeeze my eyes shut tight.

"Yep, and that's humiliating."

My stomach burns that she's not taking ownership of her confession. Because what's my excuse? I didn't have a lick of alcohol yesterday.

"Can we please forget that ever happened?" she whispers.

"Sure," I mutter in the phone before ending the call and pulling out onto the main road, my tires squealing.

14

ROSIE

*J*t shouldn't matter what I wear. It's just pizza at Golden Pies. And I'll be third-wheeling it again.

With that in mind, I tug on a pair of wide-legged light-wash denim jeans and a light green tank top. Charlie wanted to wear a dress. She said she wanted to look pretty for her daddy. Her new vocabulary is going to take some getting used to. The identity of her father has only been known by a few people in this world, but having it out in the open is still strange.

"Mama," Charlie calls from the back door where she's been peering out the small window. "He's here. He's here!" She runs to the living room where I'm sitting on the footstool and sliding my feet into a pair of strappy sandals. Snatching her stuffed mermaid from off the couch, she tugs my arm. "C'mon, Mama."

I exhale a light laugh. "I'm coming, I'm coming."

She takes off in a skip heading back down the hall, her red hair flowing behind her. "Hurry. I don't want him to leave without us."

I grab my purse and a thin sweater from the counter and meet her by the back door. "Don't forget your jacket." I nod toward the rack by the door.

"That's not going to match with my dress," she argues with a little pout.

"Denim goes with everything." I flash her a smile.

She ignores me, pushing back the sheer curtain hanging over the little window on the back door. Her feet shuffle in place. "He's not getting out of his truck. What if he leaves?"

"Hey? Charlie?" I call her, attempting to draw in her attention and focus on me. She glances at me over her shoulder. "It's okay. He's not going to leave. He'll wait for us." I touch her arm softly and lift my chin. "Get your jacket and then we can go out and meet him."

With that, she hops to snatch it off the hook, then swings open the back door. I follow her out and lock the door before hurrying down the steps. Beck steps out of his truck and rounds the front of it to meet us at the bottom of the steps.

His brown hair is wavier than usual and isn't hidden underneath a ballcap. Dressed in a pair of tan Carhartt pants and a black Carhartt T-shirt, he might as well be ready for a ranching or hiking photoshoot. We lock eyes and the air in my lungs stick. But what freezes us both is when Charlie flings herself at him and wraps her arms around his waist.

"Uh...hey, Charlie."

"Hi, Daddy. I thought you weren't coming," she rushes out, pressing her face into his side.

He flashes me an accusatory look before crouching. "Of course I was coming. I told your mom I would be here, didn't she tell you?"

I'm still standing here, paralyzed by Charlie not only hugging Beck, but calling him *daddy*.

"Yes, but it took you forever."

He checks his watch and chuckles. "I guess I am a few minutes late. Sorry about that."

"It's okay. What do you think of my dress?" She spins in front of him and my heart pushes against my chest. But it's like whiplash when another feeling hits me. My core tightens as he takes her by the hand and spins her around again.

He smiles wide, his brown eyes glittering as he beams at her. My knees wobble at the sight of this moment of vulnerability. "Your dress is beautiful."

"Mama picked it out," she admits, once she's finally done spinning.

"Well, your mama has good taste." He glances at me, and my cheeks burn. "All right, little girl, ready to go?"

"Yes!" She jumps up and down.

Beck opens the back door of his truck, and she climbs inside. I give him her booster and before he takes it, he leans in. A blast of smoky cologne hits me when he whispers, "Or I should say, she *had* good taste. But now she thinks rich guys in business suits are more attractive than blue collar guys."

My mouth pops open and we hold a look before he takes the car seat and turns around, leaving me stunned and dare I say a little turned on.

Golden Pies is just as I remember it. Same wood wall paneling, large black-and-white-checkered tile flooring, and red Formica tables. The lighting has a golden glow to it, but I appreciate the haze. It means when I look at Beck, his features are fuzzy and softened. Because the very last thing I should be doing is checking him out.

We peruse the menus while seated across from one another on a wraparound bench. Charlie is in between us and sits up on her knees to reach for the children's menu printed on a coloring page. She sets her stuffed mermaid on the bench next to her and chooses a blue crayon.

The bench vibrates beneath me, and I don't need to look to know Beck is jiggling his knee. I study him over the top of my menu. He glances from his own menu and back at Charlie.

"You okay?" I ask him.

"Huh? What?" He fiddles with his menu.

Charlie's crayon stops and she looks at him too.

"Your knee is shaking the whole booth."

"Oh, sorry." He stops jiggling and glances at Charlie again.

She smiles at him. "I shake my knee too."

His lips tip up and he folds his arms, resting his elbows on the edge of the table. "Really? Well, look at that. Just another thing we have in common."

She giggles and returns to her coloring.

"Tell me something else about you?" he asks, leaning closer to her. "You're artistic. This is the second time I've seen you coloring. You're good at it."

She hunches a shoulder, twisting her lips to the side. "I guess, thank you."

"Oh c'mon, Charlie, you're better than good." I encourage her to keep talking.

"Emma in my class, she's really good. Miss Owens hung her art on the wall in the hallway. But not mine."

A wave of defensiveness rises in me at the sadness in her tone. Beck whips his head in my direction and gives me a look like, *what the hell?*

Turning back to her he says, "Well, I'll tell you what. If you finish coloring that before we're done with dinner, I'll hang it in my truck. That's way better than some silly hallway."

Her grin is huge, lighting up her light brown eyes. "Really? Thanks, Daddy."

His lips twitch and his eyes flicker to me. My stupid heart

spasms in my chest. It's only a moment, a blip of a moment, but it's one I'm bottling up to hold on to for safe keeping.

A server swings by our table and interrupts, which is probably best. We order a cheese pizza for Charlie and a gluten free crust pizza for me and Beck to share. Beck and Charlie get lemonade. After the margaritas the night before, I stick with water.

Beck tries to keep the conversation going with Charlie and I try not to butt in. I could sing her praises forever, tell him everything about her, show him all the photo albums of her on my phone, but I want their relationship to form as organically as possible. I already took so much from them both.

I slip my phone from my purse and text West. Maybe it's out of guilt because I'm spending time with Beck or maybe it's guilt because I haven't told him about Charlie meeting her father. But I will owe him an explanation. Eventually.

Hey, what happened to you last night? I thought we were going to FaceTime

WEST

Sorry, sweetie. I got tied up at the office. Raincheck?

Sure

WEST

Tonight?

After I get Charlie to bed?

WEST

Works for me. I miss you!

Miss you too

Genuinely I do. West has been the only man since Beck that

I've trusted with my heart. When I agreed to date him, it was a big deal. And when he asked me and Charlie to move in, I spent a month contemplating it. Yet, when he proposed, it was an instant yes. Maybe that decision had been easy because Charlie loves him. Or maybe I figured if I couldn't make it work with him, I couldn't make it work with anyone.

West is also the only other man I've slept with besides Beck. With Beck, it was safe. He made me feel safe. Even though I hadn't been diagnosed with endometriosis yet, based on my symptoms, we assumed. But he knew sex was often uncomfortable for me or even painful. But he was patient with me. We talked through it together, there was plenty of trial and error, until we learned what positions were more enjoyable. He always made sure I was okay.

Sex with West is...difficult. While he's gentle and tolerant, he's usually more interested in getting off rather than assuring I'm comfortable. I guess I've concluded that it's something that will be more painful rather than pleasureful. Even if I do experience an orgasm, it sometimes leaves me with a throbbing ache afterward while he's already snoring.

"Ready to go?" Beck asks, standing next to the table and gazing down at me.

I blink up at him for a second before hurrying to scoot out of the booth, and a sharp pain stabs into my lower stomach. I pinch my eyes shut and hold my breath until it passes.

There's a light graze of his calloused palm against my bare forearm. "Hey, you all right?"

Steadying my footing, I flutter my eyes open and find Beck's face close to mine. I exhale and force a strained smile, reaching for my purse from off the bench. "I'm fine."

Instead of forcing the subject, he takes my word for it and leaves me to tend to Charlie. I follow behind them, the earlier feeling of being the third wheel tonight cemented when I see Beck's large hand tethered to Charlie's small one.

Once we're back at Dottie's, Beck takes Charlie's booster out of the back seat and sets it just inside the house once I've unlocked the door.

"Well," he says, rising up on the balls of his feet and shoving his hands in his front pockets. "I hope you had a good time tonight, Charlie."

"I did. It was fun." She hugs his waist, and he removes one hand from his pocket to wrap around her from the side. "Thanks for the pizza."

"You're welcome. Maybe I can swing by tomorrow night and we could play a game or something?"

"Yay!" she squeals, jumping up and down.

He glances up at me and I dip my chin, giving the approval even though it's strange giving him permission to see his own daughter. But he's not the only one trying to figure this all out. It's new to me too.

"Oh, I almost forgot to give you my drawing." Charlie offers him the paper menu she colored.

Even in the dark, his brown eyes appear glossy as he gazes at it for several long moments, his lips tipping up. Finally, he draws his attention to her. "Thank you. It's perfect. It's gonna go in my truck right now."

"Okay, almost bath time," I announce from the open doorway.

"Good night, Daddy. See you tomorrow." She skips inside and down the hall.

He pinches the artwork between his thumb and finger and runs his other hand over his hair. "Thanks for tonight."

"Of course."

He turns to leave.

"Beck?" I call, and meet him on the porch.

He spins around, blinking away the moisture in his eyes.

"We're leaving at the end of the week. I know there's a lot we need to talk about and figure out, but you're welcome to see Charlie anytime you want this week."

He gives me a single nod, but doesn't move.

"I have to go meet with Dottie's lawyer. She's supposed to go over her will, so then I guess I'll know more of what her plans were with the house."

"I think we already know. She paid me to fix it up so it would be ready for you and Charlie. She wanted you to move back here."

"She never told me that."

"Let me guess, she knew you were engaged?"

I flatten my lips and bob my head.

"She probably didn't want to flat-out tell you to not marry him. She only wanted you to be happy."

"Do you really think she'd want me to move back here? There's nothing for me here," I spit out.

He dips his chin and kicks the toe of his boot into the ground. "Nothing, huh?"

My stomach pinches.

"Beck," I say on an exhaled breath, the exhaustion comes on strong. I'm too tired to have this conversation tonight.

"Never mind, just forget it." He whips around and stalks off. "I'll see you tomorrow."

"Beck, wait," I call.

He stops before he rounds the back of his truck.

"I was gonna ask if you wanted to come watch Charlie while I meet with Dottie's lawyer?"

"Yeah, sure. I'd like that." Then he's stomping off again, jumping in his truck and slamming the door just a little harder than necessary.

I wait until he backs out of the driveway and starts up the street before I return to the house. When I get upstairs, Charlie is laying her pajamas out on her bed next to all her favorite stuffies. I grin at her before going inside the bathroom to start her bath water.

West calls while Charlie is in the tub.

I answer on the first ring. "Hey, I thought we were going to FaceTime?"

"I figured we'd better wait for that until after Charlie is in bed. I need some visual alone time with you...if you know what I mean."

My core tightens and I snort a laugh. "Good call. Charlie is just finishing up in the bath. Then bed, then we can Facetime."

"Hi, West," Charlie hollers into the phone from where she plays with a whale in the bubbles.

I put the speaker on.

"Hey, how's my big girl?"

"Me and Mama had the best pizza for dinner. When you come visit, we will take you there. You'll love it."

I draw in a breath, my heart hitting against my chest.

"Visit? What are you talking about, silly girl?" he replies.

I shoot to my feet and clutch my phone, punching off the speaker and stepping to the open doorway. "Hey, I should get her out of the tub and in bed. I'll call you back."

"Sweetie, what's Charlie talking about—when I visit?"

I stare at my girl in the bath, scooping up handfuls of bubbles. "Well, apparently Dottie had her house fixed up so Charlie and I could move into it."

"What?" he says, chuckling. "That doesn't make sense. She knew you and I were engaged. And my life is here, in Seattle. *Your* life is here. And so is Charlie's."

"I know, I know. Don't worry. For now, it's just an assumption. I'll let you know what I find out after I meet with her lawyer."

He sighs into the phone. "Oh, okay, good. You had me worried you two were scheming some big plan to get away from me."

"Ha, ha." My heart beats faster. "Of course not. Okay, well, I should get her out. She's turning into a prune."

"All right, sweetie. Tell Charlie good night for me. Then slip into something sexy. I'll be waiting for your FaceTime."

I end the call, a humming in my depths. "Okay, bath time is over," I sing to Charlie.

Once she's dried off and dressed in her pajamas, I tuck her underneath the covers and sit on the edge of the bed. She's got a stack of books that have quickly become her favorites of Grandma Dottie's. I pick the two off the top of the stack to let her choose which one she wants me to read.

"Okay, which one?" I hold them up, but Charlie is distracted. She's wiggling this way and that, frantically rummaging around her in the bed. "What's wrong?"

"Mama!" she screams, and throws her covers off her.

"What? What is it?" I shoot up off the bed and clutch my palm to my lower stomach, my eyes darting around the room, unaware of the magnitude of what I'm searching for. Is it a spider or an intruder?

"My mermaid," she says on an instant sob. "I can't find her."

My stomach plummets, but a little out of relief. While I'm sad for her, a missing stuffie is something the two of us might be able handle, but an intruder—I'd say Charlie and I would be in serious trouble. "Okay, calm down. I'm sure she's here somewhere, let me help you look."

"No, she's nowhere." She's throwing back the covers all the way now, scrambling on her hands and knees.

"Where did you last see it?"

"I don't know. Mama, I lost her. Daddy is gonna be mad." She collapses and I feel the plunge inside my own body.

"No, baby girl, he's not. We'll find her."

She curls herself into a ball and sobs and I take it back—an intruder would've been better than this. Seeing my baby like this wrecks my heart.

"Maybe you left her in the bathroom when you went for your bath. Or maybe downstairs." I rush into the bathroom, frantically searching. Nothing. I hurry down the stairs as fast as my legs will allow and search by the back door. Still nothing. Charlie is right. She's not here.

I head back up the stairs and find Charlie on the bed, still crying with the covers pulled over her entire body and head.

"I'll call Beck. Maybe you left it in his truck."

She quiets down, tugging the blankets off her face just a sliver so I can see her sad brown eyes. "Okay, yeah...maybe."

Pushing the blanket off her head, I brush back her still damp hair from her tear-soaked face. "Hold on." I tap his name on my phone screen, and it rings three times before he finally answers.

"Ugh, Rosie. Are you drunk calling me again?"

"What?" Confusion swims in my head and I stare at my crying daughter who's crumpled on the bed. "No."

"Is it Charlie? Is she okay?"

"We're fine. But Charlie can't find her stuffed mermaid. You know, the one you gave her? She had it with her tonight. And at dinner...shit." My brain shifts to the memory from earlier in the night when Charlie set the mermaid on the bench next to her in the booth. "It's at the restaurant."

"You sure?"

"Yes," I answer on an exhaled breath. "Unless it's miraculously in your truck, I'm pretty sure she left it at the restaurant."

"Stay on the phone, I'm gonna go out and check." There's a groan and the sound is just enough to scrape beneath my skin in a familiar way. His breathing picks up tempo and grows louder in the phone. Followed is the sound of keys jingling.

"Thanks. She's been sleeping with it ever since you gave it to her. She's a mess over here."

There's muffling in the background until he finally speaks into the phone again. "Nope, not in the truck."

"Lovely. Guess we'll be taking a little drive tonight. I doubt she'll be able to calm down without it."

"Now, hold on." He exhales into the phone. "I'll go over there and look for it. I'll bring it by if I find it."

"It's okay, you don't have to do that. You must be tired. You have work early, don't you?"

"It's fine. It makes no sense you having to load Charlie up in the car when I'm only five minutes away.

"You sure?"

"Of course. Anything for you." He clears his throat. "For Charlie."

My insides burn. My FaceTime starts ringing on the other line—West. I ignore it. "Thanks, Beck. Call me when you find her."

15

BECK

"I got it!" I sputter into the phone after Rosie answers. "Looks like she's still in one piece."

"Oh good, thank you!" Relief sounds in her tone.

"I'll be there in about five minutes."

"You're our savior. Seriously, you have no idea."

I hang up and drive faster than I probably should. This isn't a race. But tell that to my heartbeat, because it hasn't gotten the memo. It's been going a mile a minute since my phone rang and I saw Rosie's name flash across my screen.

By the time I reach Dottie's cottage, my pulse is too fast. I force myself to take a few moments and catch my breath. I'll be no good to them if I'm out here having a panic attack.

Experiencing a kid's lost object is new to me. How dire is this situation? Because the way Rosie sounded on the phone and by the way Charlie was carrying on in the background, I'd say it's very serious.

I rush to the back door, and I don't even have to knock. Rosie swings it open and the relief on her face is visible. Her shoulders lower while she exhales an audible sigh and a genuine smile pulls at her lips. It's the kind of smile that she used to have when she'd look at me. "Oh thank God. You honestly saved the day."

"No problem. Happy I could help."

"You have no idea."

"Here." I hold it out for her but she shakes her head, and I clutch my grip tighter around the soft mermaid.

"You should take it up to her."

"Really?" I run my hand over my head.

Rosie pinches the sleeve of my flannel and tugs me inside. "Yes, really. You're going to be her hero."

"I've never been someone's hero before," I admit, not able to restrain the inflating of my chest at the thought.

"That's not true," she whispers quietly, almost like a confession. Like maybe she didn't mean to say it out loud.

We make eye contact, and warmth expands beneath my ribcage. I have to force my feet to move down the hall so my mind doesn't take a trip down memory lane. "Well, if you think it will help."

"Are you kidding," she says from behind me. "A hero moment for a dad has to be a big thing. I wouldn't know, I don't think I have one."

I purse my lips, thinking about Rosie's overachiever dad, in all areas except for being a father. We at least had that in common. We both had dads who would rather be anywhere than with their kids.

Charlie's bedroom door is open about a foot, I peek my head inside and glance around. It's not really decorated for a kid. Since framing the wall and separating the large room back into two like it used to be, Dottie decorated it in the coastal theme that matches the entire house. Dottie probably hoped Charlie or Rosie might sleep in this room if they came to live. There's framed art of seashells and coral hanging on light blue walls. Mermaid and whale statues sit on the bookcase shelves among jars of seashells.

A pile of navy and white blankets sits in the middle of the bed, which I can only assume Charlie's hiding beneath. I rap my knuckles on the inside of the doorjamb to announce my arrival, then shuffle into the room with Rosie following behind me.

"Um, hey, Charlie," I mumble, clutching the stuffed mermaid in my sweaty hand.

The blankets rustle but she doesn't come out.

"Are you missing something?"

The pile moves and Charlie looks out, her eyes red rimmed, her little cheeks blotchy, and her hair mussed. But as soon as she sees what's in my hand, her entire face brightens. She shoots out of the bed and tears the mermaid from my grip. Bringing it to her chest, she hugs it and squeezes her eyes tight, smiling a huge toothless grin.

"Oh, thank you, thank you, thank you," she repeats.

When she opens her eyes, she launches herself into my arms and I have no choice but grab a hold of her so she doesn't fall. She nuzzles her little head in the crook of my neck and my chest expands. I inhale her sweet, just cleaned smell without thinking and it does something to my insides. Something I've never experienced before. It's like a new emotion has unlocked. One I don't have the words to name or explain.

Warmth travels through my arms and legs. "You're welcome."

"I knew you'd find her, Daddy. I just knew it," she whispers into my neck.

I peer over the top of Charlie's head at Rosie. Tears are filling her eyes, and she tucks her chin to her chest while she leans her back against the wall. My own eyes burn, and there's a weird pinch underneath my ribs. Is this what just a smidge of being a dad feels like? It's suffocating but in the best way and yet it's too much too fast.

I unlatch her small arms from around me and set her back

onto the bed. "Okay, well, your mama says you were just going to bed. So, I'll let you get to it."

She smiles and tugs the fluffy navy blue blanket up to her shoulders after she lies down. The stuffed mermaid is still tight in her embrace. This thing has already become so important to her that it caused a big ruffle in her bedtime routine. I push her matted hair out of her face and when I see the dimple in her chin that matches mine, my heart balloons inside my chest.

"Okay, well, I'll see you tomorrow," I mutter and back away. There's an urgency hurtling through my body, making me want to retreat.

"Wait! Daddy, stay."

"I—what?"

"Stay until I fall asleep. Please?"

I glance over my shoulder at Rosie. She's chewing her lower lip but offers me no other options. At the very least, she could give me a hint of what I should do in this situation. But she doesn't. So I take it as a sign that I gotta stay.

"Yeah, okay." I pick up the chair that's in the corner of the room and drag it near the bed. "I'll stay till you're asleep. But then I'm gonna go and I'll see you tomorrow. Deal?"

She grins. "Deal."

"Okay, now shut your eyes," I insist. I glance at Rosie again and mouth, *Is this okay?*

She nods and a small smile pulls at her lips. "I'm gonna go boil some water for tea. 'Night, baby girl." She gives Charlie a kiss on the cheek before tiptoeing out of the room.

I cross my arms and lean back in the chair, gazing at my daughter. *My daughter.* It's still sinking in even days after learning about her existence.

Watching her little brown eyes blink closed and her chest expanding and deflating as she slips into sleep is probably one of the most relaxing things I've ever witnessed. Forget meds. Forget therapy. Just give me this. Night after night.

She's so peaceful now when moments ago she was a wreck. Just like me when I'm in panic mode. Hell, I was there tonight. Racing to the restaurant, rushing inside like a lunatic searching for a stuffed mermaid that cost me sixteen bucks. But the stupid relief I felt when I found it was something I've never experienced.

For the first time since learning about Charlie, I've got my first glimpse into what it feels like to be a father. It was terrifying. And she wasn't even hurt. I can't imagine how I'd be if she were in danger or sick.

My gut tightens and it hits me in this moment—I want this. All the time. Not part time and sure as hell not only for the week Charlie and Rosie are in Golden Harbor. I don't know how that's going to happen. But I know I need to do everything in my power to make it happen.

Rosie pops her head into the bedroom and gestures for me to come. I glance back at Charlie and my heart is torn. I could sit here and watch her sleep all night. But I don't belong here. I rise to my feet and pull the blanket up to Charlie's chin before turning around and joining Rosie in the hall.

"You want to stay for some tea? We should talk," she whispers.

She's standing so close. Too close. Her toes are practically touching mine. The walls in the hallway shut in around us and I pull in a much-needed breath.

My brain knows we're going to talk about Charlie. She's offering me tea and a chat not whiskey and sex like when we were first married. But I can't convince my hormones of that. It's like anytime I'm around her, I can't think straight. I either want to fight or screw. Maybe both. Yeah, probably both.

I swallow. "Yeah, sure. Tea sounds...good."

She smiles and places her palm to her stomach. The action sends a trigger to my brain, reminding me of her illness. I follow her down the hallway toward the stairs. "Hey, you okay?"

"Yeah," she whispers, waving her hand in a little twirl over her shoulder. "You know, the normal. *My* normal," she clarifies.

I do know. More than I want to. I didn't simply marry Rosie, I married her chronic illness. The two are not separate from one another. They can't be when the disease is that severe. But I didn't mind. I loved her. There wasn't anything I wouldn't do for her.

"Please tell me you've found some relief, some alternative medicine or surgery after all these years?"

She hunches her shoulder and we enter the kitchen. It's clean but feels empty with no sign of Dottie.

"I've had a few surgeries. The symptoms got worse after I had to have a c-section with Charlie. More tissue attached to my organs. More specifically, my bowels. But who wants to talk about that?" She reaches in the cupboard for two mugs, and I study her while she moves around the kitchen with a little stagger.

My gut twists and I clench my teeth, leaning against the counter and crossing one ankle over the other. "I'm sorry. That sucks."

"Thanks," she mumbles, filling the mugs with hot malty scented tea. "I'm still debating on a hysterectomy. But my doctor says I'm young, I might want more kids."

My gaze flickers up from the steaming mugs and I catch her eye. "Do you? Want more kids, I mean?" I don't have a right to ask. But then again, do I? Charlie having a sibling would concern me.

So I don't take the question back.

She pulls her lip between her teeth and I study the movement before lifting my gaze again. We stare at one another, heat coiling through my entire body as my heart picks up speed.

Oh hell, she's beautiful.

I don't want her having kids with anyone else. Hell, I don't want her fucking anyone else.

She shakes her head, breaking the trance between us. "I don't know. For now, I'm on birth control. But none of it matters anyway. You and I both know a hysterectomy isn't a cure. It's just a Band-Aid."

"True…" I sift through what I remember about the illness. "But it might give you more relief than one of the other Band-Aids."

Rosie brings her mug up to her mouth and blows it lightly. "How do you remember all this?"

I rub at the back of my neck. "Oh, c'mon, even though you hadn't been officially diagnosed, I knew that disease backward and forward. You don't just forget." I give her an impish grin and pick up my own mug. I don't tell her the full truth. That Dottie told me she was finally diagnosed with endometriosis a few years ago. And that I've continued to keep up on the research, including following the endo foundation account on Instagram.

"You really were the best boyfriend." She says it quietly, almost as if it was a risk to say.

But a burning sensation rises inside me. "Husband, Rosie," I correct her. "Husband."

"Yes, I know," she answers, irritation in her tone as she carries her mug in both hands and shuffles around the kitchen island.

But hell, why is she the irritated one? I'm the one who was lied to for seven years. The one who has been putting my life on hold in hopes she'd come to her senses and return to Golden Harbor. Return to me.

We sit on the stools at the kitchen island, which is probably best. Not as formal as sitting in the living room, but we also don't have to face one another.

Empty boxes sit on the floor lining one wall and a few rest on top of the table, which explains us not sitting there. I shake my knee and stare into my mug like the tea is going to save me from the awkwardness hanging in the air between us. Or at the very least, tell me how to do this. How to sit here next to the woman I pledged to spend the rest of my life with, but I'm not allowed to touch. Or kiss. Or hold.

"When did you finally get diagnosed?"

"Three years ago." Her tone is softer now. "My symptoms got worse after I had Charlie."

"Worse?" The word strains unintentionally from me. Because I'm not supposed to care. But I can't help it. I missed seven years of her life. My head is still trying to play catch-up to that fact. How my wife can be a stranger to me.

"After a few trips to the ER, and seeing four different doctors, I finally found an endometriosis specialist who didn't spend my initial visit gaslighting me and telling me it was all in my head or suggest I see a therapist. Or who didn't want to just put me on birth control and 'see what happens.'" She makes air quotes, a deadpan look on her face.

Indignation scrapes beneath my skin. The memories rush at me of the negligence she received from doctors for years.

"She finally believed me." The words push out of her, threaded with emotion that I feel in my own chest.

We sit in the stillness as she blows into her mug. Internally, I struggle with what to say. While I'm sad I missed that part of her life and want to comfort her, there's a boundary I shouldn't cross. Because if I did, there would be no coming back from it. And I'm not sure my heart can withstand another beating.

Rosie exhales a long, audible breath. "I don't know what Dottie had in mind for her cottage, or for me and Charlie. But you know we can't stay here," she says, as if we're in the middle of this topic of conversation.

"I guess," I mutter, running my thumb over the rim of the mug.

"I want to do what's best for Charlie. I hope you know that." But she can't seem to look at me while she's talking. "Now that you two know about one another, I will do everything I can to keep your relationship going."

"Then why not at least consider moving here?"

"I can't." She reaches for her left shoulder and massages it, and it only distracts me for a moment. "Charlie goes to a fantastic school in Seattle. My job, my business is in Seattle. My fiancé is in Seattle."

I ignore that last reason. "There're great schools here, in Golden Harbor."

"Ha!" she scoffs, rolling her eyes. "Okay, sure, the schools here are fine. But I wouldn't say great."

"And you can start your business here. Open a salon downtown. It's a perfect location."

"It's not that easy. Do you know how hard I worked to get a space in the salon I'm in?"

"Are you going to honestly sit there and tell me it has nothing to do with your fiancé and the fact that he's rich?"

Rosie's lips screw up and she hops off her stool. "Ya know what, I think it's time for you to go. I'm tired. And I don't feel very good."

Only a smidge of guilt pushes through me because this is my daughter we're talking about. "Fine." I stand and round the island, setting my nearly full mug into the farmhouse sink. "I'm tired too. But this conversation isn't over. That little girl up there deserves to have a relationship with her father."

I storm out of the cottage without turning back around, my heart racing and skin prickling with anger.

16

BECK

Regret is a royal pain in the ass.

I tossed and turned all night. Pride keeps me from blaming it on the words I spoke to Rosie. What I said about her rich fiancé might be true, but it didn't give me any right to say it.

Milo gives me crap again at the job site for looking like shit. We're wrapping up the kitchen island at the Hernandez cottage. The painting crew came early to do the base of the island and left the finished cabinet doors in the garage for us to attach today.

"Lucky for you, you get to leave a little early again today," I tell him as I come inside the kitchen with my screw gun in hand.

"Oh, c'mon, Beck. Don't be a dick. You're gonna cut my hours because I was messing with you?"

Rolling my eyes at him, I chuckle as I crouch in front of the island. "Not because of that, dumbass. Not everything has to do with you."

Milo blows out a breath as he hands me a cabinet door. "Okay, so what's up?"

"Rosie has to meet with Dottie's lawyer and she asked me to stay with Charlie."

"Whoa, big step."

"Speaking of big steps, you wanna come by and meet her?" I glance up at him as he offers me a hinge.

He hunches a shoulder. "Sure. She's my niece, isn't she?"

"I'm thinking of going to the island soon to see Dad." The sound of him rummaging in the container with the hinges and screws is the only thing I hear in response because he's quiet at first. When I look up at him, he's pursing his lips.

"Are you taking Charlie to meet him?"

"Nah, not yet. It's too soon. Maybe next time she comes for a visit. But I was gonna tell him about her...maybe we'll go fishing or something."

"What do you mean, when she comes for a visit?"

He's deflecting, meaning he doesn't want to talk about Dad right now. I don't blame the kid—Dad did a number on him too. I want to push him to going to therapy, but last time I brought it up, he shot me down on the spot.

"So you couldn't talk Rosie into moving back here?"

A groan escapes my mouth. "Nope."

There's a pause between us while we continue working.

"And have you considered moving to Seattle?"

The screw gun nearly slips from my grip. "Are you serious? Explain to me, Milo, how that would work?"

"Chill." He holds up a palm. "It's not that crazy of an idea."

"My business is here. You're here."

"I mean, yeah...but you can't base a decision like that off those things. You know I'm not planning on working with you forever. And if I have it my way, my new single or this reality show will be the start of something big for me. I could be in LA by the end of summer."

My gut pinches and I don't want to think about a world like that. One where Milo is a few hours away and I'm here, in

Golden Harbor, alone. It's selfish—trying to keep Milo here—but I'd miss him too damn much.

I nod, trying and clearly failing at processing everything in my jumbled brain.

"Just don't rule it out, is all I'm saying. This kid—Charlie—she's your daughter."

"I know," I grit out.

⁕⁕⁕⁕

Milo and I stand on Dottie's back porch, and I knock on the door. A few moments later, the curtain lifts and Rosie and I make eye contact through the small window. There's something recognizable in her gaze. Hurt or pain. Her vision flicks to Milo and I just now realize that I never let her know he was coming with me.

"Hey, guys. Hi, Milo, it's good to see you again," she greets after opening the door.

Milo gives her a hug. "It's good to see you too. And again, I'm so sorry about Dottie. We all loved her."

"I know." She gives him a slight nod and turns around, waving us inside. "C'mon, I'm just about ready to go."

"Hey." I grab a hold of her hand on instinct before she can walk away. Electricity jolts between us. "Are you okay?"

She gives me a pained smile. "Flare day."

My shoulders drop. Those two words are like a blast from the past. When she had a flare while we were young, we would spend the day on the couch under a blanket. I'd give her pain medicine that didn't help much, bring her the heating pad, and let her pick whatever godawful rom-com she wanted to watch.

"Anything I can do?" I find myself saying as if on impulse because it was once a habit.

"You know me, I'll be fine."

It's a crap response. But I'm not the one who should be trying to fix this anymore. It's not my job. She has someone else for that. Even if I never thought of it as work before.

I follow her into the living room and Charlie is sitting on the floor eating a snack and watching cartoons on the TV. When she sees me, her entire face brightens, and I can't see my own but I'm fairly certain mine does too. She rushes at me and this time, instead of letting her hug my waist, I crouch and welcome her into my arms. My chest balloons, cracking below my ribs.

"Hey, Charlie, did you miss me?" I chuckle.

"Mama said you came to watch cartoons with me while she goes to a meeting."

"Yep, that's right. Whatcha eating? I skipped lunch so I'm starving," I tell her.

She pulls away and notices Milo. Her brow furrows as she studies him.

"Charlie, this is my brother, Milo."

Milo pushes his long waves back and bends at the waist. "Hey, Charlie. It's nice to finally meet you. Since this guy," he says, pointing a thumb in my direction, "is your dad, and I'm his brother, that makes me your uncle. How cool is that?"

She tilts her head.

"Look at that, Charlie. You have even more family to love you."

"That's pretty cool," she finally agrees.

"Well, all right. High five," Milo says, trying just a little too hard, but it doesn't seem to matter because Charlie complies and smacks her little palm against his awaiting one.

"I gotta go," Rosie announces, wrapping an arm around

Charlie's shoulder and bending to press a kiss to the top of her head.

"You mind dropping me off in town on your way?" Milo asks.

"Um, sure that's fine," she responds. "Are you gonna be okay?" she's looking at me.

"Are you kidding? We're gonna eat some"—I find the bowl on the coffee table—"fish crackers and watch some cartoons. It'll be fun."

"Okay, if you need anything, call me. I'll rush right back."

"Mama, go to your meeting." Charlie shoves Rosie in the back, pushing her down the hall.

"Okay," she says, breathing out a laugh.

"It was good to meet you, kid. Maybe I'll see you before you head back to Seattle," Milo says as he follows Rosie.

"Seattle?" Charlie mumbles in question.

Rosie whips around and we share a look. Like maybe they haven't had all the necessary conversations yet.

"Yeah, sweet girl. Seattle," Rosie explains. "He means when we go home in a few days."

"But I thought we were staying here. At Grandma Dottie's."

Rosie rushes back, taking Charlie's hand in hers. "We are, baby girl. We're staying here for a few more days. But then we gotta go back to Seattle. You have school, I have work...West is there."

Charlie's lower lip sticks out and I hold my breath. A small part of me is hoping she's about to throw a fit over this. Okay, maybe not a small part—a big part. Because if she wants to stay, it might sway Rosie's decision to stay too.

"I don't wanna go back. I wanna live here. Daddy is here. The beach is here. I can go to a new school. And West can come here."

Wait. No. That's not what I had in mind, kid.

Tears well in her eyes but Rosie is used to this. She's good at it too. "You know what? We still have a few more days here, at Dottie's, with Daddy…" She pauses, her gaze flickering to me then back to Charlie, because that's the first time she's referred to me as *Daddy*. "And then, we're going to all talk about things and make a plan. About all of it. Okay?" She brushes a single tear off her little cheek.

Charlie nods and a little smile pulls at her lips.

"Now go sit with your daddy on the couch and share your snacks with him. He loves snacks, just like you."

"Okay, Mama. Bye." She rushes back to me and tugs my arm, so I join her on the couch.

Rosie is a good mom. I always knew she would be.

The rigid exterior that's grown around my heart softens a little more. She's the reason it's there to begin with; I suppose it would make sense for her to be the only one to wear it down.

17

ROSIE

As I leave the meeting with Dottie's lawyer, the pain radiating in my legs and my back is nearly unbearable. But it does distract me from what I learned at the will reading. Beck had been right. Grandma Dottie left me her cottage. And she wanted me and Charlie to move to Golden Harbor and live in it.

My phone chimes and panic rises in my chest until I see Stella's name on the screen. I hold it in my grip and wait to respond. I slide in behind the steering wheel of Dottie's Mini Cooper and toss my bag onto the passenger seat.

The flower-shaped air freshener, the half-drunk water bottle rolling around on the floorboard, the cross hanging from the rearview mirror—they're all pieces of Dottie. Driving her car makes me feel closer to her, but it also hurts. How could I possibly live in her house and not be sad and reminded of her every single day.

The ache in my chest moves in tandem with the constant stabbing in my thighs. It's cruel to feel pain of the body and the heart at the same time. Not that I haven't grown accustomed to it. The pain in my life has been a perpetual tug of war. I find myself contemplating which is going to take me out first. Pain in my heart or the physical pain of this chronic illness.

Resisting the tears building in my eyes is pointless. I let them unleash at their will. The anguish swells in my throat and I have a difficult time swallowing while the sobs break free.

I tell myself I'll allow five minutes of release before I rein it back in and drive to Dottie's to face both Charlie and Beck.

Beck.

How do I explain to him that Dottie has left me the house, but I don't think I can stay? Can I? There's no way West would ever consider moving to Golden Harbor with us. And we couldn't possibly do long distance. That's not the kind of family life I want for Charlie. I want to finally give her stability.

My phone chimes again.

STELLA

Well??

She left me the cottage

And her ashes

STELLA

Whoa. Sort of like good news bad news

I guess you could say that

STELLA

Did she give specifics on what she wanted you to do with the cottage?

Yep. She wanted me and Charlie to move back here and live in it

STELLA

I'm gonna take a guess that you're super confused right now?

You know me well

STELLA

You and Charlie should come by tonight for dinner

Maybe another time? I'm in so much pain. My heating pad and pain pills are calling my name 😩

STELLA

That sucks girl. Let me know if you need anything

By the time I reach Dottie's I'm exhausted. But the exhaustion isn't the worst part. It's the razor-sharp pain in my thighs that's radiating down my legs and wrapping around my back. I practically drag myself out of the car and amble up the steps and to the back door.

When I push inside, the scent of cookies hits me and warms me to my center instantly. But that doesn't make any sense. Maybe Beck lit a candle?

I slip my shoes off and shuffle down the hall with a one-track mind: pain meds and my heating pad. Except the sweet smell of sugar and chocolate has me distracted.

"Mama!" Charlie's little voice sounds out and my vision skims across the living room and over into the kitchen.

She's sitting up at the island, propped on her knees.

"Hey, baby girl." I go to her and drop a kiss to the top of her head.

"Daddy is making cookies."

My gaze moves into the kitchen where Beck is bent in front of the oven and pulling a batch of fresh cookies out. Beck's backside in a pair of Carhartts is still as hot as ever. I suck my lower lip in between my teeth. I definitely should not be checking out his butt. Regardless of the license that says he *is* my husband, I'm engaged to another man. A nice man. One who wants to take care of me and Charlie.

"Rosie?" Beck calls, his eyes wide.

"Huh? What?" I shake my head, the blaring pain in my gut and legs presenting itself tenfold—along with heat filling my face from being caught red-handed gawking at him.

"I asked if it was okay that I made cookies?"

"Oh, right. Yeah, it's fine."

"And then I asked if you were okay. Are you? Okay?" His brows are up high on his forehead. It's his worry face. I've never liked to make him worry.

"I'm okay. Nothing some meds and a heating pad won't fix." I give him a pained smile, because we both know that isn't true.

"And cookies?" He flashes me a wink and it fractures part of the barrier I've built around myself.

What's this? A peace offering...from Beck?

He takes a cookie from the cooling rack and offers it to me. "They always used to help you on flare days. Thought it was worth a try."

My heart gives a punch against my ribs. *It is a peace offering.* The smallest olive branch. I'll take it. "Thank you."

He shrugs and returns to transferring the warm cookies to the cooling rack. "I'm just glad Dottie had the ingredients."

"Me too," Charlie exclaims from her stool.

"Okay, but not too many."

"She's only had six," Beck announces, but I think I only half hear him correctly.

I whip my head in his direction. "Six?" I gasp.

He and Charlie both start laughing and it takes a moment for the terror to leave my body. "Nice. Good one guys, ha, ha, ha," I say, fake laughing.

"It was Charlie's idea." Beck gives me another wink, and a shiver races down my arms. It came across as flirty but maybe I'm reading into as that. Maybe I *want* it to be flirty. Which is so much worse—me wanting it over his meaning behind it. This is new, strange territory for us. We've never not been a couple.

"I'm going to go up and change. You're free to go whenever you want." I take a few steps backward and stumble a bit before righting myself.

"Oh," he replies. "Yeah, okay."

"I mean, unless you wanna stay. Either way is fine," I blabber. "I just don't want you to feel like you have to stay."

"Stay, Daddy. Please," Charlie begs.

"I'll stay for a bit. Just until I know you're good." He gestures with his brows at me. As if we've got some kind of secret code. But I don't shield much from Charlie when it comes to my illness.

"Thanks," I mumble. I take two more ibuprofen even though it will do nothing for the pain. If I'm lucky though, it will at least take the edge off. I shuffle down the hall and climb the stairs. Beck and Charlie's voices and giggles waft throughout the house.

My stupid self thinks about how beautiful that sound is. How maybe I could've listened to it for the past six years if I had just told Beck the truth before Charlie was born. It's a cruel thing. Regrets. Letting your mind play tricks on you and punish you for things you have no control over. It's part of my illness. Making me live a life with regrets.

After I've changed into a pair of leggings and a sweatshirt, I come downstairs with my electric heating pad. The open space on the couch with the fuzzy throw blanket is calling to me. The only thing I want is to curl in a ball with my mini-me and put on one of her comfort movies. Which have all become my comfort movies now too. It's strange how one moment, your go-to's are rom-coms and the next moment they're animated talking animals.

"I made you some tea," Beck announces, just as I'm situating myself on the corner of the sofa.

I blink up at him as he's gliding over with a mug of steaming tea. I don't know what shifted between us. But something has. Is it because he knows I'm in pain? Or is he being nice in front of Charlie and later, when we're alone, he's going to argue with me.

"Thank you," I mumble, taking the mug in both hands.

"You're welcome." And there's a smile. A genuine smile. And then a spark when our fingers graze. He must feel it too because his eyes go wide when they lock on mine.

Warmth floods my body. Or maybe it's the pain meds working a little of their magic.

He tears his gaze away and fake coughs into his fist. "It's caffeinated, so hopefully it helps kick those pain meds in gear."

That small detail is an added thoughtfulness that has me in shock. I don't know if I should trust it. I find myself anticipating the other shoe to drop.

Curling up on the couch, I pull the fuzzy blanket over my legs and rest the heating pad on my stomach and the tops of my thighs. I hold the mug in my hands and blow lightly at the hot liquid, watching the steam billow.

"Mama, want me to put on the panda movie?"

"I'd love that."

Charlie picks up the remote and turns on the TV, finding the Netflix streaming option. She's learned how to work Dottie's remote faster than I have. She finds the movie and comes and sits in the crook of my bent legs. It's her favorite spot. I've gotten so used to it, that when she's in bed and I'm up late, I miss her being cozied up there.

That thought only makes my brain spiral. What if I have to share Charlie with Beck? I have to admit, leaving him with her today so I could go to the reading of Dottie's will was a relief. But if I stay in Seattle and Beck remains in Golden Harbor, Charlie will have to go back and forth all the time. Is that the kind of life I want for her? She finally has some stability. A good school with friends, and then West; a constant male role model in her life. Even if he's not that constant.

"Come sit here, Daddy." Charlie pats the couch next to her.

Beck complies, rounding the sofa and sitting on the other end. He's so close my feet are almost touching his legs. It takes me back to all those times we sat in this very position. Him waiting out my flares and cramps, bringing me anything I needed.

The sharp pains in my gut are growing worse and I tuck my legs in tighter, bringing them closer to my chest. It's too much fidgeting for Charlie and she gets annoyed and moves to the other couch, leaving Beck and I alone on this one.

I pinch my eyes tight, realizing I'm not going to make it to the end of the movie. It's only about halfway through and I can't get comfortable. The throbbing is too much. I won't be able to sleep when I'm in this much pain. But it is almost time for Charlie to go to bed. Maybe the movement and change in scenery will help.

"Okay, Charlie. Bedtime."

"Nooo, just a little longer. The movie isn't over yet."

"Sorry, kiddo, Mama is in pain, and I need to try to get some sleep too."

"Fine," she huffs.

"Want me to put her to bed?" Beck asks, shooting up to his feet.

I smile at him through the agony. "We can do it together?"

He nods and we head upstairs.

I tell Charlie she can skip her bath tonight and maybe we'll go to the beach tomorrow. Even though I have no idea how I'm going to feel and if we'll make it there at all. It's enough for her to brush her teeth, put on her pajamas, and hop into bed faster than usual.

She picks out a book and gives it to Beck. "Will you read to me tonight?"

"I'd love to." Beck's cheeks blush.

"Mama can help with the voices. She has this one memorized."

Beck glances at me and I raise my brows with a head tilt. Like, *what can I say, I'm that good.*

Sitting on the end of her bed, I listen while Beck reads and the sound is soothing in a way no medicine is. It's as if part of my brain is linked to the memory of how it once comforted me through my pain. Charlie stops him part of the way through and corrects him, telling him that's not how the voice of a frog would sound and that he needs to start over. I giggle behind my hand while Beck gives me a pitiful *help me* look.

Is this what it would be like or feel like—the three of us, a real family. Because in this moment, Charlie tucked in and looking peaceful, her daddy and I reading her a bedtime story together...it's perfect.

After I kiss Charlie good night, I go straight to my room and into the bathroom. The pain is intense, coming in waves, and it's unbearable. I start the bath water, making it as hot as possible. While the tub fills, I drop onto the floor and let the tears that have been threatening to break free finally release.

A few moments later, there's a knock on the door. "You okay?" Beck calls from the other side.

There's no point in lying. "No. But I will be."

"Is there anything I can do?"

Swallowing, I pinch my eyes tight and go against what my heart wants. "You've been great. But you can go now. Thank you."

I pull my knees into my chest and cry harder.

Again, there's a knock. "Hey, I'm coming in, so you better be decent."

The door swings open and Beck finds me in a tight ball on the floor, leaning against the tub.

His sharp inhale of breath is noticeable as his chest expands. "It's a bad one, huh?"

I nod through the tears still streaming down my cheeks.

He moves to the tub and waves his hand under the water, flinching and then turning the temperature down. "You trying to burn yourself?"

"I need it hot," I whine in between the sobs.

He crouches in front of me, cupping the back of my neck and searching my face. "Yeah, *hot*. You're not trying to boil yourself, are you?"

I hunch my shoulders, having reached the stage of desperation. "Whatever takes this pain away."

He shakes his head like he's irritated with me. He takes my hands in his and pulls me up. "Need help getting undressed?" Our eyes click; his are dark and possessive and heat blooms in my cheeks. "You know what I mean."

I can't help the small smile that tugs at my lips as I nod. "Close your eyes," I instruct, wiping the tears off my face.

His head rolls back as he groans. "You serious? I think I'm capable of helping you without looking."

"You sure about that?" I challenge, then bite my lip in regret as fire burns in his eyes as his gaze sweeps over me.

"What? It's not like it's something I've never seen. I hate to break it to you, but I've seen all your bits."

A shiver races down my back at the reminder. Crossing my arms, I rub my palms over them. "But not in a long time. And not since I was pregnant. Or had the surgery. My body…my bits…have changed. And I have scars."

He bends his six-foot frame to try to encourage me to look at him. But I can't. Not when it's me and him and we're having this conversation in this intimate space. I draw in a breath as the steam billows around us. "We all have scars, Rosie. Some just aren't visible. And scars don't make someone less beautiful. If anything, it does the opposite. Because it means you've lived. You're still living."

"Yeah, tell that to my brain," I mutter, and flip my wrist. "Now, if you want to stay in here and help, then close your eyes."

"Fine," he huffs, pinching his eyes tight with exaggeration. "But I hate to point out the obvious once again—"

"Yeah, yeah, I know. You've seen me naked before," I grumble, interrupting him and taking his hands in mine.

"No. I mean yes. But I was gonna say, you're my wife."

"Oh." My stomach flutters at his words. And now I'm fumbling with his hands as I guide them to the hem of my sweatshirt with his eyes closed. "Okay, here. Now lift slowly," I whisper.

He listens to my command, grasping the hem of my sweatshirt on both sides and gliding it up my body with care. "This guy—your fiancé—he's never…he's never made you feel like your scars…are…I don't know, a big deal, right?"

"What? No." My brows shoot up and his eyes flutter open. "Beck!" I warn with a shriek.

"Shit. Sorry, sorry," he mutters and pinches his eyes closed again. "And good. That's good. I just…I wanted to make sure." He drags my sweatshirt the rest of the way up my torso. His fingers brush against my bare skin and a shiver wriggles through me.

"West…West isn't like that." My words are unintentionally

laced with doubt, because he has made me feeling self-conscious about them.

"That's good." He tugs the sweatshirt over my head slowly.

I hold my breath until I have eyes on him once again and can ensure he's not peeking. "Can you just help with the clasp on my bra? Then I should be good."

He pulls his lower lip in between his teeth and bites on it, giving a slight nod with his chin.

I steal a second to admire his face while he can't see me. His dimpled chin covered by a three-day beard is something I've missed. As my gaze travels up to the mustache taking shape above his lip, I rub my thighs together.

"Ready?"

I spin around, facing my back to him. "Yep," I croak. And now my eyes are closed as I await his hands on me.

Warm fingers trace my skin before they work at the clasp of my bra. "Because if he's ever made you feel less-than because of your illness or your body—"

"Beck," I interrupt, catching his darkened eyes in the reflection of the mirror. He holds my gaze captive for a moment, a look of defiance staring back at me. My bra comes undone and my breasts release when it falls to the floor.

He shuts his eyes and takes a step away from me. "Sorry," he mumbles.

I slide my pants and my underwear down my legs at the same time. The quicker I get my clothes off the quicker I can get in the tub without him seeing me naked. I step over the ledge and into the steaming tub. It's almost too hot to get all the way under, but I don't have time to allow my body to get accustomed to the temp first. I lower myself beneath the bubbles, ensuring they're covering my chest fully.

"Okay, I'm in," I announce.

He turns slowly and when his gaze travels across the bubbles, lingering over my chest and my neck before finally landing on my face, I can't resist locking eyes with him again. Heat flares in his pupils and his jaw clicks. It's like a lit match between us, the fire burning brighter than it ever has before. We've spent seven years apart, and yet, in this moment, time and distance disappear and we're Beck and Rosie again. It makes zero sense.

His tongue darts out and he licks his lips, and I track every one of his movements. Including his palms as he wipes them down the fronts of his pants.

I tear my gaze away first. Shit, one of us has to before we say something we'll both regret. Or worse—*do* something we'll both regret.

He shouldn't even be in here with me while I'm in the tub. What would West think? Would I think it was appropriate for West to be in this situation if our roles were reversed? Absolutely not. But Beck isn't a random guy. He's *the* guy. And maybe that's more of a reason for him to not be here right now.

He clears his throat. "Um, do you need anything else?"

"No, I'm okay, thanks. You don't have to wait with me."

"Uhh..." He drags out the word, his tone uneasy, glancing over his shoulder at the closed bathroom door. "Do you want me to go?"

No is what I want to scream. I don't want him to go. He used to be my favorite person to be with when I was in pain. No one else brought me comfort like he did.

"I mean, if you need to go." I give a little shrug with one shoulder, afraid to move too much and show off parts of me I shouldn't.

"Rosie." He breathes out my name and goosebumps skim across my skin. "Do you want me to go?"

Biting my lower lip, desire aches low in my belly, but it's mixed with the constant throbbing, and I shake my head.

And that's all it takes.

Beck lowers himself onto the bathmat and sits next to the

tub so we're facing one another. He smiles and gives me a wink, as if to say, *don't worry, I got you.*

Just like he always has.

It's almost enough to distract me from the pain that's like a barbed wire coiled around my legs and stomach. Almost. I smile and exhale as I close my eyes and lean my head against the cool tiled wall.

18

BECK

Gazing at Rosie in the tub takes me back to both simpler and harder times. It's like no time has passed at all and we're suddenly right back to where we were all those years ago. She's beautiful, with her dark auburn waves pulled up, exposed freckles on the tops of her shoulders, and her eyes closed.

Just...breathtaking. I'm a dick for thinking it. I'm even more of a dick for looking.

But no matter how many times I tell myself she's taken, that she belongs to another man, in my heart—she's mine.

My fingers fidget in my lap and I drop my eyes to try to focus on them because continuing to stare at her is pure torture. "So your fiancé—West—I'm assuming he knows all about your illness and is supportive?"

"He's as supportive as he knows how to be," she admits quietly, releasing a low breath after the words have escaped.

Cautiously I lift my gaze to her, and I can't help the defensiveness that rises in me. "What does that mean?"

"He always makes sure the kitchen is stocked with tea and ice cream. And he'll take care of Charlie if I need to go to an appointment. Unless he's working. Then he's hired a nanny to help out."

"A nanny?" My brows lift.

"Yes, Beck. A nanny."

Intensity rises in my gut. "Why can't he make it a point to just be there? For Charlie, for you?"

"I don't know. I guess not every guy is as perfect as you," she bites out, then clamps her mouth shut like she's sorry for it.

I don't know whether I should be offended or flattered.

"Ha," I bark out, leaning my head back too hard against the wall. "I'm far from perfect. You and I both can attest to that."

She doesn't respond.

Staring up at the ceiling, I try to focus on the dust in the fan while I speak. "If I were perfect, I would've put my ego aside and chased after you when you left." I'm not even sure I should be saying what I'm saying. But I keep going anyway, lowering my gaze to meet hers. "Hell, I should never even have let you leave in the first place. If I hadn't...well, if I hadn't, I would've known about Charlie sooner. I could've been there for her...for you. We could've been a family. Like we always planned."

"Beck," she finally says, and my name echoes in the hollow of the bathroom.

I'm tempted to keep going. To say all the things I should've said to her seven summers ago. But she's giving me the look like I shouldn't. So I don't.

"You're here now," is what she whispers, and her words hum across my skin.

I dip my chin and swallow back all the things I want to say, all the remorse.

We sit in silence for a few torturous moments.

"Want a cold washcloth for your forehead?"

"That would be nice, thank you."

I hop up and pull a washcloth from the cabinet and run it under the cold water for several long beats, watching her reflection in the mirror. She adjusts in the tub and I get a peek at her tits before forcing myself to swallow and look away.

I wring out the excess water and shuffle back over to the tub, where I fold the washcloth before setting it gently on her forehead. Her beautiful green eyes disappear as they flutter closed and she releases a moan. The intoxicating sound sends a zing straight through my core and my dick twitches. I'm in caretaker mode, but I can't shut off my hormones. Being this close to Rosie, while only a layer of bubbles separates her naked body from my eyes...I'm about to come unglued.

Crouching near her, I drag the wet washcloth across her forehead and lift it to dab at her temples. I brush her wisps of loose curls off her face, and she lets out another little moan. I'm desperate to continue drawing out these adorable mewls. I must be down bad for her still, because I can't stop.

"How's that?" I whisper hoarsely.

She gives a little nod. "It's good. But I need more."

The hint of her begging has my dick hardening and straining against the front of my pants. I'm thankful this tub ledge is separating her view of me.

Her eyes fly open, and she stares into mine with abashment shining in hers. "Colder. I need it colder," she rushes out in correction.

My lips pull up in the corner, amused. "Okay. I'm on it." I run the cold water again and repeat the process, taking several deep breaths in and out so I don't send myself into a panic attack.

When I return, her eyes are closed. I lay the washcloth across her forehead again, but this time, I abandon it and return to my place on the floor. Her eyes blink a few times before she studies me, and I force myself to look away.

"Thanks," she finally whispers. "For staying," she elaborates.

"No problem. I had nothing else going on." I cross one leg

over the other and make myself focus on the framed art of coral hanging on the wall above her head.

"So no hot date tonight?" she teases.

I shoot her a mock glare. "Nah. Funny how fast word gets around in a small town that I'm still married."

"Oh, right." She winces. "Sorry."

I hunch a shoulder. "Whatever," I mutter. "It's fine."

"I really am glad you're here tonight."

When I glance her way, she's smiling and worrying at her lower lip, and we hold eye contact for a long time. Maybe both of us saying all the unsaid things in our minds that we'll probably never get the courage to say out loud.

❧❧❧❧❧

*W*hen Rosie is ready to get out of the tub, I leave her to get dressed and go downstairs to make her some chamomile tea. I unplug her heating pad from near the sofa and take it and the hot mug back upstairs. I push open the bedroom door with my foot. She's already tucked in under the blankets on the bed.

A smile brightens her face. She already looks better.

"I found your heating pad and made you some tea."

"Beck," she says on an exhale. "You didn't need to do that."

"It's fine. I didn't want to leave you without making sure you have everything you need first." I set the cup on her nightstand.

"You're leaving?"

I rub at the back of my neck. "Yeah. I should let you get some sleep. It's been a long day."

"It has. I haven't even had the chance to tell you about what happened at the reading of Dottie's will."

"Right," I mutter, like it hasn't been at the forefront of my mind since she returned earlier. "Anything exciting?" I crouch in front of the nightstand and plug in her heating pad. When she doesn't answer, I sit up on my knees and look at her.

She's got a bottle of pain meds in her grip that she's fiddling with.

"Rosie? What happened?" I snatch the bottle and open it for her before handing it back.

Our fingers graze slightly and she sighs. "Well, it turns out, Stella was right about a few things. Dottie did want me and Charlie to move back here. She left us her house. Charlie and me."

"Oh." My mouth goes dry as I stand and cross my arms like I need to prepare myself. "And? What are you gonna do?"

Her gaze lifts to meet mine and I catch the uncertainty in them. "I don't know."

"C'mon, Rosie, you gotta give me something." I pace in the bedroom. "You must have an idea of what you want to do."

"I don't." She shakes her head. "I'm too exhausted to think clearly right now."

"No shit," I sputter. "Since you let me in there while you were taking a bath."

"Whoa." She straightens, propping herself up in the bed. "What does that mean?"

"That you're not thinking clearly. You're engaged to another man but then you asked me to stay in there...while you took a bath." I stop pacing and throw my hand up. "And I think I know why."

"Yeah? You think you're so smart, huh?" With her eyes narrowed, she shields herself by pulling her knees to her chest and hugging them. "Okay, tell me why."

"Because," I shout. "Because I think you still have feelings for me."

The look on her expression shifts, almost like she's been punched.

"Just admit it."

"So what if I do?" she cries out. "So what? You still have feelings for me," she accuses.

"I never said that," I bite back.

"No? Then tell me otherwise." She lowers the blankets and rises to her knees. "Tell me you don't still love me."

"You tell me you don't still love *me!*" I holler back, stopping at the foot of the bed.

"You're the one who's still holding on to a marriage that hasn't been anything more than a piece of paper in seven years."

With my hands clenched in fists at my sides, I open my mouth, but then clamp it shut again, my heart hammering in my chest. *This could be it, Beck. This could be the moment you finally admit your feelings and set this life on track again.*

"Mama?" Charlie's voice sounds out and I whip around and find her standing in the open doorway, squeezing her stuffed mermaid to her chest.

"Hey, baby girl. You okay?" Rosie asks.

"I'm okay." She rubs a clamped fist over her eye. "Are you okay, Mama?"

"Of course, Beck was just getting ready to go. He got me some tea and plugged in my heating pad for me first."

"Daddy, do you really gotta go?" Charlie asks, and the question nearly splits my chest in half.

I crouch in front of her and take her little hand in mine. "I do. But I'll try to come by tomorrow. To see you and check on your mom."

"Okay." She wraps her free arm around my neck, giving me a hug.

"Now, why don't you go cuddle with your mom. I'm sure it will do her some good."

"I like the sound of that. Come up here with me, Charlie." Rosie opens the covers, and Charlie runs over and crawls into the bed with her.

"I'll check in with you tomorrow," I announce.

Rosie dips her chin. "Thanks."

I turn and walk out of the bedroom, not able to look back for fear it'll break me. "Good night," I mumble over my shoulder before I rush down the hall and stairs. Leaving my family is more difficult than I ever thought it would be. Except they aren't mine.

And maybe that hurts the most.

19

BECK

How are you feeling?

ROSIE

Much better. Thanks again for yesterday

Welcome

Mind if I come by tonight? To see Charlie?

ROSIE

Charlie wanted to go to the beach today. Want
to meet us at Jensen Beach?

If you don't mind me tagging along

ROSIE

Of course not. I want you to be able to see
Charlie as much as possible before we go

So you're still planning on going?

ROSIE

We can talk more tonight

Fine

I'll text you when I'm on my way

I end the call and have the urge to chuck my phone into the ocean. Instead, I shove it into my pocket and throw my head back and release an untamed groan.

"That good, huh?" Jack's voice sounds out and I turn around.

He's standing on the porch holding out a coffee from Seashell Bookshop. I snatch it from him and grunt again.

"You're welcome." He takes a drink of his coffee, like him being here on my jobsite on a random weekday dressed in a suit is normal.

"Thanks," I mumble, eyeing him below a furrowed brow. "What're you doing here? Shouldn't you be at work?"

"I'm the boss. I can do whatever the hell I want."

"Huh. Well, I'm the boss too but here I am at work."

"You need to hire better employees."

"My brother works for me," I argue.

"My point."

I lean against the railing, facing Jack and the house, and lift my coffee to my mouth. "It's the middle of the day. And you never just show up at my jobs. You okay?"

His jaw ticks. "Thought I should check on you. You've had a lot going on lately."

"No shit." I take a swig and shake my head.

"Hey, don't be an ass just because you've got a boner for your ex-wife and she's moved on."

"Wife," I correct him. But what's the point? Why do I have to keep correcting everyone? Including the woman holding the title.

"That—that's your problem right there." He stabs a finger at me. "She's not your wife anymore. Dude, she's engaged to someone else. Face it, she's moved on."

"Ya know what? No one asked you to come by."

"Again, you're welcome."

I take a drink of my coffee. He's right. Though I won't admit it to him. "Rosie's leaving in a few days."

Jack drops his chin and shakes his head. "That sucks, man. I'm sorry."

"What am I supposed to do? I don't know how to stop her. She's going back to Seattle and taking Charlie with her and then when am I gonna see her? Some random weekends I can get over there? Or maybe some holidays?"

He shrugs. "I guess."

"Well, that's not good enough." I pound my fist on the top of the railing.

"Did you tell her to stay?"

"Yep," I drag out, almost as if I'm afraid to admit it.

"Then there's nothing more you can do. My advice is—"

"I didn't ask for your advice," I interrupt.

"Tough shit, I'm gonna give it to you anyway. Sign the divorce papers and let her go. And take every opportunity you can to see your daughter." He slaps my shoulder. "I gotta get back to work. But let's hang out after they're gone."

I push off the railing and tip the cup at Jack. "Sounds good. Thanks for the coffee."

"Welcome. See ya later." He lifts his chin in a nod before rounding the house.

Milo peeks his head outside. "Coffee? Where's mine?"

"At Seashells Bookshop," I reply with a grunt.

"Smart-ass," he mumbles. "C'mon, I'm ready for you in the house."

"Yeah, yeah, coming." I take in one last look at the beach, inhaling a deep breath.

My mind wanders to the beach near Dottie's house. It's a similar view but has the perfect alcove. The one Rosie and I spent countless hours hiding in while we made out. Dry humping on a beach is a lot messier than one might think. Sand goes everywhere, regardless if you've got clothes on or not.

         ❧❧❧❧

I skip out of work early. Jack was right about one thing: when you're the boss, there should be no reason why you can't leave early. Plus, Milo owes me for planning to cut out early Thursday and taking Friday off. My nerves are extra jittery. Probably just anxious to see Charlie, but I can't help but stress over the conversations Rosie and I need to have.

We came so close last night to either completely ending things between us or confessing our love to one another. I'm not sure which one I fear more. I still love her. God only knows why. The woman broke my heart seven years ago and then showed up here with my child. I should hate her.

But how do you hate your first love? The only person to ever love you who didn't have to. No blood. But she might as well have been. I've never loved anyone else. Not like this. And I fear I never will.

If I let her leave again without telling her how I really feel, I know I will regret it. But the words Jack said to me today play on repeat in my mind as I drive to the beach to meet Rosie and Charlie. *Sign the divorce papers and let her go. And take every opportunity you can to see your daughter.*

Jack is probably right. I had my chance with Rosie, and I blew it. But she blew it too. And maybe that should be our sign.

If we were meant to be, we would've stayed together. It wouldn't have been easy to let her go.

Except it wasn't easy.

Letting Rosie go was the hardest thing I've ever done.

My phone chimes as I'm getting out of my Chevy at the beach parking lot.

ROSIE

We're about a half mile past the boardwalk

I yank off my boots and socks when I reach the sandy path that leads to the beach and hook my fingers in the back of them. It's busier than I'd like, but it's not surprising. Golden Harbor is becoming a tourist trap, quickly evolving into one of the coast's top small towns to move to. Now, if it appealed to the only person I care about moving here, then I wouldn't mind our little town making it in the news.

The boardwalk comes into view. I shove back the memories and focus on the present. Because the past is the past. And Rosie and Charlie are here now. And that's all that matters.

When I finally spot them off in the distance, my heart gives a squeeze. I take a mental picture because it may be all I have in a few days once they're gone, and I'm left here alone. The raw, unfairness of that reality claws up my throat.

Charlie sees me first and when she does, it's like her entire body smiles. I smile back and crouch, opening my arms wide as she runs toward me. When she reaches me, I clutch her against my chest and close my eyes tight. Unexpected emotions rattle me and tears prick my eyes.

Damn. I'm not a crier.

I swallow. "Hey, big girl. How's today?"

"Daddy, I'm so glad you're here!"

I draw back and stand when I spot Rosie approaching. But Charlie isn't letting go so easily. She wraps one arm around my leg.

Rosie is dressed in a yellow tank sundress that's low-cut with pockets. Her hair is down and wavy as the early evening breeze blows through it. A shock of intoxication pulses through my veins upon seeing her like this. Her coloring looks better than it did yesterday.

"You found us," Rosie says, a small smile slipping. "How was your day?"

The question throws me off. Like she's trying to be the dutiful wife and I'm the working husband and we are one big happy family spending an evening at the beach. But it's all a fucking mirage.

"It was fine," I answer. "The more important question is, how's the beach today?" I glance down at Charlie and she finally unravels herself from my leg, taking a hold of my hand with her tiny one. "Find any good shells yet?"

Her face lights up, showing off her toothless grin as she digs her free hand deep into her pocket and presents two colorful shells.

"Those are awesome."

"Mama found a piece of blue sea glass. Show him, Mama."

Rosie removes the sea glass from the pocket of her sundress and opens her palm. "Pretty, right?"

"Yeah, that's a good one."

"It's the first time I've found sea glass."

"But, Mama, you have a necklace with sea glass in your jewelry box. It's green and a heart."

Rosie and I both lift our gazes from the sea glass and meet one another's eyes. Blush tints her lightly freckled cheeks and I hold my breath.

"You kept it?" My voice is like gravel.

Tilting her chin, she breaks our eye contact. "Of course I did."

"But...why?" It comes out accusatory.

She runs her fingertips down the front of her neck, turning

to face the ocean. "Hey, Charlie. How about you show your dad how fast you are at playing tag with the waves?"

"Okay. Watch me, Daddy." Charlie runs backward until she sees me looking in her direction and she spins around to run toward the water.

"Why?" I ask again, while I watch Charlie.

"I can't believe you're asking why. That piece of sea glass was like a promise. A placeholder for the engagement ring you gave me later. Don't you remember?"

"Of course I remember," I mutter, squinting through the breeze.

"Then why ask?"

"I guess I just don't get why you'd bother keeping it."

"Despite what you might think, I did love you."

"Did?" I say, without thinking it through first.

"I did," she confirms, and my bare feet feel as if they're sinking deeper in the wet sand. "I still do."

I whip my head to face her and my heart thrashes against my ribcage. She's smiling, her cheeks aglow and her golden-rimmed green eyes sparkling against the low setting sun. She attempts to push her hair behind her ears as it blows crazily in the wind.

"Don't look so surprised." She rolls her eyes playfully.

And I can't sort through my emotions fast enough. My hands tremble and I wring them out. Is this genuine, or is she fucking with me? Because my heart couldn't handle that.

"Last night—"

"My pride didn't let me admit it," she interrupts. "Not before you did. But then when I woke up this morning and found myself face-to-face with the urn holding Dottie's ashes, I was reminded just how short life can be." She takes her eyes off Charlie for a second and glances my way with something that resembles pity reflected there. "But, Beck..."

"No buts," I interject, the muscle in my shoulders stretching taut as I draw in a breath.

"I'm engaged to someone else. When he proposed and I said yes, I made a promise to him." There's pleading in her misty eyes.

Hot blood rushes through my veins as anger builds in me. "Yeah, and you made a promise to me too."

"I know." She bites her lip, nodding. "I will always love you. That will never change. But I think it's time we come to terms with the truth. We both played a part in our breakup. The fact that I left and you didn't come after me—that I left *at all*— should tell us that our love wasn't enough."

"That's not fair," I bite out.

She bobs her head. "It's not. At least we agree on something."

My throat goes thick, and I can't think straight.

"We need to just focus on what's best for Charlie now."

I turn and watch as she runs to the waves, taps the water with her toe, and then spins around and races back toward us. I squeeze both of my fists into tight balls, stretch out my fingers, and squeeze them again in some sort of attempt to keep the anxiety at bay.

"Can you please do something for me?" I don't wait for her to answer, or maybe I don't hear her as there's a blaring pounding in my ears. I turn to look at her intently. "Promise me you'll really think about moving here."

"Beck." My name slips out of her mouth like she's exhausted with me.

"Not for me. For Charlie. Please."

She purses her lips before finally nodding. "Okay."

Then I turn and tug my phone free from my pocket and take pictures of my daughter as she plays in the waves. Because these photos of her—now—in Golden Harbor may be the only ones I'll ever get of her here. That thought is almost enough to send me spiraling. But I repeat the mantra in my head that Dr. Sam taught me.

Inhale. Hold, hold, hold. Exhale.

Inhale. Hold, hold, hold. Exhale.

Inhale. Hold, hold, hold. Exhale.

I refuse to miss this precious moment with my daughter because of a damn panic attack.

20

ROSIE

It shouldn't have been hard to let Charlie go with Beck. He is her father after all. But he still doesn't know her that well. He's never dealt with her having a meltdown or a spiral. And what if he can't tell the difference? Between a typical child tantrum and an anxiety-induced spiral. Just because he lives with anxiety and panic attacks doesn't mean he can see it in another person.

It's only ice cream. They'll be gone for an hour or two tops. She'll be fine, I tell myself as I fix a charcuterie board for girls' night with Stella and Daisy. The distraction will do me some good.

There's a knock on the back door and after I open it, Daisy and Stella squeal and rush inside Dottie's seaside cottage. Stella gives me a hug and holds out a bottle of wine. Daisy's arms are full as she carries in ice cream and more wine.

We all go into the kitchen and Stella starts opening drawers. "Where's Dottie's wine opener?"

"Second drawer to the right of the fridge." I point.

"Got it," she singsongs, holding it up.

"Yum, everything looks delicious." Daisy studies the goodies on the charcuterie board.

Stella twists the wine opener into the cork. "So do we want to watch a movie, or do we want to talk?"

"I don't care." I take the ice cream from Daisy and put it in the freezer.

"I'm up for anything. Have either of you seen that new rom-com on Netflix?" Daisy plops down on a stool at the kitchen island.

"Are you kidding? I haven't seen anything that's dropped in the past few months." I pull a stack of plates out of the cupboard and set them on the counter.

"Sounds like we should watch a movie. Girl, you're missing out."

"I don't even know how you find the time. You're at Peace of Cake twenty-four seven." Stella finally pops the cork.

"Not twenty-four seven. But yeah, I'm there a lot. Willow needs me more right now."

"Maybe if her prick of a nephew had stuck around instead of ditching her and the business, you wouldn't have to work so much."

Daisy dips her chin to her chest, tucking her blonde hair behind her ear. "It's fine. You know I don't mind. I love what I do."

"And it loves you. You're so good at it," Stella says.

"I can't believe Christian never came back." A few high school memories play through my mind. "I guess I assumed he would've come back after college. That was his plan, wasn't it?"

Daisy rolls her eyes. "Was—key word. Instead of using his business degree to come back to Golden Harbor and take over Peace of Cake as planned, he used it for evil. Got some hot-shot job in LA making the big bucks. Guess when you get used to looking at an income with that many zeros, you no longer want to take over the family business."

"Willow has been real sick," Stella explains.

"Oh no, I'm so sorry, Daisy. I didn't know."

"She has good days and bad." She sniffs.

"But if something happens to Willow, Peace of Cake will be in good hands." Stella gives Daisy a pointed look.

I glance back and forth between them. "You?" I gesture with an empty wineglass at Daisy.

"That's the hope. I've been there since practically day one. My mom and Willow have been best friends since college."

"And she works her ass off."

Daisy waves off Stella. "Anyway, bingeing my shows is all I have in this life."

"Not true. You have us." Stella pours the dark red wine into the glasses.

"For now," I correct her.

"What do you mean for now? Stella said Dottie wanted you to move back to Golden Harbor and that she left you the cottage."

I shoot a look at Stella.

She hikes her shoulders up toward her ears. "You never said it was a secret."

"It's not. It's fine. It's just...things are complicated." I rub at my temples.

"What kind of complicated? Like Beck-complicated?" Daisy waggles her light brows while smirking.

My mind drifts back to the other night when Beck was in the bathroom with me and then afterward when I nearly confessed I was still in love with him. "No," I finally say, accepting the wineglass Stella's holding out for me.

"That was a long pause," she accuses.

"What's going on with you two?" Daisy brows lift in interest.

"Nothing."

"No, girl, you can't lie to us. This is you and Beck. Things with you two have always been more than complicated."

"Well, if that's true, things got more complicated. Not just with Charlie, and Dottie leaving the cottage to me. But then learning what Dottie's wishes were." I shake my head, pushing back unwanted emotions.

"Maybe it's time for a pros and cons list," Daisy says over her shoulder as she leads the way toward the sofas in the living room set up into an L-shape.

"Oh, yeah because that always goes over well in romcoms," Stella chimes in, carrying the charcuterie board.

"Making a list is pointless. I can't move here. West would never." I plop down on the end of one of the sofas and hold my glass out so wine doesn't swish out.

"If he really, truly loves you and wants to spend the rest of his life with you, he should at least consider it. That's love. That's marriage. It's full of compromise." Holding her glass up at me, Stella gestures with her chin before swirling her wine around and taking a sip.

I know she's right. I should be able to talk to West about all of this and not make the decision on my own. But what kind of job opportunities would he have in Golden Harbor? His current job is too involved to do remotely. And I'm not a fan of long-distance relationships.

"What about Charlie? Has she said what she wants?" Daisy asks, plucking a cracker and a piece of cheese off the tray before tucking her legs underneath her.

"She's six. What do you think she wants?" I glance at her. "She wants to stay here, by the beach, with her dad"—I mimic a child's voice when I say the last part—"but she also said West can come visit. She doesn't understand."

"Maybe he can. Maybe he comes on the weekends."

"Call me old-fashioned, but I don't want a husband only on the weekends."

"Well, you've had one that you haven't seen for seven years and that hasn't seemed to bother you."

I shoot her a glare.

"Damn, Daisy," Stella drags out, eyes wide.

"Sorry." She winces. "I didn't mean it how it came out."

"No, no. I deserve that." The food choices spread out on the charcuterie board no longer look appetizing.

Daisy pats my leg. "No, you don't. And I am sorry. I know it was hard for you to stay here. Thinking you'd lost the baby..." She shakes her head. "I can't imagine."

"And we're glad we got to spend these few days with you. Charlie too." Stella smiles at me and warmth blooms in my chest. "We'll support you in whatever you decide. As long as you don't go seven years without seeing us again."

My lips tug up at the corners of my mouth. "Deal."

<div style="text-align:center">~~~~</div>

After Beck brings Charlie back, Stella and Daisy leave and the three of us watch a short show on TV like a regular family. She asks if he can read to her and tuck her in. I try not to allow the hurt to show on my face when I tell her it's fine and kiss her good night from the couch.

Respecting their time together should come easier, especially since they're up there saying goodbye. Even though we'll be back in about a week, I'm sure it's hard on Beck. He's just learned he has a daughter and now I'm taking her away.

I clean up the dishes, handwashing the wineglasses while my mind processes the conversations from the evening with my friends.

Footsteps sneak up behind me and I whip around. "Beck. You scared me."

He rubs at the back of his neck, shielding his wet eyes from me, and there's an instant ache in the center of my chest. "So, I'm gonna go."

It's a silly question, but I ask it anyway. "Are you okay?"

There's a moment of silence. He pinches at his eyes with his thumb and finger and deflects the question. "Do you need me to drive you to the airport in the morning?"

"No, Stella's already offered."

"Oh...okay." He takes a step backward. "So?" I ask and wait, looking intently at her. "Have you thought more about moving to Golden Harbor?"

"I have. And I can't."

A grumbling sound escapes his lips as he drops his head.

"I need to go back to Seattle and let Charlie finish her last week of school and get some other things straightened out. I need to talk with West in person. And tell him that Charlie has met her father. I can't have this kind of conversation over the phone. I also need to reschedule appointments for my clients with other stylists. Then Charlie and I will come back to Golden Harbor once she's on summer break."

Beck lifts his gaze, and we lock eyes. His chestnut brown's glaze over and he doesn't speak.

"It will give Charlie some more time to make memories here at Dottie's...and with you. And it will give me time to pack this place up and get it listed."

Sadness washes over his expression.

"Don't give me that look, please. For now, it's the best I can do."

His eyes appear heavy. "I guess that's something."

"Then we'll make plans for you to come visit Seattle in the fall. Charlie will be in school, so maybe over one of her breaks. Or Thanksgiving. Maybe start looking at hotels now."

"I guess," he mutters.

"Well, you weren't expecting me to offer you a room at West's, were you?"

"Honey, if you're living there, planning to marry the guy, maybe it's best time you start calling it your place too?"

I narrow my eyes. So we're back to the nickname again.

"Seems like you've given this a lot of thought."

"I have." I try to push confidence in my tone.

He takes a step closer and his short beard and mustache have me imagining what it would feel like having it touch my bare skin. His defined chest is visible in the solid black T-shirt he's wearing. *What is he doing?*

"So you're sure this is what you want?" His voice is gravelly and sexy.

What am I saying—sexy?

I nod once and swallow. "It is. It will be best for Charlie."

"And what about you?" He takes another step closer.

Heat races straight through my core and I mindlessly trace my fingertips over the front of my throat. "What about me?"

"What do you want, Rosie?"

My eyes search his, just trying to place what I'm seeing reflected in his darkened brown stare. Craving? Tenderness? "What I want doesn't matter."

"That's BS and you know it," he mutters.

"Well, maybe I don't get what I want," I fire back, pushing up the sleeves of my sweater. "I'm a mom. My job is to make sure she has a good life."

"And you don't think the two can coexist? Her having a good life and you too?"

My eyes burn. "It's too late for me."

He shrinks the distance between us and we're standing so close now. The scent of his woody and smoky cologne is strong and goes straight to my head. A whoosh of dizziness hits me, but I don't tear my gaze from his. He lifts his hand and it trembles slightly before he sets it against my cheek. "I can give both her and you a good life, Rosie."

"Don't do this now," I plead, tears breaking free from my eyes.

He grazes the side of my face, the roughness of his calloused hand sending a quivering rush between my thighs. "If not now, when?"

"Seven years ago," I blurt.

His head rears back while his eyes dance over my face with indignation.

I force down whatever sensation has been building inside of me. "Why didn't you fight for us then?"

Beck swallows, and I watch the lump bob. "First of all, I wasn't aware there was an *us*. And second, I've already apologized for not coming after you." He moves his hand up to my hair and brushes a strand behind my ear. "I'm here now. And you're here."

My phone chimes, startling us both.

"I will be back in a few days," I repeat, withdrawing until my back hits the edge of the sink and putting some much-needed distance between us. He lets me go even though it looks like it's the very last thing he wants to do. My phone rests on the counter, and I stretch to glance at the screen.

West.

"Fine. If this is what you want." He exhales a long breath as he wrings out his hands. "I'll see ya in a week, I guess." Beck spins around and stalks down the hall toward the back door.

I follow behind him, gripping my phone and waiting for him to leave before I answer. Explaining a growly Beck in the background to West was not how I envisioned tonight going.

He leaves without a goodbye or good night. Just when I think we've made some kind of progress, we end up taking two steps backward again. But while my heart longs for a man I loved long ago and possibly yearns for this new man I'm just getting to know, my brain is always on Charlie. She will always come first. My heart must take a backseat.

I once again put on a brave face, inject strength into my tone, and answer the phone. "Hey, West," I say, but all I want to do is run out that door and chase after the man who will always hold my heart.

21

———

ROSIE

*I*nstead of waiting at the airport with open arms, West sends his assistant, Piper, to pick us up. I don't let my mind wander too far or think too long about how beautiful she is. What with her twenty-something perky breasts and glued-on eyelashes and perfect Pilates body.

Piper drops us off in front of West's building with a quick apology for being unable to help us with our bags. She says it's on the account that she needs to get home and start her red-light therapy and skincare routine because she and West have an early meeting. Which I suppose lets him off the hook for not coming himself to pick us up.

We wheel our luggage through the lobby and into the elevator, my body feeling a lot like this suitcase—dropped down a chute onto baggage claim, spun around on the conveyor belt, and then picked up and dragged. It doesn't feel much better when Charlie and I are welcomed by a dark, quiet apartment. Not even a hallway light left on for us.

Charlie is beyond tired, and I don't have the energy to argue with her about the importance of washing the airport and plane gunk off her; I put her straight to bed. After she's settled and falls asleep, I don't give myself the same luxury. Despite my body aching, I jump in the shower and wash the day away. I slip into the king-sized bed alongside West, still exhausted but at least feeling clean, and he stirs.

His eyes flutter open, and a sleepy smile appears on his lips. "You're home." He cups my face with his palm and gives me a small kiss. "Guessing everything went smoothly with Piper."

"Mmm...yep," I mumble softly, even though I want to argue that it should've been him to pick us up.

"That's good." He grazes my cheekbone with his thumb. "Hey, you wanna bang one out real quick?"

My mouth pops open while irritation burrows in my gut. "Can't. I'm on my period," I'm quick to reply. But it's not a lie.

"Again?" he groans, his palm slipping from my face. "Wasn't it just your time of the month?"

Agitation builds across my shoulders. West and I have been together for over a year, and he still hasn't learned that my body doesn't care what the calendar says or what doctors or the textbooks say about the average woman's cycle. When you have endometriosis, there are no rules. It decides when and how long you're going to bleed, and if you're going to have the cramps from hell or the ones that threaten to kill you.

I try to keep my cool as I answer him. "You know my body does what it wants."

"Yeah." A long, drawn-out sigh blows out between us. "I'm beat, let's talk tomorrow night. We'll have dinner," he whispers before rolling over and putting his back to me. "Good night, sweetie." It's only seconds and he's back into rhythmic snores once again.

I try not to cry. But the loneliness creeps in, and I can't shake it. I hadn't anticipated falling back in love with Golden Harbor. But being near the ocean again, with old friends and familiar places, had me feeling more like myself than I've felt in a long while.

And I've missed me.

Sneaking out of bed, I tiptoe to my jewelry box and pull out the gold necklace with the green heart-shaped sea glass. My mind is flooded with the memory of when Beck gave this to me. Our first wedding anniversary. Back then, I never took it off. Not even when I showered. I clasp the hook at the back of my neck and wrap my fingers around the smooth rock as I slip back into bed.

West is right—we do need to talk. But I'm not sure he's going to like what I have to say. If he truly loves me and still wants to marry me, he'll agree to the break I'm about to ask him for. I need time and space to figure out what I want to do. And what is best for Charlie. And right now, my heart tells me that's being in Golden Harbor.

We've been back in Seattle less than twenty-four hours and everything feels off. Or wrong. I feel off and wrong. Physically, my body is here, but my heart is somewhere else entirely.

The noise, the rain, the busyness. It's all too much. And I'm fairly certain my body is reacting to the dampness in a way I never noticed before.

Charlie is happy to be back to see her friends before school ends for summer vacation. But she looks sad. She misses Beck. I tell myself that I don't. I couldn't possibly. And he has absolutely nothing to do with me wanting to get back there in a hurry.

I told Beck I was only coming back to Golden Harbor for a

week to finish packing up Dottie's house and to spread her ashes, but the truth is, I don't know how long I plan to stay.

The loneliness is still here today, ebbing through my veins as I work and chip away at my full schedule of clients. All regulars except for one. I'm not even sure how that one managed an appointment when I'm typically booked three months out.

One of my clients is an elderly woman with almost white hair and is wanting a perm. While the chemicals are working their magic, I step outside to catch a breath of fresh air. Only, it's raining so I have to stay under the covered awning and the only people out here are my smoking colleagues. Hair stylists in downtown Seattle must be the only remaining smokers. It's like stepping into a '90s grunge music video.

So much for a breath of fresh air.

I return inside and plop down on one of the chairs in the small shared kitchen where some of us hide from clients and scarf down our lunches in between back-to-back appointments. But I can't eat. My stomach has been upset since the popcorn I ate on the airplane had me throwing up last night.

Tugging my phone free from the front pocket of my apron, I see a few texts from Stella. A smile pulls at my lips. I'm glad we've rekindled our friendship and now it's her name I see on my screen.

STELLA

Ran into Beck at Seashell's this morning. He's down bad

I'm sure he's missing Charlie

STELLA

No way. That was a man down bad for a woman

Doubtful

STELLA

So?? You break up with Mr. Richy-Rich yet??

I never said I was breaking up with him

STELLA

Fine. Are the two of you on a break yet?

What are we sixteen?

STELLA

Worked for Ross and Rachel

Did it though?

STELLA

Good point

Anyway break up with him and get your butt back here. We all miss you

Miss you too

"Hey, Mrs. Miller is asking about you," Hannah announces, popping her head into the kitchen. "She thinks her head is burning."

"Did you tell her that's just the chemicals?" Bracing my hand on the table to hold my weight, I pull myself up. I give a small stretch, but it sends a jolt of pain zinging down my lower stomach straight to my butt. Wincing, I pull in a breath and hold it for a second or two before releasing it and shoving my phone back into my apron.

"You okay?" There's a concerned look smeared on Hannah's face. She's the only person in the salon who I've talked to about my endometriosis.

"Fine. Just the usual." I put on a brave smile.

"Good. Well, should I tell her that it's literally the chemicals burning her scalp?" Hannah snickers.

I roll my eyes. "I'm coming. Don't want to lose one of my best clients."

"Hey, speaking of, you haven't even updated me on your trip and now you're planning on leaving me again? Like maybe for the entire summer?"

"Yeah, sorry. I'm not sure how long I'll be gone this time."

"Take me with you," she pleads, tugging on my arm. "Sun, sand, surf, ahhh...sounds like heaven."

Laughing, I give her a sympathetic smile and walk backward as I say, "If I'm gone too long, you better come visit me." And then I return to my client before her head melts and her hair falls out.

Charlie comes out of the doors of the school with her peers, and I rush to her with my umbrella open, as do about thirty other parents. She's shuffling her feet along today, instead of her usual skipping.

"Hey, Charlie, how was your day?"

"It was okay," she mutters.

"Just okay? Not great? Not the most fun ever?" I give a tug to one of her braids as I bend, attempting to get her attention.

Charlie just looks at me with big eyes, her lips in an almost pout. She loves school.

"What's wrong?"

"I miss Golden Harbor."

Pursing my lips, I release a sigh. "Me too. But we'll be back there in less than a week." Taking her backpack from her, I hike it over my shoulder and wrap her up in a side hug, hiding underneath the umbrella while we rush to the car in the rain.

When we get home, we leave our wet boots on the rug by the door to dry out and I hang up our jackets and the umbrella. With the threat of a flare looming, I don't have the energy to *Mom*. Lucky for me, Charlie doesn't know life any differently than what I've been able to handle. I try not to dwell on the fact that that might not be a good thing.

"What do you say I make us some hot chocolate and we watch a movie? It's the best thing to do on a rainy day."

Charlie beams and races to her room to most likely get her favorite blanket and stuffies. I change out of my work clothes and throw on a pair of yoga pants and a hoodie. When I return to the kitchen, Charlie is already seated on the couch with the remote in her hand. I heat water on the stove and fix us two mugs of hot cocoa.

"Extra marshmallows please?" Charlie calls.

"Yeah, yeah, I know how you like it." I laugh while rolling my eyes. I reach for my bottle of pain pills in the cupboard and take a few, hopeful they'll kick in before the pain that's already generating in the tops of my inner thighs has a chance to spread to my back and lower stomach.

My phone dings from where it's resting on the counter. A smile tugs at my lips when I find a sweet text from Hannah checking in on me. After I respond, I bring our warm mugs of hot cocoa into the living room and set them down on coasters on top of the glossy coffee table.

Charlie scoots to the edge of the sofa and picks up her mug, inspecting its contents. She gives an approving smile. "My daddy knows just how to make the best hot chocolate too."

"Well, who do you think taught me?" I smile and her whole face beams at my response.

*W*est surprises us by getting home earlier than normal. Even Charlie is still awake and I'm searching the contents of the freezer for something to whip up for dinner.

"Hey, how are my best girls?" He rounds the corner into the kitchen with a bag of Chinese takeout in his grip.

"Hi, West!" Charlie runs to him and when he crouches, she shoots into his arms.

And dang it if my heart doesn't shift in my chest.

"I missed you," he says into her hair. "How was the beach?"

"It was so fun! I'm going to get my shells to show you."

While Charlie races off to her room to retrieve her treasures, West scoops me up in his free arm and presses a forceful and possessive kiss to my lips that leaves my head spinning. Pulling back, I search his expression to read what this mood is.

"I missed you the most," he says, but his smile is tight.

"Yeah, me too." I take the bag from him and set it on the counter to pull out the contents.

"You look tired."

Gee, thanks. Love that for me. My fiancé basically pointing out that I look like crap.

"Guess the beach wasn't as restful for you as it was for Charlie." He loosens his tie at his neck before slipping his suit jacket off his shoulders and hanging it on the back of the stool pushed up to the island.

There's an obvious buzz of distress in the air between us.

"Actually, the beach was amazing. But Dottie's service, the reading of her will, and going through her things was exhausting." I'm not sure why I have to remind him why I went to Golden Harbor in the first place, but here we are.

"I bet. I'm sorry you had to do that. And alone."

That added *alone* scrapes underneath my skin. Is he expecting me to admit I wasn't exactly alone? Or is this a sad excuse for an apology for not coming with me? With West, who can say.

"But you're home now." He rounds the kitchen island and squeezes my arm, pressing a kiss to my cheek. "Let's eat. I'm starving."

"Thanks for bringing dinner. And getting off early."

"Of course. I want to hear all about your week in Golden Harbor." Yanking his tie over his head, he unbuttons the top two buttons on his collared shirt and waggles his brows at me suggestively.

I force a smile and pull a few plates from the cupboard. Even though it's takeout, West doesn't like eating out of the cartons. "I was hoping we could've talked last night. Ya know, after we got home."

"Yeah." He waves me off and fills his plate. "I was super tired. My day was stacked with meetings. And I had one early today."

"So Piper mentioned," I quip, waiting for an explanation.

"You know those drain me, sweetie."

I bob my head along while he talks. "Well, it's just that there's something really important we need to talk about."

"Okay, sure. After dinner."

"But—"

Charlie runs into the kitchen with her fist full of beach treasures and the stuffies Beck gave her underneath her arms.

Crap.

"Let me see what you got there."

"Look at these pretty shells I found. And look, West. This is sea glass. And I got two new stuffies."

"Wow. Your favorite."

"My daddy gave them to me," she says, her eyes gleaming.

Double crap.

West's expression goes stony. His jaw ticks and he glances at me with a sharp look in his blue eyes. Without tearing his gaze from me, he asks, "Your dad?"

"Yeah. I met my daddy! And guess what? I'm just like him. We even have the same chin. With a dimple and everything."

"Is that so?" West finally detaches his stare from me and pays attention to Charlie. "Hey, why don't you take your plate into the living room and put on that show you like with the blue dog."

"Really? I can eat in the living room?"

"Yeah. Just sit at the coffee table and be extra careful, okay?"

"Yay!" She jumps and I offer her a plate I've filled with her favorites. She takes it cautiously and shuffles into the living room slower than I've ever seen her move.

I can't read West's expression when he returns his focus on me. Is he hurt? Angry? Just plain tired?

"So, Charlie met her dad?" His tone is subdued.

"She did."

"And when were you going to tell me about this?"

"Well," I begin, pushing my plate away because I've lost my appetite. "I had planned on talking to you last night after we got home but you couldn't be bothered to pick us up at the airport. Or even stay awake until we were home."

"No, don't put this on me." He rises to stand. "Because the way I see it, you had plenty of chances to tell me."

"Okay, first of all, we hardly talked while I was gone. West, you're busy all the time."

"That's bullshit," he bites out, and glances over his shoulder at Charlie. "We shouldn't be talking about this here." Taking me by the arm, he all but drags me down the hall and into the bedroom. "Don't bust my balls because I have to work and provide for us."

Shoving down the offense I'm taking over his statement, because I work too, I continue. "I wanted to talk to you in person. Which is why I was hoping to talk last night after we got home, and Charlie went to bed."

"Fine. We're talking now. Mind filling me in on what the hell is going on?"

Releasing a deep breath, I begin. "Charlie's father lives in Golden Harbor. We met when I went to live with Grandma Dottie while I was in high school. And when we were twenty, we got married."

His brows shoot up to his hairline, but I keep talking or I worry I'll never get it all out. "I found out I was pregnant really early on...I started cramping and bleeding." Anguish builds in my chest at the memory. "Beck and I assumed I had miscarried. We were devastated. It broke us. It broke me. I couldn't stay there. Everywhere I looked, I saw the life we could've had. So...I left." Tears fill my eyes.

Pacing in the room, his fingers are interlocked and clasped at the back of his neck. I've never seen him like this. "And then what?" he finally asks.

"A few weeks later I went for a checkup, and she confirmed I was still pregnant. But by then, Beck and I hadn't spoken since I left. He never came after me. And I never told him. And... well...here we are."

West finally stops pacing and looks at me. "You didn't tell him about Charlie until now?"

I shake my head and the tears release, rolling down my cheeks.

"What does he want? To have a relationship with her?" His eyes are dark and when I don't answer right away, he strains out, "With you?"

"I don't know," I answer honestly. Because who knows what

Beck wants. I'm not even sure if Beck knows what Beck wants. "I mean, yes, he wants to have a relationship with Charlie."

"But with you?"

I clutch at my sleeves and answer, "I don't know. But it doesn't matter. Because that's not what this is about."

"The hell it isn't."

Taking small steps toward him, I lower my voice. "I love you. Nothing will change that."

He throws his palms up and backs away. "Whoa. What are you saying? Are you...are you ending this?"

"No," I'm quick to say. "No. But..."

"But?" The word flies out of him.

"But...I need to go back to Golden Harbor."

"Go back? But you just got home." Confusion smears his expression.

"When Charlie finishes school at the end of the week...I'm gonna go back. Maybe for a few weeks or maybe...for the summer."

"The summer?" he snaps, and he's back to pacing again.

"Grandma Dottie left her cottage to me. I need to go back there and get the house ready to sell. And spread her ashes."

"So you're not breaking up with me?"

I bite my lower lip.

West dips his chin and blows out a breath. He moves across the room toward me and wraps his arms around my waist. "You and Charlie are the best things that have ever happened to me. Don't do this."

I catch the mist glossing over his eyes when I say, "I'm just asking for some time."

"And then what?"

"And then...I don't know." Honesty wins and pride moves through me. Seven years ago, I wouldn't have been able to do this. Heck, the Rosie from *one* year ago couldn't have done this.

"I don't want to make you any more promises I'm not sure I can keep."

"I don't want to lose you." His words croak out like a confession.

"I'm sorry. I don't want to hurt you. But I have to do this. I owe it to Charlie. And to Beck. I can never give them back those years I took away, but I can do this for them."

"I suppose that makes sense. Even if I don't like it."

He releases me and I work at tugging the ring from my finger. I set it into his palm, closing his fist around it. "I think you should hold on to this."

Without speaking, he tucks it in his pocket and backs up while his eyes scan me from my head to my toes and back up again. A shiver runs through me. "Just taking a mental picture of you before you leave."

"West," I whisper, not really sure what else to say.

"I'm going to go eat with Charlie. And I'll do her bedtime routine if you don't mind."

"Of course."

"I'm sure gonna miss my girls."

I'm tempted to correct him and tell him we aren't his girls. That the phrase he always says is starting to irritate the hell out of me. But I don't.

"Oh, and Rosie," he calls before exiting the room. "I think it will be best if you sleep in the guest room until you leave."

My mouth pops open but then I think better of it and clamp it shut, not having the energy to drag this conversation on further. I just watch him leave the room. And then I collapse on the bed, releasing quiet sobs as worry about whether I'm even doing the right thing wracks my brain.

22

BECK

$\mathcal{N}$ow that Rosie and Charlie are back in Golden Harbor, each day that passes is like a ticking time bomb. I want to enjoy every second I have with Charlie, but how am I supposed to do that when we're racing to a finish line I don't want to reach? I've only just met her, am finally getting to know her, and I'm going to have to say goodbye again. It's unfair.

How can it be that I found out I was a father less than two weeks ago, and now I can't imagine my life without this person? It's like I've been missing this piece of me for the past six years and I'm finally whole. How am I supposed to just let her go? Especially when she wants to stay too.

But I know it's not my place to ask Charlie. The last thing I want is to confuse her. Rosie is right about one thing—she's only six, she can't possibly know what she wants.

I cut out of work early. It pisses Milo off, but he understands. I'm no help anyway because all I can think about is seeing my daughter while she's in town.

"You owe me," Milo hollers while I'm hopping into my rig.

I shoot him a glare. "Boy, your whole life is an open bar tab."

He chuckles and shakes his head, knowing good and well I'm joking. But also right.

I send a quick text to Rosie.

On my way

ROSIE

Okay. Charlie is ready

I put the truck in drive and tear off in the direction of Dottie's cottage, my head swishing with all the things that are up in the air. Keeping my anxiety at bay proves to be even more challenging while my relationship with Rosie is still unsettled. My brain knows I need to sign the divorce e-doc sitting in my email inbox, but my heart says *not yet*.

Call it hope or call it plain stupidity, but I'll know when it's time. And now just isn't it.

When I pull into the driveway, Rosie and Charlie are sitting on the back steps. They both stand as I park and jump out. I round the back, and Rosie is already handing me the car seat.

"Hey, here's her booster." Her long, auburn hair shields her face, like she doesn't want to risk making eye contact with me.

Did I miss something?

"Thanks." I take it and Charlie flings her arms around my leg. I crouch so I can bring her into my chest. "Hey, Charlie girl. I missed you."

She giggles against my chest and my heart expands. It's like she's always meant to be right here. In my arms, face pressed to my heart, where I can keep her safe and hear her sweet laughter.

"Looks like you're ready to go," I say, more to Rosie because she's acting like she can't get me out of here fast enough.

I stand and Rosie gives a backpack to Charlie, but she says to me, "I packed some snacks for her. And her favorite blanket."

"Hey?" I call to Rosie and bob my head around until I've caught her attention. Her green eyes are striking, but wary. "Is everything okay?"

"Fine." Her lips flatten.

I scrunch my brows together and tilt my head, not buying the BS she's serving up. She forgets—I know her.

"You're fine with me taking her, aren't you?"

"Of course," she mutters, but her gaze flicks away again and she crosses her arms, her green tank top hugging tighter against her chest. Like a moth to a flame, my eyes can't help but be drawn to her luscious cleavage.

I clear my throat and take Charlie's backpack from her. "Charlie girl, why don't you go climb in the truck."

"Okay, bye, Mama." She gives Rosie a big hug and races to the back door of my rig.

I lean in closer to Rosie, her floral but citrusy scent filling my nose. "You do trust me, don't you?"

She forces a smile and replies, "Yeah, I trust you."

Still not buying it, I try a different angle. "Are you mad?"

She frowns. "Mad? Why would I be mad?"

I hunch a shoulder. "I don't know. Because I'm taking Charlie. Because I'm not taking you. Hell, I don't know."

"Pfft," she releases under her breath. "You're crazy. I'm not jealous, if that's what you're insinuating."

"No, not jealous." I scratch at my stubbled chin.

She turns around and ambles to the back door. "Just promise me you'll bring her back in one piece," she calls over her shoulder.

"I thought you said you trusted me?"

She spins to face me. "I do. I do." But it sounds to me like she's trying to convince herself.

I give her a half smile before heading toward my Chevy, the

car seat in one hand. But I stop and call, "Hey, does Charlie know how to swim?"

"What?" Rosie gasps. "I thought you were taking her to the cove to look at the sea lions?"

I chuckle. "Yeah, I am. Just asking in case..." I let my words trail off, my skin tingling with amusement.

"In case what?" she blurts.

But what was humorous only moments ago suddenly kicks me off my feet as the reality hits me. These are the things I should know as a father, if my kid can swim or not.

I rearrange my expression. "I was only teasing."

She shakes her head, rolling her eyes. "Not funny," she mutters. "But, to answer your question, yes, she knows how to swim. There was a pool at the apartment we lived in before I met West. And he's paid for her to have private lessons for the past year."

Learning about her and Charlie's past feels surreal. My mind can't help but wonder if this was a nice apartment. And where did they live before that? Did Rosie have enough money to take care of Charlie?

The guilt slams into me and my heart races. I tighten my grip around the armrest of the booster seat. What if Rosie is only with this West guy because of the financial stability? I've been saving money. I can afford to take care of her and Charlie.

"Rosie." Her name whooshes out of me on an exhaled breath.

Her brows knit together in worry. "You okay?"

I try to inhale and hold it, then release it. But the air constricts in my lungs. This isn't the time to have this conversation. Charlie is in my truck waiting to have a fun day.

I swallow. "I'm fine," I force out. "But later we should talk about...child support."

Her mouth pops open and her expression constricts. "I

never asked you for anything before, and I'm not going to start now."

I shake my head. "It doesn't matter whether you're asking or not."

"Just focus on your time with Charlie. We can talk later." She smiles. But it's the forced kind, not the one she used to gift me with.

She's noticing my shortness of breath, my tightening grip. She can probably hear my heart thudding hard against my chest from where she's standing. She's giving me an out and like a coward, I take it. Having a panic attack now could result in canceling my day with Charlie and I can't risk it.

"Yeah, okay. Later." I give her a nod and head straight for my truck without looking back.

A fter I park in an angled spot at the lot for the cove, Charlie hops out and I take her by the hand. Milo is only a couple years younger than me, but as if engraved in my memory, I'm back in that mode.

Originally, I had wanted to take Charlie to the beach for her first surfing lesson. I missed out on plenty of her firsts and can't stand the thought of someone else teaching her, but I thought I better save that for when she's a little older.

"Have you seen sea lions before?" I ask Charlie as we walk hand in hand down the pathway.

"Yep. But only at the zoo." She does a little skip and a jump.

"You're gonna love these guys. They're pretty cute. And there's always a lot of them. If we're lucky, they'll put on a good show for us."

"Yay, I can't wait."

We round the corner and walk down to the cove. It's already crowded. But not surprising. Once someone posted about this place on social media, it completely popped off. It's only a matter of time before the population of Golden Harbor outgrows the town. There's only so many houses and restaurants, and our roads in town aren't wide enough to accommodate much more traffic.

We aren't close enough to see the sea lions yet, but the echo of their barks sound out around us. The mist from the ocean disappears the further we step into the dank cove and a fishy scent infiltrates my nostrils.

I glance down at Charlie, and she's got her hand cupped over her nose. I chuckle. "Just wait, I promise it will be worth it."

Her eyes are little slits peeking above her palm and they look hopeful.

When she withdraws her palm, a gasp escapes her. The sea lions are on the rocks, showing off with playful claps and barks. Some are swimming, gliding on their sides, or floating on their backs.

Charlie giggles. "They're so cute."

"Told ya." I smile and squeeze her hand.

I help her weave in between a large group so she can get a closer look. I slip my phone out of my front pocket and take a few pictures while she's watching the sea lions.

She spins around. "Take a picture of me for Mama."

"Okay, smile big so she knows you're having a good time."

I take a few and choose the best one to attach in a text to Rosie.

"Daddy daughter day out, huh?" a guy nearby says.

I glance up. "Uh, yeah."

"She looks just like you," the woman standing next to him chimes in.

I rub at the back of my neck, watching Charlie as she claps along with the sea lions. My heart shifts in my chest. "Yeah… but she looks like her mama more. And her mama is a knockout."

The woman smiles.

I don't know why I said it, but I don't take it back. Because it's true.

Charlie rushes in through the back door of Dottie's cottage and I follow behind her, carrying the booster seat under one arm and her backpack in the other. I set them both on the floor in the entryway.

"Mama!" Charlie calls, kicking off her sandals and racing down the hall, now with a stuffed sea lion in her grip and the stuffed mermaid is shoved in her backpack. So quickly her loyalty has changed. That mermaid didn't even see it coming, the poor bastard.

I shuffle down the hallway and when I step into the kitchen, Rosie is sitting at the table with photos and albums scattered all around her. Charlie is pressed to Rosie's side, and her arm is draped around her. Charlie holds up her stuffed sea lion and talks a mile a minute. My chest expands, her excitement about the day easing my worries if she had a good time or not.

"And now a stuffed sea lion." Rosie's green eyes sparkle.

"What?" I shrug and pull a seat out at the table, dropping onto it.

"You're spoiling her," she says, but she's smiling.

"One time won't hurt the girl." I could turn this into an

argument. Remind her how I haven't had the chance to spoil her for six years. But she already knows that, so it's pointless.

"Sounds like you had a good time."

"It was the best day ever!" Charlie does a little jump. "After the sea lions, we went to a gift shop and got saltwater taffy and I got to watch how they make it. Oh! Mama, did you see the pictures of me with the sea lions?"

"I did. I'm so glad you had fun."

"Daddy, where's my backpack? I need to get my mermaid and introduce my new stuffies to their friends."

"It's by the back door." I pat the top of her head before she zooms down the hall, my attention flickering to the photos scattered around the table. Charlie's footsteps bound up the stairs. But I'm distracted by the familiar faces haunting me.

A young Rosie and a young Beck, dressed up for prom. Rosie in that spectacular sexy green dress and me in my stupid penguin suit and cheesy grin. Little did that idiot know he was about to get laid for the first time. There's another photo of us on the porch swing out front. Too many moments spent on that damn porch swing. Too many memories.

I pinch the corner of a photo of Dottie with Rosie on one side of her and me on the other after she won first prize at the quilt show in Ojai. We'd driven up for one night and Rosie and I snuck out of our rooms with a hotel comforter and a complimentary bottle of wine the sponsors of the show had gifted Dottie. We'd lain on the grass beneath a dark sky full of shining stars. We whispered promises to one another about our future. Promises I'd forgotten about until this moment.

"What happened to those kids?" I ask before thinking, studying the younger versions of us.

"They grew up."

I glance at her and see my life flash by. "Did we? Because how come we're still having the same arguments?"

"What arguments would those be?"

Her expression is tired. She's probably having another flare day and I'm making it worse by pressing these conversations. But if not now, when?

"If two people love each other, is that enough?" I ask, holding eye contact even as emotions and questions glaze over hers. "What happened to those promises we made each other?"

"Again, we were kids." She finally tears her eyes away from mine and shuffles the photos into a stack. "What did we know about love?"

"A lot," I mumble, and her fingers still for a moment.

"What did we know about the real world? About life?"

She has a point there. Maybe we'd been naïve to promise we'd stay together forever. We were eighteen. But we did stay together for a few years. Made it through some difficult times together. Got married at twenty. Even when she left three years later, I never doubted that she was the one.

"That's fair." I toss the photo back onto the table while she continues stacking them. "That was a fun trip though."

She glances at me and her lips pull up, her green eyes sparkling. "It was. Especially when Dottie searched for that bottle of wine then asked the organizers to give her another one, all the while knowing full well we'd been the ones who drank it."

I smirk. "Yeah, she was a cool lady."

"She was." She taps a finger against her chin. "Speaking of..." Her voice trails and when I glance up to meet her gaze again, she gestures her chin in the direction of what looks to be an urn on the edge of the kitchen counter.

I swing my attention back to Rosie. "Is that...?"

"It is." She presses her lips together.

"When did you get those?"

"At the reading of the will when I was here last. I knew most of Dottie's wishes after she died, so I had to do a lot of the decision-making from Seattle before I came. I knew she wanted to be cremated but I didn't know until then that she wanted me to spread her ashes in the ocean."

There's a silence between us. Charlie's soft voice is muffled from upstairs while she talks to her stuffed animals.

"You haven't done it yet?"

She shakes her head and puts a stack of albums into a box.

"Did you want some company? While you do it, I mean?"

She gives me a smile despite her eyes glistening. "No, I should do this on my own. I'm gonna spread them Saturday morning."

"Do you want me to stay with Charlie? I was going to go fishing with my dad, but I can reschedule."

"No, that's okay. I've already asked Stella."

"It's no problem, I can go fishing with my dad anytime."

"Beck, it's okay. Besides, Stella and Max want to see Charlie too."

I glance down at my fidgeting hands in my lap, my breathing quickening. The desperation to help her but the inability to do so is paralyzing me.

"Hey," she hedges, forcing me to focus on her calming eyes. "You can't fix everything." Her smile is forced, but more importantly it's pained.

All of this is painful.

23

ROSIE

Dropping off Charlie at Stella's goes smoothly. For not using a babysitter often, Charlie has taken to being cared for by Stella and Beck easily. Despite it being early, Stella and Max are wide awake.

"I should only be a few hours," I assure Stella when I pull her into a hug.

"Don't worry about it. Take your time. You can't rush things like this."

"I know. Thank you." I wave and hurry back to Dottie's little car.

Of course I couldn't spread Dottie's ashes in the ocean by her cottage. She specifically requested I spread them in the waters on the island. It's a process to get there. I have to take the ferry.

At lease it isn't crowded at this time of the day. Mostly fishermen and people who work on the island but choose to live in Golden Harbor. After I park my car and ensure it's secure, I climb out and lock it, then head to the upper deck in search of coffee.

After I order and pay—and pray it's good—I take my coffee

and stroll to the end of the ferry to look out at the water. The sun is already rising and golden hues paint the sky. It's beautiful. The spray can't be felt this high off the waters, but I close my eyes and allow the light and cool morning breeze hit my face. After an inhale and exhale, I open my eyes again and take a sip of the coffee.

It's hot and nearly burns my tongue, but it's good. No Starbucks like I've gotten used to living in Seattle and West reloading my app constantly. But it's not bad.

I glance around and spot a few fishermen My curiosity is getting the best of me, wondering if Beck is on this ferry or if he left even earlier. Or maybe a part of me does wish he were here with me to make this easier. He's always been good about centering me. Just like I've always been good about calming him.

I slide my phone from my pocket and I'm tempted to text him. But when it lights up, the 'SOS Only' signal appears on my screen. *Great. No service on the ferry.* It's probably best this way. I shove my phone back into my pocket and gaze out at the island in the distance. Even if he's almost all I can think about.

Being in Golden Harbor, in Beck's orbit again...He and Charlie spending time together—it's thrown me into more of a spin than I expected. While I knew some lingering feelings might resurface, I hadn't expected them to be this strong. Or that Beck would still be harboring feelings as well.

I groan aloud and take a slow sip of my coffee, being extra careful this time. The sweetness of the honey hits my tastebuds this time and the heavenly brew touches my soul in a way that's unexplainable to a person who doesn't drink coffee. How do people not drink coffee?

I don't want to rush today. Like Stella said, this is important. Dottie specifically asked me to do this. I need to take the time that's needed to do it right. To remember and honor her. I may not be able to fulfill her request of moving back to Golden

Harbor and living in her house, but I will make her final wishes happen.

<center>~~~~</center>

After the ferry reaches the port and I'm back in the car, I follow in the line, inching my way off and onto the two-lane road that will take me into the main part of the island. I recognize most of the places I pass. A grocery store, a taco stand, a bar. Except the bar has a new sign. A fresh coat of pain. A new name too: *The Thirsty Turtle*.

It's Beck's dad's bar. I pull into the lot without thinking and park the car haphazardly. My heart rate picks up speed and like a dummy, I contemplate knocking on the door. They're closed now, but Beck said his dad lives in the upstairs apartment.

There's a truck parked out front, but my brain finally plays catch up with my heart and I remember. They're fishing. Probably at the marina, which means I'll be spreading Dottie's ashes on the opposite side of the island.

My phone buzzes as it connects to service and when I check it, my heart does a little jump in my chest.

BECK

I know I'm not your first choice but let me know if you need anything

But I don't trust myself to respond. I only heart his message and swipe to my other texts.

HANNAH

I miss you already!

It's been pouring since yesterday 🐢

> Better get the spare room ready for me. I need some sun in my life!

Smiling, I tap out a reply, telling her she's welcome anytime.

STELLA

> Charlie is currently teaching Max his colors with crayons. Mind if I keep her for a few days?

> Guessing you're still on the ferry and don't have service

> If you bring me some seafoam chocolate I'll be your best friend 🙏

> You already are my best friend 😊

I pull out into traffic again and onto the main road that leads to the beach. The traffic is picking up now that it's later in the morning. Folks getting kids to school, getting onto the ferry, getting to work. Everything moves the same here as in Golden Harbor, the same as in Seattle really. Just on a smaller scale. Maybe even a simpler scale.

There are a few beaches down off the main road. But I'm trying to find the perfect one. In Dottie's mind, it apparently exists. But could she specify and help me out—no.

When I was young, Grandma Dottie brought me to the island a few times. As a child, I found the ferry ride exciting and the shops off the main road overwhelming, filled with beach toys and trinkets. But the stretch of one small beach after another was my favorite. The shell selection is better on the island than in Golden Harbor.

As a teenager, I came to the island with friends. Beck and Stella, sometimes Jack, Daisy, and Christian. Back then the island allowed bonfires on the beaches. We'd stay late and sleep in our cars even though we weren't supposed to. But the last ferry leaves strictly at five year-round, long before the sun goes down.

Since it's still early, I stop at a strip mall with several coastal shops and a fish and chips shop on the corner. When I enter the first shop, it's packed full of stationary, painted wooden block signs with silly quotes, and stuffed animals that Charlie would go nuts over. I can't resist looking at and touching everything. I'm so used to bringing Charlie with me and reminding her to not touch anything that it's like I'm making up for it.

I pick up a card for Stella that has two sea turtles sipping margaritas. And because I don't want to leave Daisy out, I find a Slug Bug keychain and buy it for her. In the next store, there's a coloring book I know Charlie will love. I pick it up for her instead of a new stuffed animal, since Beck has gotten her some recently.

My mind goes to Beck, but I try to push him to the back of it. Maybe it's because he's on the island now. Knowing he's so close is keeping a continued buzz in my brain. It's tempting to text him. To take him up on his offer to meet me so I don't have to be alone while spreading Dottie's ashes. But I can't keep relying on him to do the hard things. And things are too awkward between us right now.

After I purchase the coloring book, I push out of the store and onto the sidewalk where the scent of the ocean and deep-fried seafood fills the air. It's been forever since I've had fish and chips. West doesn't like seafood, so we never get it.

I walk to the corner and order my lunch from the window. While I wait for my number to be called, I scroll social media and sit at a wooden picnic table where the blue paint is weathered and chipping. A woman with an apron tied around her waist and a pencil behind her ear approaches my table. In one hand she has a cardboard basket with fish and chips and in the other a bottle of water. "Here ya go, dear. Guess you didn't hear your number being called."

"I'm so sorry." I bite my lip and accept my lunch from her.

"Ah, no worries. You looked a bit distracted." She wipes her palms across her apron and gives me a sweet smile. "Enjoy."

"Thank you." I return the smile and gaze at my food with appreciation as my mouth waters.

Say what you will about seafood, but you can't go to the beach without eating it. Even if it upsets my stomach, it will be worth it. I've got no plans but snuggling Charlie on the couch tonight and watching one of her favorite movies.

My phone vibrates while it rests on the wood tabletop.

> **WEST**
>
> Just wanted to check if you made it to the island and see how Charlie liked the ferry ride

> I thought it would be better if I did this alone so I didn't bring her with me. I left her with Stella

The bubbles appear and then disappear. They appear again but same thing, they disappear. Apprehension settles in my stomach and I pick up a piece of fish, breaking it in half and dipping it into the tartar sauce. It's perfect. Flaky but not dry and not smelly. That's key to good, deep-fried fish. That it doesn't actually smell like fish.

I try a few of the fries and the greasy residue doesn't stick to the top of my mouth. They're hot and delicious.

My phone buzzes.

"Ugh." I groan out loud when I see West's name across my screen again. It's not as if we agreed on a no contact arrangement, but I suppose I assumed it.

> **WEST**
>
> You should've asked me first before leaving Charlie with a stranger

My eyes widen and my stomach bottoms out as I reread his text several times before I finally respond.

> Stella isn't a stranger. I've known her for years. And Charlie is comfortable with her

WEST

> She's a stranger to me

A shiver of anger races across of my skin.

> Did you ask me if you could leave Charlie with Piper before I met her?

WEST

> I don't want to fight with you

> Then stop texting me

WEST

> Regardless what happens between us, I still expect to have a relationship with Charlie

> I'm about to go into a meeting I'll call you later

> Please don't

I slam my phone down on top of the picnic table. The lady who brought out my food meets my gaze and raises a quizzical brow. I force a smile despite the tears swimming in my eyes and glance down at my basket of food that moments ago looked like the best thing I would experience today. Now, my stomach recoils at the sight.

Swiping the bottle off the table, I retrieve a few pain pills from my purse and chug the water, having difficulty swallowing them down. Anger sears my skin, and I blink long and hard to fight the impending tears. Who does he think he is? Charlie is *my* daughter. I could've argued that point with him, but I had been letting him help with some of the parental things.

My phone rings but I quickly silence it. Letting the both of us cool off and get our heads on straight before we communicate again is probably a good idea.

I eat the rest of my fries, wash them down with my water, and then chuck it all into the trash before I follow the sidewalk back to where Dottie's car is parked. Once I'm safely back inside and buckled in, I burst into tears.

It takes parking and scoping out three beaches before I pick the one that feels perfect. I have to silence the voices telling me that Dottie might not agree. That she might complain about something or everything about the beach I've chosen.

But what does it matter? I'm half tempted to keep her ashes and bring them back home with me to Seattle. She won't know if I spread them or not.

Or maybe she will. Maybe Dottie's looking down on me from heaven right now. And maybe she's giving me those disapproving drawn-on eyebrows and faulting me for not choosing to stay in Golden Harbor. For not choosing to find a way to piece my family together.

Honestly, I'd give anything to have her here with me right now, telling me what to do.

24

BECK

*D*ad comes out of his apartment and shuffles down the stairs slow. Signs of both his age and years of addiction are showing, but I try to shrug it off. He's got his fishing gear in one hand and a small cooler in the other. My shoulders stiffen, the anxiety swirling over what he's got in that cooler. Even though, by now, I know it's not booze—tell that to my nerves.

He swings open the back passenger door of my truck and sets the small cooler inside. "Hey, son. How's it going?"

"Morning. Whatcha got there?" I grunt, gesturing my chin at the cooler.

"Water. Gatorade. Electrolytes?" he says the last thing in question.

The intense strain across my shoulders eases. "Good thinking."

He rolls his eyes but doesn't say anything. This rebuilding trust and a relationship between us is still new. After decades of damage, it's not going to happen overnight. We both know that.

"Help me with the fish cooler, will ya? It's sitting just inside the bar. Already filled it with ice." He tosses his fishing gear in the bed, and I hop out and meet him at the bar's entrance.

After he unlocks the door, I follow him inside. The Thirsty Turtle looks different when it's dark and not filled with people. Dad gave it a new name when he took over ownership—still not sure where he got the name, but it sounds like one of those name generator outcomes—yet he left the '70s lighting and original brown wood paneling on the walls. We each grab an end of the cooler and take it out to my truck, shoving it in the bed along with our fishing gear.

After I climb back inside and Dad hops in, I offer him a coffee. "Grabbed your favorite."

"Oooo nice, thanks, kid." He accepts the paper cup and takes a sip, a wide smile spreading underneath his thick, graying mustache. "Did you tell Jenny hello from me?"

"Sure did." I snicker.

"Good, that's good, kid."

"She even threw in an extra shot of espresso for free." I back out of The Thirsty Turtle's parking lot after he's buckled. "You ask her out yet?"

"Shoot. Cut your ol' dad some slack. You don't just ask a girl out like that all willy-nilly. It takes time. It takes work. Not like you kids these days."

I chuckle. "I feel you on the taking work. Sadly, that still hasn't changed in the dating world for people my age either."

"Yeah?"

I don't glance his way because I don't need to. I already know what expression I'll find on his face. Hopeful.

"Sorry, still not dating anyone." I take a sip of my coffee, the bitterness mixed with the sweet vanilla an explosion of deliciousness on my tongue.

"What happened to that one gal? You know, the cougar?"

I choke on my coffee. "She wasn't that old, Dad." I swallow.

"And she was fine. But I guess, yeah, the age thing was a problem. For her, not me," I clarify.

"Aw, that's okay, son. The right one will come along."

The right one did come along, I wanna say. She came along and I snagged her. I had her. But then I lost her. And even though she's walked back into my life, it feels like she's slipping through my fingers again.

"I know what you're thinking," he says, and now I do glance his way. "If you and Rosie are meant to be, you'll find a way back to each other."

I chew on my lip.

"You never mentioned it, and I didn't have the heart to ask... Did she make it to town for Dottie's memorial?"

I swallow the rising lump in my throat. "She did."

"How did it go?"

"Actually, she's still here."

"Really? Is she planning on sticking around?"

"For about a week."

Dad blows out a whistle. "A week, huh? Sounds like...a chance," he says at the same time I say, "like trouble."

I groan out a *pft* and mutter, "whatever."

Dad's quiet for a moment next to me and I've almost reached the marina. This feels like as good a time as any to tell him about Charlie. "Dad?"

"Mhmm?"

"That's kind of why I asked if you wanted to come fishing today. I've got some...news."

"Oh? So there was an ulterior motive? Not just a casual father/son fishing trip?"

I park my truck in the first open spot at the marina, worried if I waste any more time, I won't be able to spit out what I need to tell him. I ram the shifter into park so fast we both fling forward before rearing backward. Dad's head ricochets off the headrest.

"Whoa, what's going on? You okay? You're scaring me." He rubs at the back of his head.

I turn to look at him, clenching my teeth and trying to ignore the other fishermen likely beating us to the best spots.

"Are you in some kind of trouble?"

I shake my head and exhale a wobbly breath. "Rosie didn't return to Golden Harbor alone."

A sullen expression overtakes his face and his lips droop. "Oh, son. I'm so sorry. She brought a boyfriend with her?"

I scratch at the scruff on my chin. "No, not exactly."

His graying brows draw together. "No?"

"She brought a kid with her...My kid."

"I don't understand." He rubs at his forehead.

"Rosie was pregnant when she left Golden Harbor seven years ago."

"Woah, and you didn't know?" he asks, tilting his chin.

I shake my head, choosing not to go into the details with him now.

"So are you trying to tell me she had a baby? Your baby?" He points at me.

"Yeah. That's exactly what I'm trying to tell you." A smile grows on my face. "She's six. Her name is Charlotte. Well, Charlie for short, she actually hates Charlotte." I chuckle thinking about how the first time I met her and how she corrected me. "I'm trying to tell you...you have a granddaughter, Dad."

Emotion stirs in my gut as his eyes glisten. "Wow. Well, this is something."

"Yeah, you can say that again."

"How are you handling all this?"

I adjust my hat on my head. "Better now. It was a shock at first."

"Well, yeah of course."

"But I've been spending a lot of time with her. She's a good kid. Real cute too. She looks like me. She's a Stone for sure." I tug my phone free from my front pocket. "Let me show you a picture."

He takes it and swipes through my album. "Yep, definitely a Stone. What a sweetie. Looks a lot like your mom."

A rock drops in my stomach. This was a response I wasn't expecting.

"Really?"

"Are you kidding? That smile? That's your mom's."

I take my phone back from him and stare at a smiling Charlie. "I thought her smile was Rosie's."

Dad shakes his head. "I don't know what that kid got of Rosie's side, but it sure can't be much. Her red hair, that's about it."

I continue staring at the photo, my heart aching and expanding at once.

"Let me guess. Now you're stuck having to make a decision. Stay in Golden Harbor and be a part time father or go to Seattle to be with them?"

I push my thumb and finger into my eyes. "I wish it was that easy. She's engaged."

"Ahh. That does make things more complicated."

"Ha." I bark out a sarcastic laugh. Complicated doesn't even explain half of it. He doesn't know that Rosie and I are still married. Which adds another layer of *complicated* to this mess.

～～～～

Dad and I sit out on his little boat for half the day. We catch nothing more than kelp. We drink his Gatorade and eat the protein bars I packed. But the sun is too high and fishing this late in the day while it's this warm is pointless.

"We better call it," I announce.

He's got his pole cast and is watching and waiting expectantly. "C'mon, you gotta have patience."

"Fine," I groan. "A little longer. But the last ferry leaves at five and I need to be on it. I was hoping to see Charlie tonight."

"That's always been your problem. So impatient."

I glare at him from across the boat, the muscles in my shoulders going taut. What does he know about me? He was drunk my entire childhood and into my adulthood. But my therapy sessions with Dr. Sam have taught me that I can't continually bring up what I've already forgiven him for.

"Not impatient, Dad. Just anxious is all."

"That, too. Why are you always so anxious?"

I raise my brows and blink at him. "You're kidding, right?"

"You can't blame me for that too. For your anxiety. You going to therapy for the trauma I caused from being an alcoholic makes sense, but the other stuff, how's it my fault?"

"Maybe the two go hand in hand," I spit out.

"Fine." He holds up his palms in surrender, and the boat rocks. "I've apologized, you've apologized. We don't need to do this again."

"At least we're in agreement there."

"But, son, at some point, you gotta start taking responsibility. You gotta stop blaming everyone else and start being an active participant in your own life."

Anger sears my skin from the inside out. "I don't want to do this with you. Not here, not now."

"Why? Because you know it's true?"

"No," I snap. "Because...because..."

And well, shit, he might just be right.

"You've missed out on six years of knowing your daughter. Do you really want to miss out on six more?"

"Of course not."

"Then I think that's your answer. Rosie or no Rosie, if she's not staying in Golden Harbor, you gotta go to Seattle. Learn from my mistakes. Don't repeat them. Go be a father for your girl. If you don't, you're gonna regret it."

My phone buzzes in my pocket. I tug it free and hold my breath when Rosie's name shows up on the screen.

ROSIE

Are you still on the island? Can you meet me?

25

ROSIE

By the time Beck reaches me, I'm a fully-fledged mess. It's been forty-five minutes since I texted him and explained where I was at. To say he was surprised to discover I was on the island as well is an understatement.

An hour ago, I collapsed on the dock in a heap of tears. I stayed strong at Dottie's memorial. Before and after it. During the past two weeks while I've been sorting through her personal items at her cottage, I've been dealing with my own life drama.

But spreading her ashes and saying goodbye was apparently my breaking point.

Through my hazy vision, the image of Beck appears. Any last bit of strength I've been clinging to dissipates in this moment.

"Oh, damn, Rosie." There's urgency in Beck's voice and his movement as he rushes to me.

Dropping down to his knees, he wraps me up in his arms and I allow it. I sink into him, sobbing and digging my fingers into his taut back, trying to cling to something tangible. The solidity of his chest and the strength of his arms as he embraces me gives me the stability I'm desperate for.

"Shh," he hushes, his warm breath brushing the cuff of my ear. "I've got you."

And it feels like he really does.

"I think I missed my ferry." I cry harder into his chest, my cheek pressed against the soft cotton of his T-shirt.

"It's okay, we'll figure it out." His palm caresses my hair before he cups the back of my head. "Why didn't you tell me you were going to be on the island?"

"I wanted to do this alone." My words come out broken.

He sighs through his nose. "You don't have to do everything alone. I told you I'd come."

I sniff, nodding with my face still tucked close against him. "I know."

We stay like this for what feels like a long time but is only a few minutes. Reluctantly, I pull away from him and wipe a knuckle under my nose. Beck tugs a bandana from his pocket and wordlessly takes my chin in his rough hand while he gently wipes the wetness from my cheeks. He peers into my eyes, his gaze dancing over me, and my core tightens. It's sweet and somehow intimate. Until now, we've been practically at each other's throats.

A nervousness ticks in my veins below my skin, and I swallow. "Did you wipe your fishy hands on this?"

He chuckles, and my comment finally breaks whatever trance we were just stuck under. "Do you really think I'd do that and then wipe your face with it?"

"I mean, I'd hope not. But you have been pretty pissed at me."

"Yeah...I guess I have. But I'm more pissed at this fucked up situation." Pushing my hair off my face, he tucks it behind my ears.

"I know. I'm sorry." I gaze at him through wet eyes to find

him staring back at me with the gentleness that's always there when he looks at me. Soft, and kind. New sobs break free from my chest.

"Hey, hey, c'mon now. You're making a mess of your face again." A weak smile pulls on his lips.

"I...I can't help it. I don't deserve you," I whisper, immediately lamenting the words once I've spoken them.

His eyes meet mine again and they dance around as if he's questioning if he heard me. I hope he didn't, but I also don't take them back. More tears slide down my cheeks and he catches them with the bandana again.

"Are you kidding? I've been an asshole you since you got here."

"I deserve it," I mumble, blinking up at him.

"Maybe." He purses his lips and continues drying my face.

I expected him to deny it. But it's better he doesn't. I've been beating myself up over this secret—this lie—for too many years. It's time someone else did it.

"There." He studies my face with a confident smile. "Good as new."

My face is hot, my eyes are dry and burning, and I'm well aware of what I look like when I've been crying. There are some women who are pretty criers. But I am not one of them.

"Doubtful," I mutter. "But...thanks." I bite my lip, and he stuffs his bandana back into his pocket.

He fidgets his hands when we pull apart, and I comb my fingers through my hair as I glance out at the water. Grandma Dottie's urn sits next to me on the dock, the lid shoved back on tightly. I inhale a few deep breaths.

"Thanks again for coming."

"Of course."

"Was your dad mad?"

"Nah. Today was a crap day for fishing. Too hot."

I wince, glancing over my shoulder at him. "Sorry."

He waves me off. "We may get along better these days, but let's just say I'm still not quite ready to take his advice."

"Oh yeah?" He meets my gaze, and he looks me over too long that my body heats under his stare. "Did you tell him? About Charlie?"

He tears his eyes from me and focuses on a boat in the distance as it glides over the water. "I did."

Biting my lower lip, my stomach tightens. "What did he say?"

Beck sighs, low and long. "That I should put her first. Change my whole life for her or I'll regret it."

"Oh, Beck, I—" I clamp my mouth shut, then open it again when he doesn't speak. "You know I don't expect you to do that, right?"

"I know you don't," he spits out, his tone growing harsh. "But you haven't left me with much choice, have you?"

"Whoa." I hold up my palms.

"Just...I don't want to do this. Not here, not now." He adjusts his hat on his head. "This is about Dottie. You asked me to come, and I'm here."

"Geez, Beck, don't do me any favors." I roll my eyes.

"What? What is it then that you *do* want from me?"

I stare at him, my eyes watering again as disbelief fills me. Beck never used to raise his voice at me. He's never looked at me like that either. But then again, the years we've been apart have piled up on each other. People change. We've changed. I suppose we've drifted apart further than I knew.

"I'm sorry."

He throws up a hand. "There you go apologizing again. Just stop, will you?"

"I was going to say I'm sorry I asked you to come today. I thought...I don't know...that maybe we could find a way to move on. To make this work. Whatever this is. But I was wrong."

"No, you don't get to do that. You don't get to keep playing the victim."

Young Beck, the old Beck, never would've said these things. He never would've talked to me like he is right now. And it only solidifies what I already knew—we aren't the same people from seven years ago.

And we're over.

"Why don't you just go? I'm fine now."

"No," he mutters, and stands up. "I'm here. And you're clearly not fine."

I pull myself up to stand, my body groaning as I do. "I will be. I'm just gonna do this and then..." Except I don't know what comes after this. Because I missed the last ferry. Meaning I'm stuck on the island.

Beck bends and picks up the urn.

"Beck," I snap, stretching to snatch it back. "Hey, give that to me."

He holds it out of my reach. "No, I came to help. So let's get this over with."

"You're such an ass—*let's get this over with*?" I stand on my tiptoes and try again, but with him standing well over six feet, I'm no match. He holds the urn high above my head in an outstretched arm. "You're so immature. Cut it out."

"*I'm* immature?"

"Yeah. Give me the ashes, now." I hold out my palm.

"Let me start, then I'll give them to you."

"Why would I let you start? She was my grandma."

He brings the urn down against his chest to screw open the lid and I reach for it again, getting my hand gripped around it. In one swift motion, he twists his body away from me, wrenching the urn from my grip. I ricochet off his shoulder and the motion has me tripping backward.

I'm too late, even as I attempt to catch my footing.

Beck calls out, "Rosie!" and reaches for me.

The shriek that slides out of my throat is swallowed up by the ocean when my head goes under. I'm only in the water for a few seconds before an arm hooks under my chest.

"Rosie? Are you all right?" Beck asks, his lips close to my ear. "Rosie?"

Kicking my feet and flailing my arms is harder while dressed in jeans and a T-shirt. I sputter after my head shoots above the water. "What the hell was that?" I scream.

"I'm sorry. Are you okay?"

Once I know I'm out of danger, I wrestle out of his hold and splash water at him. "You're sorry? Ugh," I groan. "You're such a child."

"Hey, I jumped in and saved you, didn't I?"

"Yeah, and you wouldn't have had to if you hadn't been acting like a complete ass."

He swims to the edge of the dock and hoists himself up easily. Like the weight of his wet clothes makes no difference. Flipping around on his stomach, he holds his arm out to me. "C'mon, give me your hand."

I glare at him but quickly assess my options and ultimately give in, accepting his help. He slips his hand over mine and guides me to the dock. I brace myself on the edge as he pulls me out of the ocean. He wraps his arms around me, and I shut my eyes, squeezing out the world.

With his chin resting on the top of my head, he mumbles, "I'm sorry."

And even though I know he is, I can't help but wonder how we got here.

Here as in the two of us. Not necessarily here in this moment. Though this is not how I saw things going either. This day—hell, this life—is not turning out how I expected.

26

BECK

It takes Rosie several minutes to get over the shock of what just happened. I don't know what I was thinking. I probably wasn't thinking at all. Which isn't like me. I usually overthink things. I'm not reckless. I've never been able to afford to be reckless.

"Hey, where's your phone? We need to try to dry them out."

"Shoot. I forgot." She frees hers from the back pocket of her jeans.

I yank mine from my front pocket. It's soaked. And I've got nothing dry on me.

"I'm sure I've got a sweatshirt in my rig. That's about it."

She's frantically running her palms over her phone, but they're still wet too.

"C'mon, let's go to my truck. We can put the heater on and try to dry them out. And you can put my sweatshirt on."

She sets her phone down onto the dock. "I can't leave. Not yet."

"But Rosie—"

"I'm not leaving until I spread Dottie's ashes. That's what I came here to do." She gives me a determined look, her jaw clenched.

"Okay." The urn is resting on its side on the dock. I pick it up and give it to her. No more games.

She doesn't look at me when she accepts it. I don't blame her. It's my fault we're in this mess.

Unscrewing the lid, she unzips the bag that holds the ashes. "It's funny," she begins. "I didn't want to be alone while doing this, but I didn't have anything planned to say out loud."

"That's okay." I lower myself down, dangling my feet over the calm water. "You don't have to say anything."

After a few moments, Rosie sits next to me. "Isn't that weird?"

"I think...by you coming here and doing this, that's enough. You're doing what she asked."

"Not everything she asked."

When I glance over my shoulder to look at her, she's staring at me. Our eyes meet and I don't know what to say. I'm so afraid to say the wrong thing. The last thing I want to do is upset her. Again.

"Just because she asked, doesn't mean you have to do it. You gotta make your own choices. This is your life."

She rolls her eyes and flicks her attention away. "My life." She exhales a breath. "That's funny. Because all my life I feel like I've been living for other people."

"All your life? That doesn't really seem fair. Who were you trying to please when we got married? Me?" I wince, not sure I want the truth when she answers that question.

"Fine. I guess not all my life. Because that decision was for me."

My heart expands in my chest, fighting against the wet shirt. "And you wanting a divorce...Is that decision for you too?"

"Now that's not fair." She shakes her head.

"You're right. Sorry." But I do want to have this conversation.

Even if now isn't the right time. Our time is running out quickly. "But I guess to get remarried, you kinda have to divorce me first."

Her eyes flick up to mine and we hold a shared gaze of sadness and maybe remorse too. "I guess."

I nod and return my gaze to the glistening water as the sun lowers. From my peripheral, Rosie is waving her hand in the air, ensuring it's dry before she reaches inside the urn and pulls out a closed fist of ashes. She holds it tight, outstretching her arm and hovering over the water's surface for a few moments. At last, she opens her hand, spreading out her fingers and letting the ash drift into the ocean below.

While Rosie repeats the same process again, my mind sifts through memories of Dottie. Most of them from when Rosie and I were dating in high school, spending time at her cottage. Some after we were first married and spent Sundays with her at the beach or having lunch after church.

A few pop into my head from after Rosie left. When Dottie would call me to come over and fix something. A leaky faucet, a running toilet, a broken cabinet knob. Dottie was independent. I don't know if she really needed me to tend to those things or if she just missed having me around. But I never questioned it. Because I missed her too.

⌒⌒⌒⌒

*R*osie is even more mad at me than usual. Apparently, I'm to blame for her missing the last ferry of the day, even though she's the one who stayed on the island too long. But I will take full responsibility for our clothes and phones getting wet.

As Rosie tries calling Stella after we climb inside my truck, I rummage in the back seat for one of my work sweatshirts. I find one and give it to her before turning over the ignition and blasting the heat despite it being warm outside still.

"Hey, Stella?" Rosie speaks loudly into the phone. "Can you hear me?"

Stella's voice is muffled on the other end. I grasp the hem of my wet T-shirt and peel it over my head. The instant warmth from the heater hits my bare skin. Rosie glances my way, her eyes traveling across my chest and my abs. I catch her gaze with mine before they dart away.

"Stella? Yeah, how's Charlie?" She kicks off her sandals. "Good, that's good. Listen, you're not going to believe this. But I missed the last ferry. Yeah, I know. Thank you. But I'm so sorry. No"—she glances at me again—"not alone," she mumbles. "It's a long story. I'll fill you in tomorrow. Since it looks like I'm stuck here for tonight. I'm not sure. But if you need anything for Charlie, there's a key to Dottie's under the flower pot on the porch."

"Ugh." I throw my head back against the headrest. "Seriously? Because no intruder would ever think to look under a flower pot," I mutter under my breath.

"I have to go and figure out what I'm going to do. But I will be on the first ferry in the morning. I'll try to call later so I can tell Charlie good night. And, Stella? Thank you," she says before hanging up the phone.

"I thought you said Golden Harbor is a safe town?" she quips.

"Yeah, but that's like rolling out the welcome mat."

She shoots me a glare and I fire one back. Rosie and I are like oil and water these days.

"Can you look away so I can take my shirt off?"

"Oh, you mean like how you looked away when I took mine

off?" I smirk. But she's not amused. I roll my eyes and turn to face the window. "Fine. Happy?"

After a few moments of rustling, she sighs. "I'm good now."

When I turn back around, I find her drowning in my Stone Company sweatshirt. And damn. She looks hot dressed in my clothes. A fantasy of her dressed in nothing other than this materializes in my mind.

Her branded with my name.

And now I can't think of anything sexier. My mouth waters and a shot of arousal jolts in my groin. I swallow. "Any better?"

"A little. Thanks. Now, can you take me to a hotel or something?"

"We can stay at my dad's place." I'm already driving in that direction.

"Your dad's? You mean...the bar?"

"You don't have to say it like that. He has an apartment above the bar. So no, you're not gonna have to sleep in a bar."

"Are you sure he won't mind?"

"He's my dad. What's he gonna say? No? Dude owes me more than a night on his couch, don't ya think?"

She's quiet next to me, biting her lip while she taps on her phone.

When we reach The Thirsty Turtle, I park near the back steps that lead to my dad's apartment. We hop out and I round the front of the truck to the passenger side and gather our wet clothes in my arms.

"I'll throw these in the wash for tomorrow, but we'll have to bum some clothes from my dad for tonight."

"Oh yay, a Willie Nelson T-shirt, can't wait," she mutters, rolling her eyes.

I chuckle, because she's not wrong. That's my dad's wardrobe. "At least it will be dry."

"Yeah." She bites her lip.

"What's wrong?"

"Why don't you head up and fill your dad in. I need to make a phone call."

I lift my brows. "The boyfriend?"

"Fiancé," she corrects.

"Right. Fiancé." I take a few steps backward, holding the wet clothing against my bare chest. "Good luck." I spin and jog up the stairs, running through my own conversation I'm about to have with my dad.

I knock a few times on the door before trying the handle. It turns and I push a shoulder into it and step inside Dad's apartment. It's small and lacks enough windows to let much natural light in. There are a few lamps scattered around. The hint of a seafood scent is attempting to be masked by a lit vanilla candle.

"Hey, Dad?" I call, "You in here?"

He shuffles into view from the hall that leads to the bar downstairs. "Hey, son. What are you doing here? And what happened to your shirt?"

"Long story. We missed the last ferry. Mind if we crash here for the night?"

"We?"

"Yeah." My eyes dart around the apartment. "Rosie and me."

His brows shoot up. "Oh. Well, talk about a turn in events."

"No, *no*. No turn of events. Rosie was here spreading Dottie's ashes. We missed the ferry. That's it."

"Mind explaining why you're all wet?"

"Uhh..."

"That would be your son's fault," Rosie says from behind me.

I spin around and she's peering around me, taking a step and approaching Dad with her hand out. "Hello, Mr. Stone. It's good to see you again."

"Likewise, dear." He takes her hand but yanks her in for a hug and she stumbles into him.

My heart shifts in my chest.

"Your son here thought it would be a good idea to go swimming. Our phones too." She holds hers up. "Now I'm only catching half of a conversation."

"Well, that was stupid, kid. C'mon, give me your phones, I've got some rice."

"That doesn't actually work," I mutter under my breath.

"Does too. I'm a fisherman, you don't think I've dropped my phone a time or two? Give them here."

We both do and Dad retrieves a bowl and a bag of rice from the cupboard.

"Mind if I do a load of laundry?"

"'Course not. Need to borrow some dry clothes too?"

"Please," Rosie says sweetly.

"I have to say, if someone would've told me that you two kids would end up at my place for the night, I would've told them to go fly a kite." He sets his hands on his hips and glances back and forth at us. "But here you are. At my place, soaking wet, spending the night together."

"Not together," both Rosie and I blurt in unison.

Dad chuckles. "Uh-huh. Sure."

27

ROSIE

*M*r. Stone feeds us a simple but yummy dinner of rice with chicken, broccoli, and an herb dressing and is nice enough to offer me his bedroom. He says he'll share the pull-out sofa with Beck in the living room. But I tell him that's not happening. First, I'm not about to kick a grown man out of his own bed. And second, I'm not going to sleep in a random man's bed. Besides, he's a bachelor; who knows when the last time was that he washed his sheets.

We change into dry clothes. I hate that Beck doesn't look bad dressed in his dad's gray sweats and T-shirt while I feel like I'm drowning for the second time today, wearing an oversized shirt and plaid boxer shorts I've had to fold over a few times so they don't fall off. Beck's dad tells us good night and slips into his bedroom, leaving Beck and me alone.

"Forget the pull-out, we can each just take a sofa," I suggest, pointing at the two that are placed in an L-shape in Mr. Stone's living room.

"You're joking, right?" Beck deadpans.

"Well, I'm sure as hell not sharing the pull-out with you, if that's what you're suggesting."

"I wasn't suggesting it, but it makes more sense than the two of us scrunched up on the sofas. I mean, you might be fine, but not all of us are five foot nothing," he grumbles. "I've got long legs."

As if I need a reminder about how long his legs are. Like I don't have memories of those very legs wrapped around me like a human pretzel after hours of making love in the bed we shared. Those memories practically haunt me every time I close my eyes and allow my mind to wander back to the years we were happily married.

I start grabbing the throw pillows and tossing them onto the coffee table. "I'm five five. How do you not remember that?" I mutter.

"That's what you want to argue about here. Not the fact that we're two grown adults who should be mature enough to sleep in the same bed, but instead we're going to sleep on these cramped sofas?"

"Oh, I'm mature enough. But the question is, are you?"

"Do you not trust me? Is that it?"

"Can I?" I raise my brows at him.

"You don't think I can possibly keep my hands off you? Gah, you're so full of yourself." He chucks a pillow at me, and it hits me in the chest. "The way you get under my skin and piss me off, you have nothing to worry about. But I don't think that is what you're worried about."

I throw the pillow back at him, but it hits the floor instead with an unsatisfying thud. "What are you talking about?" I shove my hands on my hips.

He grabs one of the back cushions of the sofa and takes a step closer. I suck in a breath. "I think you're worried that I *won't* touch you," he challenges, his eyes not wavering.

My chin wobbles. "What? Why would I *want* you to touch me?"

"Because. I think you remember just how good it felt. And you're craving it again."

I wave him off despite the humming between my thighs. "You're delusional."

"Guess what, honey?"

I glare harder and step closer to him. "What?"

"I think you've forgotten, I know you. I know what you're thinking. I know what you're feeling." He closes the gap between us and I swallow, my gaze running over his face and paying close attention to the dark, animalistic look in his eyes. "You're my wife."

With that, my shoulders give in, and I lose the fight in me. He's right. He knows everything about me. Despite how much I think I've changed during the years we've been apart, I'm still me.

But I can't give in. Not to him. And not to the yearning that's stirring in my depths.

Because we will always be Rosie and Beck. Incompatible.

"I'm tired." I avert my gaze and move to the stack of blankets and pillows Mr. Stone left on the coffee table and snatch one of each, dragging them with me to the smaller sofa.

"Yeah? I'm tired too," he grits out, tossing a pillow onto the longer sofa and flopping himself onto it.

As I curl into a ball and try to get comfortable, fluffing the pillow and pulling the blanket up to my neck despite not being cold, Beck stretches out on the other sofa. Without covering himself with a blanket, he interlocks his fingers behind his head and crosses his ankles.

I wait several long minutes before I even move, keeping my eyelids pinched tight. The sound of his breathing is loud and raspy, like he's not calm at all. And I feel the same way. Besides the warmth in the room and the emotions from the day, the tension buzzes in the space between us, keeping me wide awake.

It's too bright in the small apartment. The bar's parking lot lights shine through the sheer curtains. And it's loud. The booming from the bar still full of life below us reverberates off the floor. It's tempting to sneak down there for a drink in hopes it will calm me enough to be able to sleep.

I can't help but watch him from the corner of my eye. The way he lies there, so nonchalant like he doesn't have a care in the world, grates underneath my skin. His eyes are closed, so I give myself the freedom to catalog his features. His facial hair is shorter than when I was here last week. My thoughts take a detour, imagining how incredible the roughness would feel against my skin. Between my thighs.

The brown Willie Nelson concert T-shirt he borrowed from his dad stretches across the muscles of his chest as it rises and falls. My mouth waters as I remember back to his shimmering wet pecs and abs while he sat shirtless in his truck earlier today. As I lower my gaze to the gray sweatpants, the bulge in the front sends a hum tightening in my core.

"Get a good look?" His voice echoes out into the space between us.

My eyes snap up to his. "Wh-what?"

His lips curl with amusement and indignation rises in my stomach. "I've never minded you looking."

"I don't know what you're talking about," I mutter as I roll onto my back, my heartbeat picking up speed.

The chuckle he releases is cocky and laced with satisfaction. "I actually loved it when your eyes were on me."

"Just stop." Flames lick at my cheeks.

"You're still cute when you're all flustered and turned on."

"What?" My head flies up and I prop it in my hand. "I'm not turned on."

He mimics my posture, his eyes darkening from across the room. "It's okay, honey, your secret is safe with me."

"I'm annoyed, that's what I am." I glare at him.

"Annoyed...and horny."

"Uggggh." A groan drags out of me and I fling my head back down on the pillow.

He cackles again and the sound pulses through me, waking up parts of me I pushed away so long ago. Places only Beck could reach. And satisfy. Dampness pools between my thighs and my breathing becomes shallow.

It's quiet again between us. The time ticks by in my head slowly. The heat surrounding the room dissipates. But I still can't sleep. No matter how long I lie here with my eyes closed.

After what feels like forever, the rumbling in the floor settles.

"I could really go for a drink," I whisper, not even sure if Beck is still awake.

"You're in luck," he replies quietly. "It just so happens there's a fully stocked bar downstairs."

"There's no way I'm going to a bar dressed in your dad's underwear and an old Wranglers T-shirt."

He breathes out a light laugh. "They should be closed by now. There's a noise restriction law on the island. All bars have to shut by one a.m."

"I remember that."

There's rustling across the room, and I turn to glance his way. He's already sitting up with his feet on the floor. "C'mon, let's go get that drink." He stands and gestures with his chin for me to follow.

I hop up and pad after him, trying to be light on my feet so as not to wake Mr. Stone. Though I'd be surprised if our arguing hasn't already woken him up.

"This doesn't mean things between us are good," I warn.

"Yeah, yeah. I guess we can call a truce while we get that drink. Deal?" he says over his shoulder, a fiery look in his eyes and a mischievous grin on his lips as he leads the way down the stairs.

"Fine. Deal." But deep down, I know this is a very bad idea.

Beck closes the door at the bottom of the stairs behind us, and I follow him down a hall. There's restrooms and a storage room off the hallway before opening into the restaurant. Beck flips on a few lights.

The bar is much as you'd expect it to be in a small island town in California. Wood-paneled walls with posters and a neon sign. Pool tables, dart boards, and tables pushed to one side with chairs flipped upside down and resting on them. An L-shaped bar fills an entire corner and practically one side of the restaurant.

Behind it, a variety of alcohol bottles line the shelves. Beck rounds the bar and reaches for two glasses, setting them on the countertop. He takes a few ice cubes from the machine and drops them into the glasses with a clink.

I prop my elbows on the countertop, watching him with interest. As he turns around to peruse the bottles, my gaze betrays me as it glides across his wide back and down to his backside in the grey sweats.

He spins around and I'm too slow to tear my eyes away from the view of the peak in the crotch of his sweats. Caught again. Damn. He snorts a laugh, but I don't let him get the upper hand. I can't.

"Were you gonna ask me what I wanted to drink or is this another thing you just assume about me?"

"Whiskey," he says as he holds up a bottle.

He might've known me at one point. But he doesn't now

I hold my chin up higher. "I don't drink whiskey. Not anymore."

"Oh, c'mon, you're kidding."

"Nope. I don't drink much at all."

"Not even whiskey? You used to love it. Especially Jack." He twists the bottle open with a little quirk in one brow.

"Yeah, well, I have a kid to take care of. Clients. A fiancé."

"Besides the kid, I don't see how the other things are relevant."

"I don't expect you to understand," I mutter.

Groaning, he gives me a glass. "Don't start talking to me about responsibilities again. Because I'll call bullshit. Here."

I roll my eyes but take the drink. Anything to shut him up. I bring it up to my lips and he does the same. We don't take our eyes off each other, and the burn is fierce and searing as the once familiar liquid runs down my throat. The warmth and sweetness on my tongue evokes images of my youth. Beck and me. It was always Beck and me.

He could've chosen any other kind of alcohol from those shelves, but he chose the one that used to be my favorite. The go-to liquor we'd sneak from his dad's stash and drink on the beach while we watched the sun sink into the ocean.

Well played, Beck.

"So what's the deal, your rich boyfriend doesn't let you drink anymore?"

"Fiancé," I correct for about the thousandth time. But it's more of a reflex because I guess West isn't my fiancé. Not anymore. "It's not about *letting* me. I drink wine sometimes."

He lowers his head to catch my attention. "Again, he can't be your fiancé when you're still married to me," he growls.

"Whatever." I roll my eyes, turning around to face the pool tables. "I thought we were calling a truce?"

"Fine." Beck moves from behind the bar and shuffles toward the closest pool table. He pushes a ball and it rolls into a corner pocket. "But wine? Really?"

I breathe out a light laugh. "Yeah, wine. It's good, once you acquire a taste for it."

"No offense, but I don't need to force myself to drink to get a taste for it. Have you met my alcoholic dad?" He chuckles dryly.

"Recovering alcoholic dad, right?"

He bobs his head. "Right. Two years now."

I take a pool stick from the holder on the wall and fidget with it. "How does that work? Him owning a bar when he's a recovering alcoholic?"

"I don't know." He rolls another ball across the table, but it bounces off the side. "He says it's about discipline. A constant reminder of all he's lost that keeps him from drinking."

"And your mom?" I'm almost afraid to ask.

"She moved to Florida after the divorce. Started a new family. Haven't seen her in several years."

"I'm sorry."

He shrugs, taking the pool stick from me. "I'm not. She made her choice."

I watch as he lines up a shot with the cue ball and then stretches across the table. "So that's it then? She made her choice, so you just write her off? That's just what you do, don't you?"

He throws his head back, groaning. "What do you want from me?"

"Nothing, just forget it." I snatch the stick from him, giving him a little pout. I'm tired. Tired from this long day. And honestly, tired from going round and round with Beck about the same things.

"No, I won't forget it." He slides between me and the pool table. "You want to talk about the choices you made? About you leaving?"

"Do you want to talk about the choices *you* made? I'm not the only one who made choices. Yes, I'm the one who left, but, Beck, one of us had to."

"No, that's bull and you know it. We could've made it work... together. That's what husbands and wives do."

"And I've apologized for my choices, for my fault in what happened between us. Have you? You could've come after me."

He drops his head. I'm not sure if it's because he's getting ready to apologize or if he's getting emotional or angry. But that's the problem, we seem to have lost the ability to communicate.

I set the stick down on top of the pool table and toss back the rest of the whiskey, my mouth numbing to the burning liquid. I strut back to the bar where Beck left the bottle sitting and refill my glass.

Beck shuffles over next to me and fills his again. "Truce, remember?" He holds his glass out to me.

I glare at him without speaking but relent and clink my cup against his. I tip the glass back and swallow a big gulp, my nostrils burning. "How many more times do you think we're going to have to call a truce before we're done with this drink?" I ask.

"Well, technically this is our second drink."

I roll my eyes again and amble back to the pool table, my body loosening up from the alcohol and dulling the ache in my back. I set my drink down and the retro jukebox in the corner of the bar catches my eye. It's one of those old Encore CD jukeboxes instead of the digital ones most bars have now.

While I search through the selections, Beck sidles up next to me, holding out a five-dollar bill. I'm tempted to refuse the offer, but I don't have any cash on me, so I reluctantly accept it. Flipping through the mix of genres, it's clear Mr. Stone curated the selection choices himself. I decide not to overthink it and pick enough songs to eat through the five bucks.

Returning to the pool table, I hop onto it and sit on the edge, letting my legs dangle off. The first song begins, and it's a love ballad between two country singers, which I chose unintentionally. The tone of their voices has a hum travelling through my body, turning me inside out the more the acoustics fill the space.

I try and fail miserably at not looking in Beck's direction, but I can't fight it. We make eye contact as he watches me curiously over the rim of his glass, the glimmer in his brown eyes setting fire to my bare skin. The sexual tension returns and stretches between us like a resistance band. My gaze flicks away and I pick up my drink again and run my thumb over the side of the glass.

We can't let the band snap.

Beck sets his drink down and struts over to the dart board. It's a worn, old-school one. He plucks the darts out from the board before stepping back and planning his attack. He throws a few and they reach the target but no bull's-eye.

While he continues taking his aggression out on the darts, I twirl my glass. The whiskey and ice swishing around distracts me until Beck lets out a grunt. I glance up at him and take another sip of my drink.

Tonight, he's a lot like I remember him. Maybe not in the gray sweats and the 1988 Willie Nelson "On the Road Again Tour" T-shirt. But somehow, the style still suits him.

His hair is a little messy after his shower and flops back over his ears every time he pushes it away. The brown in his eyes change in different lighting, just like Charlie's do. Right now, under the half-lit florescent bar lights, they're more chestnut brown. But out in the sun, they have golden undertones.

As he focuses on his next throw, he bites on his lower lip. He probably doesn't even know he's doing it. But I know he does this when he concentrates on something. I used to think it was sexy. And dammit, I still do.

Which is downright silly. Except this is Beck. My first love. My husband.

And is it so wrong to be attracted to my husband?

28

BECK

Rosie's green eyes take on a sultry hue beneath the bar lights. They draw me in while she peers at me over her glass. My skin heats under her intense gaze and I can't seem to resist staring right back at her.

She's killing me right now with how tempting she looks sitting atop the pool table, pushing her disheveled auburn hair away from her face and sipping her whiskey. Rosie dressed in a pair of my dad's boxer shorts and a worn black Wranglers T-shirt should be a turnoff. But instead, the view of her is sucking me in.

She bends a knee and rests her leg on the pool table, causing the shorts to ride up further and reveal even more tanned skin. The way the oversized shirt is slipping off one lightly freckled shoulder is distracting and sexy as hell. She's gotta know what she's doing to me.

At last, I break eye contact and return my focus on the dart board while the music fills the dead air between us. I throw a couple more darts, but my head is spinning. Being back in Rosie's presence has me questioning all life's choices.

What if I hadn't been so stubborn? What if she hadn't left? What if I'd known about Charlotte sooner?

But the thought of Charlie evokes irritation, and my shoulders tighten. I abandon the darts in the board this time and turn to face Rosie. The whiskey must be working its magic because she appears relaxed, content even.

"So the boyfriend," I say, using the word choice purposefully. It gets a little scoff from her but this time she doesn't correct me. *Hmm, progress maybe.* "Is he good to Charlotte?"

"Of course," she hisses. "I would never be with someone if they didn't treat her right. Never."

"Good, good." I shake my head, not really sure where I'm going with this. Yeah, I wanna know, but I don't want to piss her off again. Especially when we called another truce. "And she...likes him?"

Rosie shifts so she's sitting cross-legged, drawing my attention to her bare skin that's been kissed with freckles. I fight back a groan as my dick twitches in my pants, and I fold my lips in between my teeth.

"She does," she answers. "But she hasn't fully let her guard down around him yet. It takes her a while to trust someone enough to be herself around them. I suppose that's my fault. We didn't stay in one place long enough for her to build steady relationships. Not until now."

"So now, with *him*...it's permanent?" This time I don't intentionally emphasize my words, but I can't help it. Because even though I've never met him, I know he's not right for Charlie. Or for Rosie.

"I did say yes when he proposed."

I move across the room and decide it's safer to create distance. I lean my back against the pool table across from the one she's sitting on. "But you're not married." I point out.

"Well, no. Not yet." She purses her lips. "Because I'm still married to you."

I cross one ankle over the other and smirk. "Oh, right. That."

"Yeah, that," she deadpans.

We lock eyes again and I dare to ask, "You sure he's right for you?"

She tears her gaze away from me and dips her chin. "You don't get to ask me that, Beck. You lost those privileges."

"Fine. You're right. But I have the right to ask about Charlie," I say. She whips up her head, worry smearing her expression. "Is he right for her?"

"That's not fair."

"No, what's not fair is finding out I have a kid six years after she was born."

Her lower lip wobbles. "Beck," she whispers.

"So many decisions were made without me. Now that I know I'm her father, I should at least have a say in where she lives. Who she lives with. Don't you think?"

"You're right. And I know we need to have this conversation. We need to have a lot of conversations before I head back to Seattle. But I don't think tonight is the right time. It's been a long day. My body hurts. And we've been drinking."

She's right. I know she's right. But I almost push it. I almost choose now to argue my case on my rights as Charlie's father. That I want her here, in Golden Harbor. That I want Rosie here too.

But she leans back on her hands, and it causes her chest to thrust forward like it's on display. Damn she's tempting. Sitting there like a delicious meal waiting to be devoured on top of that pool table. A guttural groan slides up my throat as I try to ease my erection. I'm like a teenager because it distracts me from my anger and frustration. She's always had this effect on me.

"Truce?" I find myself questioning.

A small smile slips onto her lips, and she dips her chin. "Truce."

I return the smile in agreement and sling back what's left in my glass. The once sweet and burning liquid is watered down from the melted ice.

The sound of Rosie humming the song that's reverberating through the speakers whirs in my chest. Two shots of whiskey aren't much but it's enough to cause a buzz in my head. I refuse to believe it's from the seductive woman across from me.

"Besides just looking like you, she's a lot like you," Rosie says softly, and I train my eyes on her, trying to listen and not look at her tits. "She's cautious like you. Doesn't warm up to just anyone. So if it feels like it's taking her a while, be patient with her. She'll come around."

I nod along with her while she continues talking but I don't speak.

"She loves art. Which you've already noticed. Guess she gets that from you too. She's been drawing and coloring since before she even knew how to write her name." She lets out a little laugh. "Once Charlie colored on some of Weston's papers for work. He wasn't very happy, but after that he came home with an easel and large white sheets of paper."

My chest rises and falls rapidly. It's like learning about someone you hardly know but somehow you have this connection to.

"She can't hardly go anywhere slow. You've seen her. She skips everywhere. Oh, and she loves candy but hates chocolate."

"You're kidding? Are you sure she's *your* kid?" I deflect and chuckle. My heartbeat quickens and I try to inhale a measured breath through my nose.

"She can be anxious too. No panic attacks yet, luckily."

My gut twists at learning this. She's only six and already she's showing signs of anxiety. It kills me that I would pass that on to her. "Why...why are you telling me this? Now, I mean. I've been spending a lot of time with her."

Her eyes go wide and guilt flashes across her expression. "I just thought you might want to know more about your daughter."

"Well, it sucks."

"I'm sorry...I didn't mean to..."

"I mean that it sucks that she got that from me."

"Oh...I know, right? Who doesn't like chocolate?" She smiles.

But I don't find any of this amusing. I shove splayed fingers through my hair, pushing it back. "Not that," I bite out.

"You mean anxiety? We don't know if that's hereditary or not."

My limbs tingle and heat rises in my core, spreading down my arms and into my face. My heart rate accelerates and the beats punch against my chest.

"Hey? Are you okay?" Rosie's voice is soft and muffled, almost like she's under water.

"I'm...f-fine," I stutter, the simplest words being forced out.

I tell myself to stop focusing on what is happening with my body and instead, make myself breathe. Just like Dr. Sam taught me. But when the panic hits me this hard, my body and my mind betray me. That's the thing about anxiety: you don't have any control over it. It controls you.

"Beck, look at me." Rosie speaks louder, attempting to break me free from this before I spiral.

"Jus-s-t...keep talking to me. You know, like you used to?" I whisper.

She straightens and I move closer to her. I've got no right, but Rosie doesn't hesitate to reach for my hand. Her cool touch zings like electricity straight to my veins. But it's not enough to ground me. I squeeze back the tears welling in my eyes.

"Open your eyes and look at me," she commands.

It takes a few moments for my brain to signal my eyes to

open. My gaze flutters, taking Rosie in with a glossy view. My breathing releases in tiny, rumbling gasps.

"Good," she coaxes, holding my hand in hers and brushing her thumb across my knuckles. "Now take a deep breath and hold it for a few seconds."

My heart continues to race and I'm panting now like I've just run several miles.

Rosie fists the front of my T-shirt, hauling me closer to her until our foreheads press together. The intensity of the physical contact triggers my senses. I suck in a breath and hold it for a few seconds before releasing it.

"Good. Now another." Her gaze is earnest.

I inhale another breath, and this time I hold it longer. Rosie mimics me, matching her breathing with mine, and it anchors me. With one hand splayed next to her on the pool table, I reach my other around her back. The yearning to hold something tangible is so powerful I don't think; I only act. I glide my hand down until I reach her ass and grasp it in my palm.

My awareness of our close proximity heightens and threatens to send me further into this spiral. But as we lock eyes, I stare into the familiar green hue and see everything I've ever known to be good and right in my life. I see my person. I see my lover. I see my...home.

Rosie doesn't release her grip from my shirt. Or the pressure of her forehead from mine. She reaches up to the back of my neck and rakes her fingers through my hair. It sends a shiver racing through my body.

As my breathing evens, my heart continues to gallop in my chest for an entirely different reason. Rosie is in my arms. It's something I hadn't realized I've been longing for until this moment. All this time I've been holding on to anger and resentment, and it's blinded me from my true feelings.

I still love her.

Rosie's grasp tightens around my neck and I draw back

slightly, pressing my lips to her forehead. Her skin sears my mouth beneath the kiss I give her. Soft, lasting, purposeful. As her eyes flutter closed, she releases a throaty exhale. The sound awakens a numbness of emotions and arousal I've been fighting to depress.

With my hand still gripping her ass, I haul her against my hard length. She draws in a sharp breath and her eyes fly open, the green now dark and feral. I drop my gaze to her full lips. They're rosy and alluring and I've never been more tempted to smash my mouth against hers.

I want her. She *knows* I want her. And yet—I know I can't have her.

As she tips her head back, she gives me a shy smile and my hope shatters. She releases the clutch on my T-shirt and slides her palm down from my neck and across my chest. And suddenly I'm blaringly aware of just how close I came to kissing her. How close I came to grazing the cuff of her ear with my lips and murmuring, *Are you wet for me, honey?*

Instead, I'm doing the very last thing I want to—withdrawing from her. "Well, it's a good thing Charlie has you," I whisper and release my holding of her. My knees wobble as I take an agonizing step backward and exhale a shuddering breath. "You always know how to handle a panic attack."

"Yeah." The word vibrates from her chest. "I'm glad I was here. I mean...I'm glad I could help." She hops off the pool table and stands before me, her vision slipping down to see how bad I want her. There's no hiding it—my cock is standing at attention, hard as steel. Her gaze darts back up and pink highlights her freckled cheeks. "I should get some sleep. Tomorrow is a busy day," she rushes out as she adjusts the T-shirt to cover her shoulder, nibbling on her lip and driving me even wilder.

"Yeah, me too." I lift my arm as if I'm excusing her and giving her permission to leave.

Dipping her chin to her chest, she tucks her hair behind her ear and shuffles away. "Good night, Beck," she calls over her shoulder.

"Night, Rosie."

I let myself watch her as she walks away, shuffling down the hallway to the door that leads to my dad's upstairs apartment. It's a cruel reminder in a way. Like I'm always watching her walk away.

29

ROSIE

The kink in my neck is a keepsake of the painful decisions I had to make last night. Leaving Beck in the bar was torturous. And sleeping on separate sofas was even more brutal.

But acting on feelings isn't something I can risk. Not at this point in my life. I have Charlie to think of.

I roll off the sofa and peek at Beck who's still sleeping while I tiptoe to the bathroom. The mirror's reflection is confirmation of the lack of sleep I got last night. When I step out, I grab a blanket and my phone and sneak out the door to the deck.

My phone is in working order thanks to Mr. Stone's rice trick. I have no missing texts or calls. I release a sigh of relief and gaze at the street and shops down the street. From this spot on the deck, there's a clear shot of the ocean.

Finally alone, the last twenty-four hours play through my mind. Beck's intense gaze as if he wanted to devour me. The feel of his skin pressed against mine. Being in his embrace, his hair slipping through my fingers, the stroke of his hand against mine.

We were so close, his breath brushing against my lips. His

mouth hovering over mine. Him palming my backside and thrusting me against his stiff length.

My phone vibrates in my hand and I jump.

BECK

Where are you at?

I've got a surprise for you.

My lips twist while I consider returning inside. I was a mature adult last night. As tough as it was, I made the decision not to cross the imaginary line. Staying put out here, I'm safe. There's no worry over crossing boundaries or doing something either of us will regret. Or worse, not be able to undo.

My phone vibrates again.

BECK

I made coffee.

And that settles it. I'm back inside the apartment in less than two seconds. There's no consideration when coffee is involved. My answer is always *yes*.

"Thought you could use this." With a little wink, he offers me a mug.

"Desperately." I don't check the temp; I don't even say thank-you before I'm gulping it down. It's hot but not burn your mouth hot. And it's strong. The kind of strong that gives you a kick in the ass to wake up. "Thank you," I finally say once I've come up for air.

He shrugs and takes a sip from his own cup as he leans against the kitchen counter. He's still dressed in his dad's sweats and T-shirt, and if it's possible—looking hotter than he did last night. Maybe it's the added touch of his hat that he's using to either hide his messy hair or his eyes from the embarrassment over last night. "It's nothing fancy like I'm sure you're used to."

And we're back with the little digs. This one may be more subtle than his usual, but it's still obvious.

"What do you even know about me?" I quip over my shoulder as I stalk through the living room and back outside to the deck.

"A lot, actually," he says to my back, following me.

I didn't mean to start a fight. I'm tired, it's early, and there's a dull ache sitting around my back and lower stomach. And clearly neither of us got a good night's sleep. Because if I was cramped on the sofa, he definitely woke up feeling stiffer. My mind shifts after that last thought, wondering if other parts of him woke up stiff.

"I know you need a cup of coffee within the first thirty minutes of waking up or you get grouchy." He chuckles lightly, but not in a patronizing way.

I open my mouth to speak but clamp it shut when it appears he's not done talking.

"Or you get a headache. Which then makes you grouchy." He smirks at this, and I just roll my eyes. "I know you like to visit new coffee shops but you never like the coffee. You only like to go for the vibes. Because I know that you prefer your coffee with honey and oat milk. But if they don't have it, you'll settle for sugar and cream."

My stomach twists and to keep myself from overanalyzing his words, I take another drink of my coffee. Except the taste of the sugar on my tongue is a cruel reminder. After seven years, Beck still knows how I take my coffee.

"And I know it damn near killed you every day since Charlie was born that you hadn't told me about her. You never kept secrets from me." My insides quiver and some of the guilt I've been holding on to releases. "Pfft. What do I even know about you? How can you even say that?" He shakes his head, running his thumb over the handle of his mug. "I know a lot about you, Rosie."

I swallow another gulp of coffee. "I guess you do," I mumble.

We lock eyes and there's heat and tenderness ricocheting between us. We share a weird sort of reconciliation smile.

I move to the railing and lean my elbows on it while cradling my mug in both hands. He joins me, our arms brushing slightly, and my body fills with warmth. There's not only memory carrying these feelings. Because as much as I thought they were gone, it seems they were only stuffed down deep. Now that we're together again, those old feelings are threatening to rise to the surface.

We drink our coffee silently, probably another thing he remembers about me—I prefer to have almost a full cup of caffeine before communicating with others. Gazing at the ocean in the distance, the rising sun glitters across the waters surface.

When I glance over my shoulder at Beck, his brown eyes are pensive beneath the rim of his hat. My stomach tightens in apprehension as I consider what's on his mind.

"Ya know, I know a lot about you too."

He turns to face me, leaning a hip against the railing. "Yeah?"

"I know you're good at your work and you enjoy it."

He bobs his head but I'm not sure he believes my words.

"I know for someone who doesn't forgive easily, when you do, you're gracious and benevolent."

His eyes soften but he just shrugs a shoulder and glances down at his bare feet.

"You're patient. I always admired the way you handled the responsibilities of caring for Milo."

He plucks a splinter of wood that's peeling off the side of the railing. "I figured he could use some gentle parenting for a change."

He's attempting to play off these qualities I'm pointing out.

Like he's been so beaten down he doesn't even know how to take a compliment. And the fact I might've had something to do with that causes my heart to break.

"I've seen it with Charlie too," I say softly.

This catches his attention enough that he lifts his gaze to meet mine. His eyes crinkle slightly and the brown hue goes glossy. I smile and lift my chin, reassuring him of my words.

He clears his throat. "She's a good kid. It's easy to be patient with her."

"Yeah, well, she wasn't always easy."

He purses his lips and wrinkles his brow. I'm hit with the reminder that he didn't know her then. And it's my fault he didn't.

"The teenage years probably won't be easy either," I add.

"I hope I get to be around for those."

The blow punches me again. "Beck," I say on an exhale. "You will. Now that she knows, and you know."

"You think she's going to want to keep spending time with me?" he asks, concern smearing his expression.

"Are you kidding?" I reach for his arm without thinking. "She's crazy about you. Probably because you both are so much alike."

"I'm pretty crazy about her too." His lips pull into a smile. "And her mom." He releases the admittance like it's effortless.

Beck plucks my hand from his arm and holds it, gently caressing his thumb across my knuckles. My body tingles in response to the roughness of his calloused hand and my heartbeat picks up speed as I draw in closer to him. He locks his gaze with mine and I feel it again—that damn resistance band. When I search his eyes, I'm flooded with want and desire. I see my hopes and dreams so vividly staring back at me.

I see my future.

My brain is overloaded with questions of demographics and logistics. But my heart is pushing out strained beats against my ribs at the idea of this thing between us being a real possibility again.

"Beck, I—"

"I know it doesn't make any sense. That *we* don't make any sense. Not now. But the way I see it, we never made any sense. And that didn't stop us before. Why let it stop us now?" He tugs me closer.

"You're right, we don't make sense. Look how it worked out for us?" I say it like a question, as if he somehow forgot.

"But that's the thing, it hasn't ended. Not for me." His eyes search mine and the fire burns between us, scorching my body and reaching all the dormant parts of me. "And something tells me it hasn't ended for you either."

Tears well up in my eyes and my heart races as the energy buzzes between us. He holds me closer, and the feeling of being desired and wanted is exhilarating. Every fiber in my body is alive and craving the attention it's been starving for. The satisfaction only he can grant me.

"It hasn't," I admit on a soft sob, the confession breaking something free in my body.

With zero hesitation, he takes me by the hand and yanks me back inside the apartment. He snatches my coffee and sets both mugs on a side table. And I almost protest. Have I had enough coffee for this...for whatever is about to happen?

Before my brain has time to comprehend what is going on, he shoves me against the closed door, stealing my breath. He cups his palms to my cheeks, the roughness of his hands stroking my skin. His eyes are dark and lustful as they dance over mine with intention. Looking at me like he wants to devour me. And I think if he doesn't pull away now—I will let him.

I will let him consume all of me.

His hands skid downward where he pushes pressure with his thumbs into the sides of my neck. "You're more beautiful now than ever," he confesses on a rush of breath. "I've been wanting to tell you that since I first laid eyes on you at the beach that night by Dottie's. But you know how stubborn I can be."

Warmth expands in my chest and a smile pulls at my lips. I take a hold of his hands while they're still clasping my neck. "I know," I whisper. "And I guess I'm stubborn too. Because I haven't told you...my engagement is off."

With the release of my confession, the resistance band finally snaps. He spins his hat backward and leans in closer, the hard plane of his body pressed against mine. I suck in a breath as a blaze of yearning rushes between my thighs. Achingly slow, he lowers his mouth to mine and greediness has me pushing up on my toes to meet him partway.

At last, his lips brush mine, setting fire to them on contact. It's soft at first, almost as if he's scared to trust it. But the gentleness is intimate and has my mouth answering greedily. Like it's been waiting its whole life for this moment. For this exact kiss. Like it's never known a kiss this amazing could even exist.

My mouth moves over his with ease and desperation all wrapped into one. When he licks the seam of my lips and forces his tongue inside, a soft moan escapes me. He slips a hand inside the front of my shirt, his rough and calloused hand gliding over my ribs, and a shiver runs through me.

When his hand inches further and discovers I'm not wearing a bra, he releases a guttural groan. "You're killing me," his words grate out. He skims a thumb across my nipple before cupping my breast. My knees go weak, and I sink against the door as my head goes dizzy.

Beck pulls back reluctantly, gazing down at me with heat radiating in his brown eyes as I lick my lips. A gritty groan breaks free from him. "I need you, Rosie. I need to have you. Right now," he rasps as he sets his warm lips to my neck and plants a row of kisses until he meets my eyes again. "But if you tell me no, I'll let you go. As much as it will completely shatter me. I will." He clasps his free hand to the back of my neck and forces me to look at him. "Just say the word."

"You have me. Take me, please."

A cocky grin pulls at the corner of his mouth as he drags the pad of his thumb across my lower lip. "No need to beg, honey."

I roll my eyes and shove him in the chest. Chuckling, he leads me toward the sofa and sits, yanking me into his lap so I'm straddling him. With his large palms splayed across my back, he leans in and presses gentle and purposeful kisses to my neck, leaving a trail of fire in his wake.

"What about your dad?" I pant out.

"He's gone. He left early to go fishing with his buddies. It's just you and me."

At his words, I melt. *It's just you and me.*

Beck's hand finds the back of my neck, fingers curling around it with a hint of possessiveness that kicks my craving into drive, and he guides my mouth toward his again. But he pauses midway and forces my gaze to meet his.

"I've waited seven years for you," he whispers, the rush of breath from his words reaching my lips.

"I know, me too," I agree softly.

"No, I mean...there's been no one else...since you."

Air catches in my throat at his confession. I rear back. "Wait. What are you saying?"

"I meant my marriage vows, Rosie. Every single one."

My eyes water again.

"You're my wife," he says, his voice haughty. "You're mine."

"Beck," I whisper, a few tears slipping out. Guilt presses against my chest, threatening to cave it in. Even though there has only been West, I've been reckless with my vows. Reckless with Beck's heart.

"It's okay," he says softly. "I didn't expect you to wait.

Honestly, I didn't expect me to wait." A small smile appears on his lips. "It's not like I didn't have the opportunity. But none of them were right. None of them were you. None of them were... my wife."

And because I know Beck, and know his words are genuine, I know there's no animosity there. My chest expands again, and I thread my fingers through the hair at the back of his neck. "There's nothing I love more than when you call me your wife," I admit, then scrape my fingers over the facial hair on his cheek. "And I want you to see what you've been waiting for."

He gives me a teasing grin, leaning in close and nipping at my lip with his teeth. "Good. Show me. *Wife.*"

30

BECK

We take our time. Even though we need to catch the ferry soon. But we shut out the world and it's just me and Rosie. No one else.

She slips her hands inside my shirt, skidding her palms across my abs and chest and making me quiver beneath her touch. As she kneads her fingertips into my skin, it heats the more she touches me. My mouth can't get enough of hers, sliding, nipping, tasting. It's all familiar but at the same time, different and new.

With her in my lap, her auburn hair hangs down to frame her face and I can't stop from staring. She's beautiful. I want the visual of her, just like this, to be seared into my memory forever.

Rosie takes a hold of the hem of my T-shirt and slowly tugs it up my sides, her fingers teasing my ribs and making me chuckle. I lean forward so it's easier for her to slide the fabric up my back and tear my mouth from hers while she tugs it over my head. Her eyes drag across my bare chest, and she draws her lower lip in between her teeth. A smile pulls at my lips. No doubt she likes what she sees.

"Your turn," I say softly but with a hint of a growl. My greedy hormones are desperate to get my own look at her.

A hint of pink color swirls into her cheeks and it makes her more alluring. That and the fact she's still embarrassed over this even though I've seen her naked a thousand times.

I take the hem of her shirt and slide it up slowly, giving myself time to adjust to seeing her bare skin a little at a time. I do *not* need to go into a spiral over this and ruin the moment by having a panic attack. Or worse—come in my pants. That would be embarrassing. Like I'm a teenager. But that's how she makes me feel.

Young. Wild. Reckless.

The shirt reaches her chest, and I tug it up and over her rounded breasts. I gaze at her, studying every square inch, before I at last pull it all the way over her head and toss it on the floor.

"You're beautiful," I declare on a breath.

"Are you kidding? *You're* beautiful. How long have you been hiding that six-pack? I don't remember this from seven years ago."

I release a light laugh and give a sheepish shrug. "Just more defined, I guess."

"This is more than just defined. You looked good before, but you're gorgeous."

"It's just work. And a few nights at the gym. What's your excuse?" I gesture at her body.

She dips her chin, almost as if just now noticing she's missing her shirt. "Uh...seriously? I'm nothing special. I've got scars from surgeries and stretch marks. And I'm bigger than I used to be."

"Yeah, you are."

She whips her head up, horror in her eyes when they meet mine.

I hurry to clarify. "These curves are sexy. And where'd those tits come from?"

Tucking her hair behind her ear, she mutters, "Maybe from breastfeeding? Or because I've put on a few pounds."

"You're beautiful. I didn't think it would be possible for you to look more beautiful than you did before. But you're fucking perfect now."

She rolls her lips and makes a *tsk* sound, setting a palm to her stomach where there's a few surgery scars and a trail of stretch marks from pregnancy. My gut wrenches with the thought of missing this part of her life. And I can't hide my disappointment. I won't hide it. Not from her. "I wish I could've seen you. Pregnant. I bet you glowed."

I lean forward and press my lips to her scarred stomach. Dropping a few kisses there, I work my way up to the center of her chest. Her fingers find my hair and dig into my scalp, needy. And now I'm aching to see her fully bare.

"Take off your bra. I need to see you. All of you," I demand, gathering her hair and pulling it over to one of her shoulders.

She only hesitates briefly, a bit of shyness creeping into her demeanor, but her eyes find mine and there's a fire there. Reaching around her back, she unhooks her bra, and I grip my hands around her waist. The lacy piece of fabric falls, and she slips her arms free, tossing it to the side.

Delicate and full breasts are mere inches from my view, and I soak it all in. The beauty of her has a choke hold on me. I'm in a trance, and I can't look away. I suck my lower lip in between my teeth, biting back a groan. She's somehow the same but so much more. Confident. Sexier.

My desire for her strains against the front of my pants and I tug her hips down so she can feel it. Her eyes go round and her lips pout and damn I can't help myself; I drag her front over my length. She moans approvingly as I continue grinding her against me.

"You've got me so hard over here. Better be careful, honey, or you're gonna have me making a mess in my pants." I dive my face in between her tits and spread kisses over her silky skin.

She exhales a giggle as she throws her head back. "This is familiar."

"Yeah?" I mumble as I glide my lips up the sleek column of her neck, her skin so hot and tempting.

"Yeah. Don't you remember all the dry humping we did when we were teenagers?"

I draw back, a rueful smile pulling at my lips. "Remember? That was the highlight of high school for me."

She snorts, dragging her hand down my bare chest and evoking a tremble. Her fingers dance further until they reach my sweatpants, where she teases me by tiptoeing her fingers along the waistband. I'm tempted to get things moving faster and yanking off the pants, but I also want to take my time.

"I've missed this. I've missed you."

"Me too." I nip at her lower lip with my teeth.

She tethers her fingers through my hair at the back of my neck. "There wasn't a day in our seven years apart that I didn't think about you," she admits on a whisper.

My heart squeezes at the release of her words and I draw my head back, tightening my grip on her. "Don't," I grit out. "Don't say things you don't mean. Not now."

"I mean it. I missed you...every single day."

It's cruel for her to admit to this now. When I have her in my arms and writhing on top of me, ready for me. I dig my fingers into the soft skin of her hips. "Honey, you've got terrible timing." I chuckle as parts of me I've suppressed for too long suddenly unlock. "You left a crater-sized hole in my soul."

Remorse shines in her green eyes as she peers down at me and my gut aches. I don't want her to feel bad. Not anymore. "Beck, I—"

"I more than missed you. I missed you like you were the

oxygen I needed to survive. Shit, without you, I didn't know how to manage my anxiety. And I lied to you...I did start therapy," I confess, tracing my thumbs over her hip bones and earning a shiver. "I had to learn deep-breathing exercises. I still go see Dr. Sam once a month. She keeps my BS in check."

"So I should thank her?" Rosie gives me a teasing smile.

"Now no more of this talk. We deserve this. We deserve a chance to fill the craters we both left in each other. We deserve happiness. Now..." I pause and haul her in closer. "Show me how much you missed your husband."

I return my mouth to hers. Her tongue is needy to find mine as it parts my lips. I skim my palms up her sides and she trembles when I run them over her ribs and breasts, so full in my hands.

When she finally slips her hand beneath my briefs and finds my length, her touch is gentle. It's cool, timid, and has me practically quivering. My restraint is astounding; I should win an award.

"You're driving me wild," I mumble, my thumb brushing across her nipple. "I need your shorts off. Now."

I lift her and set her onto the sofa so together we can work at tugging the shorts off. She wriggles her hips, and I yank them down her thighs. My brain goes a bit haywire when I discover she isn't wearing any panties.

My mouth waters. "You've gotta be kidding me. Are you telling me you've been commando this whole time?"

"They were wet." Her little shrug is cute but there's nothing innocent about her in this moment.

My brain short circuits at her words. "I'll be they were. Let's see if you're wet now." Bracing one hand on the back of the sofa next to her head, I bend and use my other hand to spread open her legs. The sight of her glistening pussy has me captivated. I drag a finger through her center and she trembles at my touch.

"You're soaked for me," I pant, sliding one finger inside of her and earning an adorable moan.

A little massaging always helped me enter her with more ease and it made me feral for her too. I add another finger, curling until I reach the spot that has her bucking against my hand. I slide my fingers out and lean over her, pressing a greedy kiss to her mouth. I gaze down at her again, admiring how beautiful she looks like this; bare and exposed.

"It's unfair you've been just over here looking like this, and I've been missing out all these years."

"I'm here now. And it's all yours," she says, her eyes flaring.

Damn. I'm practically foaming at the mouth.

I shimmy out of my pants and underwear, kicking them into a pile. After I've resituated bare ass on the sofa, I grip her waist. "Come here," I demand, guiding her back into my lap. As soon as her front touches my cock, her wetness coats me and her body melts into mine. Her fingers are back to tousling my hair. My eyes flicker closed momentarily as I squeeze her hips and lift her before driving her back down again.

The intensity of everything explodes and splinters throughout my body. It's too much but at the same time—not enough. I need all of her touching me. "I want to take my time with you, but I can't wait another second to be inside you."

"Good, because I'm about to finish just like this."

"No. I need you to wait." I lift her and nudge my chin. "Is this okay?"

"Yes." The word comes out with a little hiss of breath as she bobs her head approvingly.

"I want you to guide me in so I don't hurt you."

With one of her hands splayed on my chest, she reaches down with her other one and wraps her fingers around my dick. I inhale a trembling breath and have to force myself not to blow in her hand. But the feeling of her delicate fingers grasped around my sensitive skin has me so close.

After a few strokes she drags the tip against her entrance, wetting it so it guides in with more ease. As she pushes me inside of her, I lower her hips down slowly, my grip shaking. She hisses and I clench my gut as I sit up a little.

"You okay? Does it hurt?"

"It's okay."

I kiss her neck, reassuring her before gazing into her eyes. "You sure? I don't want to hurt you."

"Still the considerate lover."

"This is a partnership, honey. I'm not about to get my rocks off if you're in pain."

"I'm okay. It feels so good. Being back in your arms. With you...like this?" She drags her fingers across my head again. "Just lower me slowly."

I do what she requests. I'd do anything for her. I ease her down over me as she exhales slowly. "How's that?"

"Gah, so good."

"Good. That's what I want to hear." I lift her again and she moans. When I bring her back down, it stretches her further and she gasps. When she doesn't speak but instead scrapes her fingernails into my scalp, I don't ask any more if she's okay. Because I know her.

This isn't just intimate, it's perfect. *She's* perfect.

It only takes her a few moments before she's lifting herself up, pushing off her knees, and coming back down harder each with each thrust. Her mouth lands on mine with desperation, her lips sliding and her teeth tugging. My hands find the smoothness of her back, the dip in her hips, and I can't stop touching her.

As her tongue darts out to tangle with mine, I nearly come unglued. Every fiber in my body is alive. I don't want this moment to end. The worry in the back of my mind that I may not get this chance again blurs with each jolt of pleasure.

Rosie's breathing quickens and her kisses get sloppy. The

delirious part of my brain is giving in and ready to let myself fill her. She's rocking against me, her breasts bouncing, and I know she's close too.

"That's it, that's my good wife. Take it. Take what you need," I coax as I kiss her and run my palms over her bare ass. I nuzzle my head in the crook of her neck, kissing the smooth skin there, and she pants louder. Moving lower, I sweep out my tongue and lick her peaked nipple.

"Are you close?" she says on a breathless whisper.

"Honey, I've been on the verge of blowing for the last five minutes." I chuckle.

"I'm gonna...gonna come."

"Do it," I encourage, and drag my tongue across her pebbled nipple.

She hisses out a breath right before a moan tears from her mouth. I bring her down on top of me as I grind her harder and faster, rubbing her clit over my length each time I glide out of her slightly.

I lift my eyes to her again. "Look at me. I want you to see who's making you fall apart." I nip at her bottom lip.

"Oh, Beck."

"That's it, it's me, your husband. Eyes on me, honey."

Our eyes lock while we both ride out the last few seconds of this blissful high. Our kissing is intermittent, our breathing is erratic, and while she screams out my name, I swallow it with my mouth. I kiss her as I surge inside of her, filling her to the brim with everything I've been holding in for the last seven years.

All for her.

When we finish and our breathing slows, she gives me a playful smile, biting her lower lip. I tug it free with my thumb and kiss her swollen lips. She collapses against my chest, and I press her bare breasts against me, the feel of her hot skin against mine makes me feel unhinged. It's like I've been somehow transported back to when we used to make love without inhibition. It didn't matter where we were, if Rosie wasn't flaring or in pain, we were doing it anywhere and everywhere.

But here we are, on my dad's sofa. And we aren't kids anymore.

"Shit," she mumbles, sitting up slightly and pushing back her disheveled hair. "What if someone downstairs heard us?"

"Now you're worried? Where was that concern ten minutes ago?" I tease with a chuckle.

"Obviously, ten minutes ago I wasn't thinking about anyone else."

"Good. That's exactly how I wanted you." I reach up and grab her hair in one fist, pulling it over one of her shoulders and tugging her toward me. Her eyes dance over my face and I admire the way her eyes have glossed over and the deeper pink of her swollen lips. I press my mouth against hers before releasing her hair.

She pushes back and there's an awkwardness between us as we take in the scene. I'm still inside her and she's straddling me. We're both still naked.

"I should probably..." Her words trail off as she glances at our clothes scattered around the living room.

"Let me help." I squeeze her waist and lift her slowly and the release of her aches deep in my gut. I instantly miss her. I stand her up between my legs and snatch a T-shirt off the floor. And as I drag it up her inner thigh swiping the dripping cum, I'm tempted to push it back inside of her.

With her eyes ablaze, she gives me a sexy smile while the corner of her lip is pinched between her teeth. "That was insanely hot."

"Yeah?" I stand and study her. Paying extra attention to her disheveled hair, her glossy eyes, and freckles that are muted by the pink in her cheeks. She's practically glowing.

"Why are you looking at me like that?" She bites her lip and pushes her fingers through her hair.

"Because looking at you after I've satisfied you, used to be my favorite thing."

Her gaze locks on mine, heat flaring in her pupils. "You never told me that before," she whispers like a revelation.

"I'm sorry. I should've." I glance down, my eyes sweeping up her naked body and admiring every piece of her, before landing on her eyes again. "There's a lot of things I should've said. Should've done...then maybe...maybe you wouldn't have left."

There's a long, delicate pause before she finally speaks. "Maybe."

I'm not sure if her response surprises me or if it's simply the guilt. "I'm sorry." I finally speak the words I've been holding in for seven years, "I'm sorry I never came after you."

Through watering eyes, she shakes her head. "No, I'm sorry. I never should've left."

I reach around to the back of her neck and grip it, pulling her close. "I get it. I understand why you left." I catch her gaze and lift my chin, trying to reassure her while I rub my thumb against her soft skin. "I spent that whole first year angry at you for leaving but I never even considered what part I played. And then...well...and then it was too late. I assumed after a year or so if you hadn't come back and I hadn't gone after you, it was over."

Tears roll down her face and she sniffs. "I'm sorry."

"I know. Me too, honey. Me too." I haul her forehead against mine and close my eyes, holding her like this for several long moments, our naked bodies molding together.

31

ROSIE

On the ferry, dressed in yesterday's clean clothes, I settle my elbows on the metal railing while Beck stands behind me. He grips the rails with both hands, his arms enveloping me on either side while I lean against the firm plane of his body. He rests his chin on top of my head while a continued breeze sweeps through my hair.

The warmth from his body shields me from the chill in the air. It guards me from the reality that waits for us when we step off this ferry. Here, in the comfort of his embrace, I'm safe.

I close my eyes and breathe in a mixture of Irish Spring from his dad's soap and a hint of his cedar and bergamot cologne that must be lingering from the day before. A rueful smile tugs at my lips, and I settle my head against his chest. There's a lingering pulse of pain between my thighs. Instead of dwelling on the discomfort of it, it's a reminder of my mind-blowing orgasms.

After we made love on the sofa, Beck led me into the bathroom where he sat me on the ledge of the tub, got down his knees, and pleasured me further. He licked, sucked, and devoured my pussy possessively. Then he turned on the water and we showered together where he washed me with tenderness. It was like a dream. One I don't want to wake up from.

We don't talk on the ferry. Maybe we're both afraid that if we do, this perfect moment will disintegrate. It's too precious. Too delicate.

We stay like this until the ferry docks and most of the passengers have gone below to their vehicles. But we take advantage of every single second. Beck takes my chin in his hand, turning my face until I can peer up at him. He licks his lips as his eyes draw me in and holds my gaze. Heat surges through my body.

He's gorgeous, just like this. Vulnerable and confident. There's a spark in his chestnut eyes that hasn't been visible until today. Or maybe I hadn't noticed it until now.

"I could stare at you all day and it still wouldn't be enough," he growls.

Warmth fills my legs, and I curl my toes. If I don't steady myself, I'm afraid I will launch myself into his arms and wrap my legs around his waist, and never let go. That's what Beck makes me feel when I'm with him. Crazed and reckless.

"This face. This mouth. You're flawless." He smiles and cups my chin, coercing my lips to his as he bends.

Our mouths crash together. The kiss is needy and passionate. It's the kind of kiss that I don't want to ever end.

I grasp the collar of his flannel in my grip and tug him closer to me, desperate to have him nearer. Like his very presence is air for my lungs. My heart races and a thrill rushes between my thighs. I find myself frantically attempting to hold on to this feeling.

When Beck draws back, I inhale a trembling breath. He grins down at me and there's a satisfied gleam in his brown eyes. Like provoking my surrender is his reward. He reluctantly releases me and wraps an arm around my shoulder, guiding me across the upper deck.

"What do you say after we get back to Golden Harbor and you pick up Charlie, you come to my place and I cook breakfast?"

"Your place, huh? I was wondering if I'd ever get to see the mysterious place you're living now."

For years, I've imagined him living in a messy bachelor pad. Only because I don't think my heart could handle him living in a nice, clean place with a new woman in his life. But I've mostly been grateful that he was forced to move out of our little place we lived in by the beach when a developer bought it and tore it down and built new million-dollar condos.

He shrugs against me. "I don't know about mysterious, but it's on the opposite side of the busy part of town, a block from the beach, and it's always stocked with the ingredients to make pancakes." An adorable smile forms on his lips.

"So, you cook breakfast now?" I snicker. This is new too. There had been plenty of times when he cooked for Milo. But it was less cooking and more being creative and preparing whatever they had in their kitchen, which sometimes wasn't much.

"I think you'll be pleasantly surprised by how much my skills have improved."

"Are you kidding, I'm already impressed by how much your skills have improved." I smirk up at him and he flashes me a boyish grin.

"In the kitchen, I meant," he mumbles, pressing a kiss to my temple as we walk. "You know if I'm any better at sex it's not from practice, that's for damn sure. Maybe it's because I've gone so long without it. Without *you*."

I clutch at his hand and stop him. He glances down at me, and I search his face for hurt but it's not visible in his expression. Instead, there's hope and appreciation.

"I've missed you like crazy," he admits, tenderness in his tone.

"I've missed you too," I confess. "I've missed...this." I draw up to him for one more slow kiss. It's laced with passion but not lust. Like we are marking this moment as it is—significant.

Pulling back, I exhale a light sigh and release my grip on him, and he groans loudly. I can't help but smile.

"C'mon." I tug his hand. "Cars. Charlie. Then home and breakfast." The words *Charlie* and *home* in the same sentence when speaking with Beck fills my heart with a yearning of family. A real family with him. Something I didn't think would ever be possible.

As we're about to take the steps down to the lower level, my gaze lands on the small parking lot near the dock. I recognize the figure standing there; arms crossed and a bewildered expression smeared on his face. My feet halt and I drop Beck's hand.

It's West. Here. In Golden Harbor. At the ferry dock.

"Hey, you okay?" Beck asks, ready to take the first step down below.

I sink my teeth into my bottom lip, barely able to look at him. I hesitantly glance up at him and shake my head before gesturing at West with my chin.

It takes a moment for Beck to skim the crowd before his eyes land on him. He instantly goes rigid. "West?"

"I'm sorry. I didn't know he was coming," I whisper.

Beck's jaw ticks. "I thought you guys were over?"

"We were. We are. It's complicated," I stammer.

"It's not that complicated. You're either with him or you're not."

I reach for his hand but he flinches and my chest spasms. "Beck—" His name cracks as it rushes out. "I'm sorry. We're not. But..."

"But what?"

"I have to think about Charlie too."

"No, you're not using Charlie as an excuse this time. Because if you did, you'd know she would want us to be together. You're doing this for you."

Glancing between him and West, I say, "I just need some time."

"You had time. You had seven fucking years."

"Beck, please."

"I love you, Rosie. But I'm not gonna be your consolation prize."

"You're not. Never. Besides Charlie, you're my favorite person," I declare, desperation in each pulse of my heartbeat.

"I don't like sharing *my wife*," he growls.

The way he says *my wife* causes a welcomed burn to radiate between my thighs. I touch his arm, and this time he allows it. "I love you."

"Prove it."

"What?"

He crosses his arms. "Choose me. Choose us."

"I am choosing you. And us... Just let me figure this out."

Sadness overtakes his expression, and he readjusts his hat on his head. "I can't do this again with you. I won't watch you leave again. I'm done."

"Beck, wait," I call out, grasping his flannel, before he can hurry down the narrow metal steps. I glance over my shoulder at the dock again, and it's now I see the small figure in the backset of West's car. Charlie. I suck in a breath.

Beck looks and sees her too. "What the hell is she doing with him?" he grits out between clenched teeth.

My head swims. "I...I don't know. She was with Stella." I tug my phone from my back pocket but I still don't have cell service.

He jogs down the steps, and I hurry after him. He spins

around, expression stoney. "She's my daughter. Not his. He's got no legal rights to her."

"I know." I nod, my mind distracted while I try to process how Charlie ended up with West.

"Take care of this. Or I will."

Tears burn my eyes. I watch him turn and walk away, my heart shattering in my chest. Once he's out of eyeshot, I rush to Dottie's car and hop in. I rummage in my purse for lip gloss and perfume. Peering at my reflection in the visor mirror, I comb my fingers through my windswept hair.

Nothing is going to make me look presentable enough to break a man's heart, but here goes nothing. I drive off the ferry and onto the dock, pulling into an open spot in the lot next to where West is leaning against the side of a black sedan.

Just as I slide out of the driver's seat, Beck's Chevy passes by and he doesn't make eye contact with me. It's probably best.

West flashes me a smile, but it's guarded. "There's my girl," he greets me as I round the front of the car.

"Weston, what are you doing here?"

When he reaches me, he leans in for a kiss, but I turn my cheek to him. There's a moment of trepidation before he follows through with it.

West straightens, and I notice now the purplish hue and swollen skin underneath his eyes. I've never seen him look so tired or ragged. He sets his hand on my shoulder and gives it a light squeeze. "I missed you. And Charlotte."

I force a tight smile. "You didn't even call first."

"I wanted to surprise you."

Mission accomplished.

"You should've called," I say flatly, peering at Charlie through the window. "And how'd you know where to find me?"

He points at Charlie in the backseat where she's distracted by something playing on a screen mounted into the headrest. "Charlie told me."

"And how'd you find Charlie?"

"I had to do some digging." His gaze shifts to the ground.

Anger sears my skin. I'm not upset with Stella. I'm very aware of how convincing West can be.

"Was that him? Charlotte's father?" He nudges his chin in the direction of the road.

"Yeah, that was Beck."

He purses his lips. "And he...went to the island to spread Dottie's ashes with you?"

He's fishing for information and I don't blame him. Seeing Beck and me together couldn't have been easy.

"Actually, no. I went alone. Beck was on the island fishing with his dad, and I ran into him." This is only a partial lie.

When he slides his hand down to my elbow, I cross my arms.

"You still haven't said what you're doing here."

"We need to talk. I don't like how we ended things."

"We could've done it over the phone."

"I thought it would be best in person." He shoves his hands inside his pockets. "Plus, you've told me so much about Golden Harbor, I thought you'd be excited to show me around." He nudges his chin. "C'mon, get in. I've only got two days and I'm sure there's lots to see."

"You took two days off of work?"

"Technically...yes. I've got a video conference tomorrow and some emails to send. But other than that, I'm all yours."

"I can't remember the last time you took off work." But I do. The memory assaults me like a shot of endorphins. He took an entire day off work and we went to Long Beach. Guilt presses down on me and pinches in my gut.

"Anything for you," he responds with a genuine smile. It's the kind of smile that used to melt my heart. Still does to a degree.

West is not intentionally a selfish guy. His work is intense and demanding, but he doesn't have healthy boundaries. It's been the root of our arguments over the last year.

"Why now?" I blurt out, not really sure I want the answer. Because will it change anything?

He frowns. "I nearly lost you," he pleads, taking my hand. "I know that now. And it's something I can't afford. Now c'mon, let's go." He tugs me, and I reluctantly glide with him until my brain catches up.

"Wait, my car," I protest, my feet halting.

"We'll get it later."

"How about Charlie and I drive my car and we meet you at Dottie's."

"Nah, I'd rather you came with me now." His jaw ticks. "C'mon, we'll get it later." With a hand pressed to my low back, he ushers me to the passenger side.

I climb in reluctantly but put on a brave face for Charlie. Spinning in my seat, I smile wide. "Hi, Charlie girl. I missed you."

"Hi, Mama!"

I pat her leg. "How was Stella's? Did you have fun?"

"Yes! It was so much fun! I taught Max how to braid. Miss Stella found her old Barbies for us."

"Wow. That does sound like fun." I face the windshield again as West slides behind the wheel.

"Mama?"

"Yes, baby?" I glance over my shoulder as I wipe the wetness from my eyes.

"What's wrong?" She's twirling one of her long braids around her finger.

Pressing my lips together, I exhale a sigh. She's not a baby. But shielding her from as much shrapnel during her childhood is my goal as a mom. "Nothing. I'm just tired." I shoot a glare at West.

"Guess what, Mama? West got me a new stuffie!" She holds

up a gray stuffed dolphin I vaguely see from the corner of my eye.

"I took her to that bookshop in town."

The car rumbles as it reverses backward and my mind races. "When?"

"After I picked her up from your friend, Stella's. We needed to kill some time since she told me it would be a few hours before the ferry docked."

"She has plenty of stuffies. And you don't have to compete with Beck, if that's what you're doing. He's her father."

"Yeah? And I'm going to be her stepfather. And the one who will be taking care of her when all this goes to shit and you girls are back home with me."

I glare at him, my gut twisting. "I don't think you've listened to anything I've said. Not now, and not back in Seattle."

My phone buzzes repeatedly in my back pocket as it finally comes to life again. I hurry and tug it free while my chest flutters. All of this is my fault. I didn't tell Stella that I broke things off with West. If I had, she never would've let Charlie go with him.

> STELLA
>
> Take your time. I'm making crepes for breakfast. Charlie says she's never had them
>
> Call me as soon as you have service again
>
> Hello??
>
> West is here! In Golden Harbor! He just picked up Charlie. He said he wants to surprise you at the dock. Please tell me you didn't spend the night with Beck on the island!

I reply to her so she doesn't worry.

> I'm off the ferry. West just picked me up

HANNAH

Just bought a one-way ticket! Coming to see
you next week bestie!

BECK

I signed the papers

We're done. You're no longer my wife

32

BECK

Checking my phone a million times does nothing to help my anxiety. But it's been half a day since I said goodbye to Rosie on the ferry. And since I signed the papers and sent her that text.

My brain is buzzing with all the scenarios where Rosie and I don't end up together. But despite how bruised and battered my heart is, it's still holding on to a shred of hope that our love is enough.

My head is too fuzzy I can't go home. I go to Milo's and sit in during rehearsal with his band. It's only somewhat of a distraction. I head to Seashell Bookshop next and grab a coffee. Consuming caffeine isn't the best idea when my anxiety is at an all-time high. Now I'm not just pacing the streets distressed, but I'm jittery as well.

I debate texting Dr. Sam. My heart feels as if it's cracking in half and my limbs are heavy. But as I walk by Peace of Cake, I see Daisy through the window where she's standing behind the counter. The weathered door sticks and rubs as I yank it open and step inside. It's been a while since I was here. Daisy and I have always been friends, but after we went on that date a few years back, things have been awkward between us.

"Beck?" Daisy calls and I spin, for some reason feeling caught.

"Hey, Daisy. How's it going?"

She frowns, her brows pinching together as her blue eyes rake over me.

My gaze drops to the display case, and I peruse the specialty cupcakes and small cakes, each one intricately decorated. "I'm just...I'm..." I don't even know what I'm doing here. "I'm looking for a cupcake," I lie.

Her lips tip to one side as she considers this. "You haven't stepped foot in here for what—three years?"

Has it been that long since that godawful date? We were such good friends; we never should've agreed to it in the first place. But Stella and Jack had us convinced we'd be perfect for each other. Except we weren't. Far from it.

Because my soulmate is currently contemplating spending the rest of her life with another man. And Daisy's soulmate up and ditched her and this town before the ink was dry on his high school diploma. Christian never wanted the small-town life. Always had dreams of something bigger.

"Has it been that long?" I scratch at the scruff on my chin. When my finger slips into the indent of my dimple, Charlie springs to my mind.

"Yep. Do you need me to refresh your memory? Because I can show you the spot where we made out in the back after our date and you left my ass with floured handprints?"

When I don't react, she snickers. "I'm kidding. Geez. You all right?" She's frowning at me again.

"Sorry." I shake my head, trying to get rid of the jumbled mess inside of it. "And I'm sorry again...about that night."

"Seriously?" She lifts her brows. "It's been three years. You think I'm still stressing over that? I mean, you're a good kisser and all, but I knew we weren't vibing."

I nod along with her as she talks. "And I'm sorry I haven't been by for a while."

"Three years," she reminds me. "You're the one who made it awkward."

"I did. You're right. We're friends, I shouldn't have let that disastrous date ruin our friendship."

She eyes me again. "Beck, are you okay?"

My head continues to whirl, the colorful cupcakes spinning and blurring. The voices around me grow louder.

"Is it Rosie? You and Rosie?"

At the mention of her name, I whip my head up and look at Daisy. "Have you heard from her?"

"Not since she got back a few days ago." She puts up a finger to her customers and waves me to the end of the display case where she meets me. "Is she okay? Is Charlotte okay?"

"Yeah, I think so...I don't know what I'm doing," I mutter. Heat sears my skin as my heart gallops in my chest. Sweat bubbles at my temples and trickles down the center of my back.

She touches my arm. "Why don't you sit down. You don't look so good."

"I'm fine. I gotta go." Taking a few steps backward, I crash into a customer and whip around. "I'm so sorry." I rush to the door and bump my hip into it, gulping in the balmy afternoon air. It does little to soothe my feverish skin. There's a bench in front of the surf shop. I shuffle toward it and plop down the second I reach it.

Pinching my eyes tight, I plant my feet flat on the ground and shove away my surroundings. The pounding of my heart and erratic breathing drown out the sounds from the busy street and shops but also amplifies them at the same time. They whir in my ears, and my head feels detached from my body.

Bringing my hands together, I interlock my fingers, and the

touch of my own skin centers me and gives me something to focus on. A smidge of light peeks through the blackness haze of my vision and sends a signal to my brain that I need to breathe. It takes several long moments before I'm able to implement Dr. Sam's breathing techniques.

After my heart slows and I finally open my eyes, I sit back, my clammy skin cool when I make contact with the bench. Locals carry their purchases out of the shop behind me. Vacationers haul rented surfboards toward the beach to one side of me, and they pass on rented bikes going in the opposite direction.

I pull out my phone and check for new texts from Rosie. Nothing. I open my email and in my sent folder, I find the document I'd been ignoring for the last year. I stare at my electronic signature and initials.

The reality hits me like a blow to my gut.

It's really over.

33

ROSIE

"How long is West staying?" Charlie asks from the backseat.

Good question.

"I'm not sure," I answer honestly. But if I have it my way, he'll be back in Seattle by tonight.

"Mama said we would go to the beach today. Do you want to go with us?"

"I didn't bring my swimsuit," West replies.

Charlie giggles. "You don't need a suit. You can just wear shorts, silly."

"I'll have to check if I packed any."

I'm not sure West even owns shorts.

"I don't think West will be here long enough to go with us to the beach, baby girl," I chime in, hopeful he'll get the hint.

But he does not.

For Charlie's sake, I hold everything in while we go to the beach and tell myself this last day with West is for her. For once, he is actually trying. He's spending real time with her. Playing in the sand, holding her hand, and jumping in the waves. I sit on a towel spread out on the sand.

Deep down, there's a gnawing at me like a throbbing reminder that this isn't normal. Whatever is happening here, with Charlie and West—it's not normal. This is his last-ditch effort to make things work between us, to convince me to come back to Seattle.

West calls my name out from the waves. I glance up and find him with his hands cupped around his mouth when he calls me again. "Rosie! Get out here!"

I shake my head. I want this moment for Charlie to be a positive one. Something she can look back on as a nice memory.

"C'mon," West tries again. "Get that fine ass of yours out here."

"C'mon, Mama!" Charlie shouts.

My phone sits inside my bag with the unanswered texts from Beck. I debate responding but I don't want to do this over text. I need to see him.

I meant everything I said to him today on the ferry. I love him. But whether it's enough for us to be together or not, I don't know. I can only hope it is.

Right now, I'm conflicted. Not with who to choose, but how to let this man down easy who welcomed me and my daughter into his life. He was open with me from the beginning, informing me that he worked a stupid amount of hours, that he'd never cared enough about a woman to ask her to move in —until me.

"Rosie!" West calls again. "Don't make me come get you," he teases.

I hop up and jog to the water to join West and Charlie in the waves. Because maybe he needs this last happy memory just as much as Charlie does before I tell him goodbye.

Back at Dottie's house, I give Charlie a quick bath while West showers in my bathroom. We drain the tub, and I wrap a towel around her, dropping a kiss to the top of her damp head. I scroll on my phone, giving her some privacy while she dries off and gets dressed in a pair of pajamas.

My heart stalls in my chest as I reread the lasts texts from Beck.

BECK

I signed your papers

You're no longer my wife

Tears spring to my eyes while I stare at it, reading it over and over.

"You okay, Mama?" Charlie asks.

I glance up and find her dressed in her pajamas. "I'm fine, baby girl. Why don't you go in your room and pick out your favorite book. I need to talk to West for a minute."

She races down the hall and when she's out of sight, I give in to the anguish that's wracking me. Sobs break free from my chest, tearing out of my mouth even as I try to cover them with a clamped hand.

I knock on the door to the bathroom and West opens it, bare chest and a towel tied around his waist.

"You should've knocked a few minutes earlier. You could've joined me," he teases, waggling his brows.

I stare at him blankly.

He bends and tilts his head. "Hey, what's wrong?"

"I need you to go," I say flatly.

Straightening, he barks out a laugh and struts past me, stopping at his suitcase that's open-faced on my bed.

I follow him, crossing my arms and leaning my hip against the mattress. "I'm serious, West. I meant what I said earlier. And I meant what I said back in Seattle before I left."

He tugs a T-shirt over his head. "Yeah, but that was before."

"Nothing has changed."

"I'm here, aren't I? That's what's changed."

"I'm so sorry."

"You're sorry?" he sneers. "Give me a break, Rosie. I dropped everything and came here to see you and Charlie." He lets the towel at his waist fall to the floor, but I look away while he puts on his briefs and pants.

"I didn't ask you to do that. In fact, I'm certain I asked you not to."

"Let's just make the best of the evening." He takes my hand in his, tugging me toward the bedroom door. "If you still want me to go, I'll leave tomorrow."

"West, no. *Weston*." I raise my voice and freeze, my feet halting. "You're not listening to me. You never listen to me." I yank free from his grasp, and he furrows his brow.

"You're serious?"

I swallow the lump in my throat and dip my chin.

He stares at me for a long moment. "Oh shit." A low audible exhale releases from his mouth as his chest deflates. "This is really over." He presses his thumb and fingers into his temples.

My heart balloons in my chest before splitting completely while I study the expression marring his face. Agony overtakes my body, and my legs fill with lead. "I'm so sorry."

"Is it him? Charlie's father?"

My head swims. It's as if he didn't hear anything I said to him back in Seattle. "What? No."

"C'mon, Rosie. That's bullshit. You at least owe me the truth." He moves his hands to his hips.

"I didn't break off things with you because of Beck." I don't even believe the words that just escaped me. "But I do still love him. The truth is, I never stopped loving him."

"Wow." He releases a whistle and shoots his attention to the wood flooring before glancing back up. "What was all this?" He gestures in the air. "Between us? Some kind of game to you? See if the rich guy would actually fall for the poor single mom?"

"What? No. You know I'm not like that. I loved you."

"Ha," he barks. "Loved. So quickly you've resorted to past tense. So easily."

"This is anything but easy. I planned a life with you. With us. And now, I have to start over. So 'easy' isn't in the vicinity."

"But this is your choice. I don't get a say here. Do you realize how unfair this is?"

The tears build in my chest. "I do. I'm so sorry."

"You're sorry," he huffs out. "You just fucked up my life and you're sorry. Whatever." He folds the top of his suitcase and zips it closed. Lifting his gaze, he locks eyes with me. "Was any of it real?"

"It was. All of it."

His lips pull up to one corner. "For whatever it's worth, I would've taken care of you. And Charlie."

"I know."

"I'll have Piper pack your shit. Just the thought of seeing it at my place makes me sick."

I deserve that. I probably deserve him tossing it all out. But he's a good guy. That's not in his nature.

"I'm going to say goodbye to Charlie. Then that's it, Rosie. Don't ever call me."

Shuffling past me with his suitcase, he doesn't look back. It's just as well. He's right. I blew up his life. Beck's life. And mine in the process.

34

BECK

I need to clear my head and calm down. I hop back in my truck. From my periphery, the children's menu from Golden Pies that Charlie colored me catches my attention. It's folded and propped in my dash covering my gauges. I pick it up and study the colorful lines. You can see the precision in each stroke of crayon. Tears burn my eyes, but I set the drawing back and blink them away.

I stop by my house for my surfboard before heading to the beach. There isn't much daylight left, but if anything can cure this ache of despair—it's surfing.

After I ride a few good waves, I shove my board into the sand so it's standing upright and plop down on my towel. I push my fingers through my wet hair and release a strangled sigh. I'm mentally preparing myself before checking my phone for a call or text from Rosie.

Maybe I overreacted signing the divorce papers. Part of me regrets it. But maybe part of me thought it might wake her up. I tug my phone from the inside of my shoe and there's nothing. Instant rage builds inside of me, and I huff out a guttural grumble. Anger prickles across my skin and I chuck my phone. It lands several feet down the beach.

All I've been doing is agonizing over Rosie and what she's doing. Is she telling West it's over? Or did she get swept up by his charm and decided to go back with him?

Maybe she and Charlie are already halfway back to Seattle by now. That last thought has me practically spiraling. Rosie and I being completely over would be devastating, but not being able to say goodbye to Charlie feels unbearable.

I've got myself so worked up that a panic attack is threatening again. A tingle travels down my limbs and the sound of the wind and the waves crashing on the beach dull. The beat of my heart picks up speed and thrusts quick successions against my ribcage. My breathing becomes shallow and fast. And it's only a matter of seconds before I'm gasping for air.

To keep me sane, I focus on the curling of the waves and tell myself to breathe. It's a simple reminder but it's desperately needed right now. With no one here to help, I have to advocate for myself.

I suck in an unsteady breath and hold it for a few seconds but I'm not sure how long. I know I need to count to three, but my brain isn't signaling my breaths. *Who is in control here?* Exhaling, I gasp and the whole process starts again. Only it's not rhythmic, that's the problem.

Somewhere in the diminished background noise, the sound of my phone chiming catches my attention. But my body is frozen—unable to move my limbs that are both weighted and feel like rubber at the same time.

After several minutes of this, it finally dissipates and is over at last. Sweat trickles down my back and bubbles at my temples. With weak arms and legs, I crawl to my phone that's popping out of the sand several feet away.

I bring the screen to my line of vision and brush the sand away.

ROSIE
Where are you?

"I'm here," I say aloud, and frantically tap out a reply.

I'm typically hardheaded, but spending time with Rosie, and learning about Charlie has put things in perspective. I'm choosing us over myself. And over my pride.

I'm at the beach

Jensen Beach

ROSIE
I'm on my way!

I can come to you

ROSIE
No. I'm already on my way. Stay there!

My central nervous system is shot. But how do I stay put when uneasiness hums inside my veins after that string of texts from Rosie? Is she coming to end things once and for all in person? Or is she coming to tell me she chose me, and we can finally be together?

I pace, sinking in the thick sand and passing my surfboard several times, threading my fingers through my hair. Every ten seconds I hold up my phone and peer at the time on the screen. Dottie's cottage is only about a six-minute drive from here. But it's been more like ten.

After what feels like an eternity, I finally spot Rosie coming up over the sandbank where the tall grass breaks and makes way for the pathway to the parking lot. She's dressed in a yellow tank top that shows off her freckle dusted shoulders, and a pair of jeans, the wind blowing her auburn hair back as she hurries toward me. In one hand, she holds her sandals and the other, Charlie's hand. My heart threatens to break out of my chest.

While worry torments my insides, I can't resist the smile forming on my lips. I may not be sure of the outcome of her wanting to meet me, but how can I not smile when I see her? I love her. I've always loved her. And no matter what—regardless of what she tells me—I'm afraid I'll love her for the rest of my fucking life.

Abandoning my surfboard, I take off in a speedwalk, then a jog, because I can't help myself. The craving to meet her halfway is intense and nothing else matters. But Rosie's pace doesn't increase. She stops Charlie and forces her to stay put before she returns her walk toward me. My heart squeezes at the visual and what this might mean. Yet it doesn't discourage me. I keep going.

By the time we reach one another, I'm nearly breathless.

"Beck," she says on an exhale. "How long have you been here? I went by your house. When you weren't there..." Her voice trails.

I reach out my hand to rub her arm without thinking first. Is she mine to reach for? To touch? "I couldn't be there. I couldn't be anywhere. But here."

"I'm sorry." Tears build in her eyes and my gut collapses.

My eyes search hers for more—for answers. "Wh...what?" The question releases from me, and I try to find my voice. "What, Rosie? What are you sorry for?" I rub her arms that tremble beneath my touch.

"I'm sorry...for everything. For today. For the last seven years." She crumples against my chest, and I catch her before she falls, guiding both of us down to the sand on our knees.

We kneel facing one another and I hold her while she sobs, consoling her as best as I can with hushes in her ear. I stuff down my own anguish that's growing inside me and tears build. I cup her cheek in my palm, coaxing her to look at me. "Rosie, you gotta give me more here. You're scaring me." I peer over Rosie's shoulder to where Charlie is still standing exactly where her mom left her. "I think you're scaring Charlie."

"I'm sorry I left. I couldn't be here. Everywhere I looked was a reminder of what I thought we lost. Every time I looked into your empty eyes, I felt guilty. And then a few weeks after I left and learned I hadn't lost Charlie; I didn't want to come back and be a burden anymore."

I brush back her hair and gaze at her watering green eyes. "Hey, never. You were never a burden."

"I know it's a lot...endo...taking care of me. And then adding a baby. This is my body that I have to live in. But you get a choice. I didn't want you to feel trapped," she says on a sob.

Gazing into her watering green eyes, I say, "I've never felt trapped with you. You make me feel like the luckiest guy in the world. Being with you is a fucking honor." I force her to look at me. "I'm a damn fool for not coming after you, I'm sorry. I love you."

"I love you, too. I'm so sorry. Will you ever be able to forgive me?"

"That depends. What am I forgiving you for?" She gives me a pitiful pout while tears continue streaming down her cheeks. "If you're getting ready to break my heart again, and go back to West, nah," I clarify, my throat constricting. "I can't survive that again."

She gives a subtle shake to her head and bites at her lower lip.

"But if you're asking for forgiveness for all the wrongs before today. Yeah, honey, I forgive you. For all of it. As long as you forgive me too." I skim my thumb underneath her eye, swiping at the wetness.

"I do." She whispers so softly I almost don't hear it.

"I do too." I smile, but maybe it's premature. "So which is it? What's going on here?"

"West is gone. It's always been you, Beck. Always."

The sigh that rips through me is years of suppression. But it feels so fragile. I'm afraid to trust this. "You sure?"

"Always. You're it for me. And I think I'm it for you."

I lift her chin with my finger, gaze into her eyes, and see my soulmate. My heart. My future. "Yeah, you bet your ass you're it for me. I love you. Always and forever." Lowering my lips to hers feels like coming home. It's a comfort I want again and again for the rest of my life. I'm desperate for it. For this kiss. For every kiss after this one.

Her lips answer mine like she's wanting the exact same thing. Her mouth parts and her tongue swipes out to meet mine. While her fingers kneed the skin on my back, my mouth devours hers. My hands are anxious to touch her how they always did—when she was mine, caressing her neck and her breasts and down to her full backside.

Vaguely I remember we're not alone. But this feels like one of those key moments that needs to be cared for. Because if this is it—her and me and this kiss—for the rest of our lives, I want her to be sure. Her decision to choose me shouldn't be questioned. Never again.

She's mine and I am hers. Forever.

Cupping her face in my palm, I caress her cheek with my thumb and slowly draw back, taking her underneath the elbow and helping her to stand. Gazing into her beautiful green eyes, I say, "There's just one problem."

Concern smears her expression. A lump bobs in her throat before she asks, "What is it?"

"We're not married anymore."

She gifts me with a cute little smile that has my core buzzing. "We had two proposals. Only makes sense to have two weddings, right?"

A smile pulls at my lips at the memory of the first time I proposed to her. So simple. So awkward. Not even a ring to give her. But I'd never been surer about anything in my entire life. "You deserved a better proposal than that. But I couldn't help myself. I knew in that moment, without a doubt, that you were my person and I couldn't wait another second longer."

"I have a confession to make." She touches her palm to the side of my face, her fingers scratching at the scruff there. "The first proposal was my favorite." Lifting her other hand up, she opens her fist and the necklace with the heart-shaped piece of green sea glass shimmers in her palm.

The smile that forms on my lips is easy. "Mine too," I whisper.

This time, it's Rosie who draws my face closer to hers while she pushes up on her toes and our mouths crash together. While my lips graze earnestly and depraved, hers slide over mine with the kind of desire that's pure and reminding me this is lasting. This is the kind of love that doesn't diminish. It's forever.

A small arm wraps around my leg and when I glance down, Charlie has both Rosie and me wound tight in her embrace. Elation expands in my chest as my heart swells. I press one more chaste kiss to Rosie's mouth before I reach down and scoop Charlie into my arms. Spinning around in a circle, she giggles, and the delighted sound reverberates through my entire body.

I set her back down and we each take one of Charlie's hands as we trudge through the sand, the wind whipping at our faces and the golden sun dipping below the dark turquoise ocean.

Glancing over my shoulder at Rosie, I find her staring at me. Her eyes squint from the huge smile stretched on her face. All the prior worries and doubts from earlier in the day have vanished. Instead of goodbye, we're getting our second chance at the life we were always meant to have.

ACKNOWLEDGMENTS

First, I always give thanks to God. Without him I would be a version of myself that I don't want to know. I've been given the gift of storytelling and the drive to keep learning how to turn those stories into books.

Thank you to my talented cover artist Claudia for putting me on your schedule and agreeing to work with me even after I reached out to you on both email and socials frantically. You have been nothing but professional and so kind. You took my character profiles and setting and a few of my ideas and turned it into the magical piece of art that this is. You far exceeded my expectations and I can't wait to work together on the rest of the series!

Thank you to my editor, Britt Tayler, for taking me on as a new client. For being highly professional and communicative through the entire process. I appreciate you for your care on such a personal story.

As always, thank you to my husband for being my partner and cheerleader in all things in life, but especially when I had a wild dream of writing a book with two main characters who have similar ailments as myself. And who still cheered me on when I was dumping lots of money to turn this book into the beautiful thing that it is. I love you always and forever!

Thank you to my kids for allowing me to bounce my creative ideas off you, for your support and asking how the "book stuff" is going, and for being proud of me and telling your friends and coworkers about your mom's books. Even if they are kissing books! As much as I love this book baby, you three will always be my best projects!

A special thank you to Starla's Hype Squad for your support, to my author and reader friends, and to my ARC readers. Thank you to Rae at House of Hearts Lit for all the support and managing my ARC team.

A big shout out to Christina Hill and all my Mountains and Manuscripts friends for the accountability and the video writing sprints. I never could've finished this book without you!

Thank you to K. Jaspersen Designs for saving me while I was stressed and spiraling, (hello anxiety/panic!) and providing a cover file for me! The real MVP!

Thank you to one of my favorite romance authors who writes lived-experience endo rep, Torie Jean. You are more than a colleague in this industry, you are a treasured friend. Endo sucks but I'm so glad it gave me you!

To all my fellow endo warriors: I believe you. Your pain is valid. Suspected endo counts. You are loved. You are more than your illness. We need better. We deserve better.

ABOUT THE AUTHOR

Starla DeKruyf is a romance author of small towns and happily ever afters. She writes books that play like movies in your head about characters you wish you could hang out with. As someone who struggles with mental health and lives with chronic illness, she often includes these topics in her books. Follow her on her socials so you can have fun and be awkward together! When Starla isn't writing, she's probably drinking coffee and spending time with her husband, kids, and her rescue pup.

ALSO BY STARLA DEKRUYF

A historical romance novella (1969-present):

Come Back: A Small Town Romance Novella

Pineridge series:

Eight Days of Christmas

We Fell in Love in October

A Little Bit Yours

Juniper Ridge series

A Pumpkin Patch and A Fling

A Women's Fiction Novel:

The Tahoe City Girls

A standalone romcom:

The Heart Rehab Experiment

The
HEART
REHAB
EXPERIMENT
A hilarious and sexy
romantic comedy
AUTHOR OF THE HOLIDAY BOX OR EIGHT DAYS OF CHRISTMAS
STARLA DEKRUYF